TWO NIGHTS IN MUMBAI

A DAK HARPER THRILLER

ERNEST DEMPSEY

138 PUBLISHING

For Mattie. My furry, little muse who was with me since the beginning. I'll never forget you, my miracle kitty.

JOIN THE ADVENTURE

Visit ernestdempsey.net to get a free copy of the not-sold-in-stores short stories *Red Gold, The Lost Canvas,* and *The Moldova Job,* plus the full length novel *The Cairo Vendetta*, all from the critically acclaimed Sean Wyatt archaeological thriller series.

You'll also get access to exclusive content and stories not available anywhere else.

While you're at it, swing by the official Ernest Dempsey fan page on Facebook at https://facebook.com/ErnestDempsey to join the community of travelers, adventurers, historians, and dreamers. There are exclusive contests, giveaways, and more!

Lastly, if you enjoy pictures of exotic locations, food, and travel adventures, check out my feed @ernestdempsey on the Instagram app.

What are you waiting for? Join the adventure today!

1

MUMBAI

The thief watched the young woman on his three-inch wrist display for the seventh time in the last two weeks. He'd grown accustomed to her routine; how she went about closing the Mumbai Museum of Antiquities every day at the same time. This was, however, the first time he'd watched her from inside the museum. While the air duct wasn't his favorite perch, it had been the most easily accessible.

The museum curator, Priya Laghari, personally checked every room and every exhibit, then saw to it that all the security systems were armed on each of the three floors, before shutting off the lights every night.

The woman carried an old-school clipboard with a simple check-list so she could make sure she didn't skip anything.

What a boring job, the thief thought.

He'd spent months preparing for this job, taking electrical service calls, air conditioning service calls, and even one call regarding a plumbing issue, all so he could infiltrate the museum undercover and rig the security feeds from every camera in the building. With complete control of the video feeds, he could see where Laghari was during every second of her end-of-the-day routine.

Gavin Harris had pulled off some amazing heists in the last few years, especially here in India, where it seemed like fertile ground for raiding museums or private collections with sometimes priceless artifacts.

The artifact he was here for, though, did have a price. At five million euros—he didn't calculate the value in rupees—Gavin's fortune would reach a new high. The money, for him, was only part of the benefit.

After all, he'd grown up around plenty of it.

A contrarian to many, half of his reason for getting into the thieving business was purely for the thrill of it. The more challenging the target, the more he wanted it. Thus far, he'd never been caught, though there had been several close calls.

He switched the screen view with a swipe of his gloved finger and Laghari reappeared, standing in a different room. This one, a square space of nearly a thousand feet, was the one he was interested in.

In the center, a white pedestal with a glass case atop it held a golden statue of Lord Mahavir, the twenty-fourth, and last, god, or *tirthankara*, of the Jain religion.

Gavin had researched the beliefs of Jainism only briefly, enough to know that he didn't care what the faithful believed, only that they often possessed valuable artifacts such as the one on the screen, gleaming in the light shining down from above. The tirthankaras were, as the Jain scriptures suggest, born as people who attained their position as gods through intense meditation, fasting, and self-real-ization.

Know thyself, Gavin remembered thinking when he'd read about how the Jain gods achieved their status.

Seemed simple enough, but he didn't understand why someone would want to waste away their days meditating. He believed the act to be highly unproductive, despite everything he'd read and seen in the media.

While people were sitting on their floors with their legs crossed and fingers curled in circles, thieves like him were stealing their deities right out from under their noses. Gavin knew the stats to back it up, too. More than a thousand ancient relics disappeared from India every year, most stolen by thieves far beneath his abilities. The resulting loss was far more than financial, though he didn't care about the loss of spiritual property. They were just idols to him, made by human hands. People could make more gods and prop them up in their temples or homes or museums to be worshipped. And with each one made, a new target appeared on the antiquities black market for an aspiring thief.

The curator walked the room, pacing from one end to the other, circling around until she'd checked off all the precious boxes on her checklist. Then she stepped out of the room, turned on the alarm, and waited until the lights switched off and the laser beams at the entryways flashed on.

Gavin couldn't see the beams, but he knew they were there. He'd analyzed the entrances to every exhibit room in the building, and it was easy to spot laser security systems. The metal housing and glass covers stood out against the white-painted backdrop of the walls, though almost no one noticed them, or if they did, they didn't tell anyone.

Most visitors to any museum didn't recall anything about the place except the artifacts and the artwork that they saw. Of course, the lure of the gift shop also helped erase any of the technical, unimportant items a visitor might behold, such as light fixtures, bathrooms, the color of the floor, or in this case, laser security systems.

Lasers could be a serious issue for most thieves, but Gavin Harris wasn't most thieves. He spent more time analyzing problems before he faced them than anyone he knew. While he enjoyed the thrill of the hunt, and the job itself, he didn't want to get caught, despite what some of the authorities might have said.

He recalled reading a piece about his last heist, where the writer suggested that he was one of those weirdos who was trying to get caught and linked that sort of behavior to a troubled past, a lack of parental involvement, or perhaps some kind of strange sense of entitlement. Gavin felt the article was purely speculative.

Although they weren't entirely wrong.

Gavin had definitely lacked parental involvement in his life. His parents were always too busy, always at a function or fundraiser, or on vacation.

He shook off the nostalgia and refocused on the screen. Laghari walked down the corridor to the stairs. Gavin switched the view again to the camera fixed to the upper corner over the stairwell and watched as she switched off the main lights before descending out of view.

Another swipe and he saw her reach the second-floor landing and disappear into the first room on the right, where she would repeat the same process to check off all the items on her list and make sure the systems were armed.

Gavin turned to the screen attached to his wrist and tapped a green button on the side. The tiny monitor blinked to life, displaying three white boxes on a black screen. The top box had a red dot in the middle, signifying the third-floor alarm system was on. The other two floors featured green dots, showing that they were not yet armed. He knew that wouldn't take long. Not that it mattered. From the foundation of work he'd laid over the last several months, Gavin had complete control of the system and could turn it off or on whenever he liked.

He knew, from his previous observations, that when Laghari finished her routine, she would check out of the building, leaving it to the security guard who kept watch over the museum throughout the night.

Gavin wondered, more than once, what the standards or training regimen was like for these kinds of guards, but he didn't complain. Their ineptitude worked in his favor. They were often willing to step aside, in his experience, than put themselves into harm's way for something that was heavily insured. Gavin knew that someday, perhaps, if he kept at this sort of work, he'd eventually run into a security guard with a military past. So far, that hadn't happened, but he wondered if the day was coming soon.

He'd seen the guy working the nightshift at this particular establishment, and Gavin had no reservations about this man's past as some kind of elite soldier.

With the curator on the second floor, Gavin knew it was time to move.

He pushed on the vent cover and quietly lowered it to the floor, leaning it against the wall to the side. Then he crawled out and onto the floor of the storage room. Stacks of bathrooms supplies lined the shelves to his left, while rows of cleaning agents and tools festooned the wall to the right.

Gavin turned the screen on his left wrist toward the door and illuminated the way out. He'd used night-vision goggles for certain jobs in the past, when the gig required it, but this wasn't one of those. When Laghari turned off all the main lights in the museum, floodlights still glowed at various points throughout the building.

Seeing wouldn't be an issue, unless the power was cut, in which case he had bigger fish to fry, but the odds of that happening were beyond slim. Even with the occasional power outages in the city recently, this museum boasted four backup generators, enough to keep the power flowing to the security system for several days with assistance from solar panels atop the roof.

He stopped at the door, glanced at the monitor on his left wrist to check the curator's position, then turned the doorknob and stepped out into the hallway. A floodlight glowed brightly straight ahead. He stood in a corner where the corridor made a ninety-degree turn and wrapped around the inner four exhibit rooms, laid out in a square pattern with paths leading between them.

Gavin pulled the blue Los Angeles Dodgers hat down over his forehead, though it wasn't because he was afraid of being recorded and recognized—it was what he did, every single job he took. Pulling the cap down was his way of saying, "It's game time. Let's do this." It symbolized focus to him and centered him on the task—the slightest slipup, the most minuscule miscalculation, could mean a long time behind bars.

He kept his eyes on the monitor of the floor below until he reached the archway leading into the exhibit where his prize waited.

The plan was simple: Pick up the idol and walk right out the back door where his car waited.

With control of the entire surveillance system, and the alarms, Gavin didn't run the risk of being seen, except potentially by the guard, but knowing where the man was, and when, meant that avoiding him would be easy enough.

He turned to the monitor on his wrist and tapped the red dot. It took weeks for him to get the code correct to hack into the system, but he'd managed, and now the reward would be lucrative.

The red dot turned green, and an audible click escaped the walls and the laser mounts fixed to the arch frame.

Gavin took a cylinder from a pocket on his left leg and pressed the button on the top. A fine mist sprayed out of the nozzle. He tucked the can back in his pocket and watched the artificial fog hover in the middle of the archway.

Had his little security hack not worked, he would have seen red beams across the opening. As he peered into the haze, he detected no sign of the lasers.

A grin slipped onto his face as he stepped into the exhibit room with his wide blue eyes fixed on the golden statue of Lord Mahavir.

He stopped short of the pedestal and looked around the room. It was a room he'd observed, studied, and analyzed for weeks, months even. While the average museumgoer wouldn't notice much apart from the exhibits, Gavin knew every crack in the walls, every detail down to how many times a week the carpet in the center was cleaned, or what kinds of drinks children spilled while visiting with their parents. He learned about the type of security system they used, the company that provided the security guards, and where the surveillance room housed the servers and backbone to the video system.

An intimate knowledge of the job was not just important; it was vital to success—and why so many other thieves ended up being caught in the act. He spared no expense of time, which was why Gavin knew he was one of the best in the business.

He reached into a black messenger bag and removed a black

device about the size and shape of a cigarette lighter. After attaching a clear suction cup, he pressed the device to the idol's glass case and pushed a button on the side. The sound of a tiny electric motor whirred just above a whisper as Gavin pulled the tool along the top edge of the glass, then down the right side, across the bottom, and then along the left edge to finish the cut.

A quick pull on the suction cup freed the square section of glass from the rest of the display case, and he lowered it to the floor without a sound.

Gavin straightened and leaned closer to the idol. He gazed at it like a hungry lion at a wounded gazelle. This would be one of the bigger prizes he'd managed to acquire, and while he already had a buyer in mind, he couldn't help but wonder if there might be someone else out there who would be willing to pay more.

He snapped his head and focused. Reaching into the display case, Gavin brushed his fingers across the golden statue. It felt warmer to the touch than he anticipated. Most of these kinds of relics were cold to the touch, at least the ones he'd stolen before.

Gavin swallowed. This moment of truth got to him every time. A combination of nerves and exhilaration coursed through his body as he lifted the heavy idol from its seat atop the pedestal.

He winced at the heft of the statue, and his arms strained to hold the weight. He'd picked up heavy items before, but gold caught him off guard every time, even after his extensive experience with moving the metal around. Gavin kept up a rigorous exercise regimen for just such occasions as this.

Quickly, he lowered the idol out of the case and set it on the floor. Then he took his messenger bag off his shoulder, set it next to the idol, and slipped the artifact into the bag. The task took less than fifteen seconds.

He glanced over at his cameras and noted that the woman was now in the second room of the same floor, running through the checklist as she always did.

Gotta love those type-A personalities, he thought.

Gavin looped the strap around his shoulder again and spun

around, ready to leave. He froze in place when he saw Priya Lighari standing ten feet away, and with a phone in her hand.

"I suppose you're wondering how I was able to make it look like I was still downstairs on the second floor," she demurred.

He didn't answer the question, but her assessment was spot on.

"You've been staking out this museum for the last few weeks," she continued. "Oh, don't give me that look. The disappointed expression, the baffled glaze in your eyes, the vein popping up on your neck. Did you really think I wouldn't notice?"

"Crossed my mind," Gavin snarled. He didn't care for weapons, especially firearms, but there were situations where having one came in handy, and right now was one of those times.

"Set the bag down," she said, keeping the phone near her shoulder with her body turned slightly, right hand at her hip.

"Look, lady, this thing is worth a lot of money to me. Now, if you let me go, I'll split the take with you. I already have a buyer." He motioned with his left hand as he spoke, to keep her distracted from the right that moved ever closer to the pistol concealed in his belt holster.

"You think me the kind of person to allow a thief to make off with a thousand-year-old piece of Indian culture, just to sell it to the highest bidder and split the profits?" she scoffed. "I don't think so, thief. I've already called the police. They're on their way. Before you reach the second floor, they will have the entire building surrounded. You have nowhere to go."

Gavin drew in a long breath and exhaled through his nostrils. His shoulders slumped and he bit his lower lip, feigning defeat. "Now, see? Why did you have to go and do a thing like that?"

With an abrupt twist of his right hand, he reached for his pistol.

2

Dak pulled the rickety motorcycle up to the sidewalk and stopped. He pushed out the kickstand and tilted the skinny bike over at an angle. Smoke trickled out of the motor, seeping from multiple seals. He looked down at the machine with a casual disregard, his green eyes flashing in the headlights of cars that passed by.

"What did you do to my motorcycle?" A man in a long maroon tunic and gray linen pants ran out of a shack that passed as a motorcycle rental office. The man held up his hands as he approached, shaking them at the sky as if the streaking clouds overhead would help him.

Dak glanced down at the bike again and shrugged. "That bullet hole was there when I picked it up this afternoon, Rith."

Rith ran bony fingers through black hair. The guy was as skinny as a lamppost. When he tilted and leaned, he almost looked like one of those whacky waving inflatable guys you see at...well, places that offer transportation. Dak had to work to keep from laughing at the gyrations Rith was making, along with the muffled sounds he kept inside while clenching his teeth.

It truly was a spectacular tantrum.

Dak prodded a little more. "And honestly, I don't know how you thought it was okay to loan me a bike with all those scratches. Just look at the smoke pouring out of this thing. That probably means it's burning some oil. If I were you, I'd be talking to whoever sold you this piece of crap."

"Idiot!" Rith finally managed. Then it all came in a word avalanche, spilling out of a cave atop a mountain. "How did you do this? My father is going to kill me! You know that, right? I'm a dead man. I can't believe you ruined this bike. We just got it last week, man." Rith slowed down to take a breath. Dak merely stood there, the setting sun warm on the back of his black Soundgarden shirt.

"You have other bikes," Dak said coolly, pointing around the gravel parking nook cut into the street corner. An assortment of similar motorcycles lined a rope that served as a fence around the closet-size lot. One "side" consisted entirely of mopeds.

Rith let out a word Dak hadn't heard before but was fairly certain to be some kind of profanity. "I can't believe you would do this to me."

"Take it easy, Rith," Dak soothed. "I'm just messing with you. Here." Dak extended his hand. He pinched a white envelope with thumb and forefinger.

Rith looked at it with suspicion, hesitant to take the envelope. "What's this?"

"That should cover the bike, and based on the quality of your inventory"—he panned the hodgepodge assortment of two-wheeled vehicles—"get you a few upgrades to boot."

The Cambodian narrowed his eyelids, still uncertain if he should take the envelope.

"Seriously, Rith. You should take this before someone else does. There's a butt load of money in there. Not a good idea to just let it hang like this."

That pushed Rith over the edge, and he snatched the envelope from Dak's hand.

"That's better." Dak extended a warning finger. "Don't flash it around out here, though. And definitely don't count it right now. Wait until you're out of sight. Okay?" He tilted his head forward, peering at his friend beneath the edge of his eyelids.

Rith nodded, though doubt still lingered in his eyes.

"You think there's not enough to cover it, don't you?" Dak put his hands on his hips, irritation spewing out of his lips with a sigh. "Seriously? You don't trust me?"

"You brought one of my bikes back, a bike I let you take for free, completely ruined."

"And I have given you the money to pay for it, and then some. Look, go into your little shack over there and count it if you don't believe me." Dak pointed at the "office" with an extended arm.

Rith considered it for a long few seconds, then cracked a smile. "I trust you, Dak," he said with a nod.

Dak's jaw let go, and his expression eased. "Good. That's more like it. Now, do you mind if we get some food? I'm starving."

The two picked a spot that served *lok lak*, a traditional stir-fried beef dish served with lettuce, sweet tomatoes, cucumber, and fresh onion, all topped with pepper and lime juice.

Dak went through two orders of the dish before he was done. He leaned back in a green metal chair and sipped a bottle of water.

"What happened to the motorcycle?" Rith asked. "And don't tell me it's none of my business. It's literally my business we're talking about."

"You mean your dad's business," Dak corrected, his words frosted with derision.

"You're so funny," Rith deflected the friendly insult.

Dak shrugged. "I was looking for someone. Things got ugly."

"What's that supposed to mean?" Rith forked a piece of beef and a slice of onion into his mouth and chewed.

"It means things got ugly," Dak repeated. "Your connection here in town wasn't exactly helpful. Your 'hot tip,'" Dak used air quotes, "led me straight into an ambush."

"So, they didn't help you find the man you were looking for?" Rith hovered over his plate.

"No. They didn't help me find him." Dak made no effort to conceal the sarcasm in his tone.

"You don't have to be rude."

"Well, sorry, but your connection nearly got me killed."

"But it didn't," Rith insisted.

"No. But it didn't bring me any closer to Tucker, either."

Rith took another bite and considered the statement as he chewed the juicy beef. "Well, I know that there was a man who came through here, an American. He looked just like the guy you described. So, if he's not here anymore, he must have left the country."

"You think?" Dak resisted rolling his eyes and instead took another drink of water.

He was tired, dirty, and frustrated. He'd received a tip that Tucker was on the move here in Cambodia and that he'd taken up residence in an apartment under a false name. That tip had led to more trouble than it was worth, and the man who tried to kill Dak—who was still trying to kill him—had slipped through his fingers.

"So, what are you going to do?"

Dak set the bottle back on the table but kept his hand on it, mindlessly thumbing the side. "I'll have to lay low for a bit, that's for sure."

"Where will you go?" Rith pressed, stabbing another piece of meat with his fork.

"Anywhere else, for the moment. Shame. Your food here has gotten much better since my previous visit." He winked at his friend.

"You didn't like the crickets? I thought you said they had a nice crunch." Rith pretended to be offended.

"Yeah, they did have a crunch to them. More of the nauseating kind. Do me a favor. Don't pitch that food to anyone in the States."

"Is that where you'll go next?" Rith diverted the conversation back on track.

"Maybe. I don't know, kid." Dak reached over and took another morsel from his friend's plate, popped in his mouth, and leaned back in the chair.

Rith didn't protest. How could he? He'd given in to the temptation and counted the money when he went to the bathroom. Dak was right; it was more than enough to buy a couple of brand-new bikes, maybe even fix up the old one that he'd damaged. The only problem now was getting it home safely—and to a bank the next day. Rith wasn't accustomed to carrying that kind of cash around, and he worried every second that someone was going to mug him and steal the envelope.

He'd managed to pass it off as paranoia. No one except his friend knew he had the cash. Other than that, Rith passed for any other middle-classer in Phnom Penh, perhaps lower-middle. His attire, his business, his economic circumstances—none of this helped him climb the caste ladder in anyone else's eyes, so he likely wasn't a target. That didn't keep him from checking his pocket every three minutes to make sure the money hadn't fallen out or somehow been pickpocketed without his knowledge.

"If I were Tucker, I'd be on the run right now, so I wouldn't have time to plan my next move. He's spooked, though. Even though he knew I was coming, and was already gone, he'll find out soon enough that his little plan fell through, and that the trap failed."

Rith considered what Dak said as he finished his meal in silence. When he was done, he picked up a bottle of beer he'd been sipping on and drank the rest of the contents. With a gratified exhale, Rith set the bottle back on the table, pausing as if pondering what to say next.

"Well, I feel bad, man. I can't help but feel like this is all partly my fault." Rith stared at the ground as he spoke.

"It is partly your fault," Dak laughed. "But no harm, no foul. You and I go back a long time, compadre. I don't think you'd try to set me up."

"The bounty on your head might put that to the test with some of your other friends."

Dak bobbed his head once. "Yeah, I know. I hope not, but it's possible. With that kind of reward out there, I'm surprised I haven't seen more mercs coming my way. The fact that Tucker has posted that kind of bounty shows that he has been skimming off the top for years. I don't have any way to prove it, but I know he was. You can't offer that kind of money for someone's head if you don't have at least eight figures locked away, maybe even nine." His voice matched his eyes, drifting, distant.

"I will keep my ears open, but I doubt I'll hear anything. I've never been in one of those secret, black market mercenary places you told me about."

"A nest? Yeah, probably best you never go in one."

"Yes, nest. Seems a funny name for a place to find underground soldiers." Rith glanced off toward the street, distracted for a second by the traffic, or perhaps by a woman's colorful dress fluttering in the wind.

"They're all over the world," Dak explained. "But you can't find them online or in the yellow pages. They keep it that way on purpose. Only people who have a connection in the network are allowed in. And if you go into one of those places without a verifiable connection, you won't walk out."

"Crazy to think about," Rith said, his eyes now fixed on the table.

Dak could see that his younger friend was imagining the seedy underground world that was Dak's playground. He meant what he said about Rith not going into one of those places. They would eat him alive before killing him. Fortunately, common folk like him wouldn't know the first place to start.

It took some effort for Dak to let go of the frustration pent up inside. He'd been so close to getting Tucker. Now the trail would go cold again, at least for a while. There would be, no doubt, another assassin coming his way. The word was out now, and Dak was a hot target.

He'd have to watch his back at all times and stay on the move. It was the way he'd lived for longer than he cared to remember. He'd slept in more strange places than he imagined possible, when he could find sleep. Unfortunately, with the anxiety of having a death mark on your head, getting decent rest came at a premium, and there was no way he'd start using one of those prescription sleep aids. While he needed to get a good night's rest, he also needed to be able to wake up at a moment's notice.

Those two necessities rarely coexisted.

"Well, I am always here if you need someone you can trust in Cambodia," Rith said. "And I will let you know if I hear anything else, but as you say, I suspect your enemies will have moved on by now."

Dak's mind lingered on the way Rith said "enemies" in the plural form. "Yeah, unless they're watching us right now." He let his eyes dart left and right, just to mess with Rith. The ploy worked, and his friend shifted uneasily in his chair.

"Yeah, could you not do that?" Rith stammered. "I already don't feel good about all this money in my pocket."

"Okay, I'll stop." Dak's easy grin disarmed his friend.

"You want a beer?" Rith asked, standing. "I'm going to the restroom, and then I'll grab a couple."

"No thanks," Dak said, raising a dismissive hand, "But thank you."

He watched Rith walk into the old building. The paint had crumbled in several spots and faded in most. He doubted the stability of the structure, in fact for many of the buildings in the city.

Phnom Penh had gone through a revival in recent years, opening up to tourists from around the world in an effort to erase the sins of past regimes, and to present their culture in a new light to the world.

Dak had enjoyed the visit, though the humidity reminded him of the Deep South back home, especially places like Charleston or the entire state of Louisiana.

He sat waiting for five minutes, then began to wonder how long it was going to take Rith to hit the john and grab a beer. At first, Dak regretted passing on the beer, but with each successive minute, he started wondering if something was wrong.

With an annoyed sigh, Dak pulled a wad of cash out of his pocket and slapped it down on the table. Then he walked into the restaurant through the same domed archway he'd seen Rith use.

Inside, a dozen tables were spread around the room. An elderly woman stood behind the counter to the room's rear. She waited behind a register, watching the room with disinterest behind wide-frame glasses that might have been twenty years old.

Dak frowned and strode toward the bathroom in a hall off to the right. He burst through the door and stepped into the empty room. He took in the scene in seconds. Two stalls straight ahead were empty, the doors hanging open. The stench of urine among other unpleasant smells filled the air, despite the creaking vent overhead doing all it could to usher the odors out into the open.

"Great," Dak muttered. "What did you do this time, Rith?"

He hurried back out the door and into the narrow corridor. There were two doors near the archway leading back into the eatery, but the hall stretched all the way to the back of the building, running parallel to the kitchen. Dim, flickering lights illuminated the corridor's pale blue tiles on the walls, and the concrete floor beneath.

Dak moved cautiously down the hall, his face blinking in and out of shadows with every electrical pulse from the erratic lights. He reached to his side for a pistol that wasn't there and remembered he didn't have a firearm at the moment.

He'd have to rectify that later.

He stopped at the end of the corridor where it veered right to a metal door. Dak looked at the seam between the frame and the door, noting it was unlocked. He didn't like going blindly out a back door, there was no telling what waited for him out there. One of his fears was that nothing was beyond the door, and that Rith had been secreted away to be beaten and robbed.

Dak reached out and grasped the door handle, then pulled.

The bright light pierced the opening into the building, and he winced for a second. His eyes adjusted faster than he'd anticipated, and he moved out into the open air.

The stench of garbage from two overflowing dumpsters to the left filled his nostrils. Dak wrinkled his nose at the odor but stayed focused. Voices joined the sights and smells. They were close. Just on the other side of the dumpsters, around the back of the building.

He took in the surroundings in a second, noting the alley stopped at the side of another building before veering off toward the main road. It was a haphazard design, but he wasn't here to judge the efficiency of the local infrastructure.

Dak tiptoed over to the corner and stopped, pressing his shoulder to the wall.

"Where did you get this money, Rith?" The male voice sneered the question, its tone thin and weaselly.

"You already have the money," Rith spat back, blood trickling from his lips. "Just take it."

"Don't tell me what to do, Rith. Your dad's a bad gambler. That's not our fault. This covers half of what he owes Mr. Lin."

"Half?" Rith complained. "He only owed ten. There's more than ten in there."

Dak peeked around the corner. The one doing all the talking shook his head. He wore a retro jacket that shimmered in an almost offensively bright green with the word *Lucky* on the back of it. Two others stood close by, in T-shirts and trousers.

For a split second, Dak wondered why the leader of the goons would be wearing a jacket in this appalling humidity. Cambodia featured both dry and wet seasons, and the latter happened to be going on at the time. He imagined the guy had to be hot in that thing and couldn't understand what sort of fashion statement the thug was trying to make.

"The leader shook his head vehemently. "No, Rith. You're forgetting about the juice. It's been running for months now on that ten. Now it's twenty."

"Come on, Ti. There's no way the juice doubled the amount."

"What did you just say to me?" The one named Ti took a menacing step toward Rith and brandished a long knife.

Rith inclined his head, his lips trembling for lack of a response.

Dak had seen enough.

He stepped out from behind the corner, staggering to his right at an angle. "Hey," he slurred. "Keep it down out here."

Dak made a show of tripping, then stumbling forward toward the harassers.

The leader spun around, at first sensing a threat but quickly tossing aside his concerns when he realized the man who'd interrupted them was drunk.

"Look at the drunk American," Ti said, pointing his knife at the newcomer. "Thought you could handle the beer here?"

Dak raised a finger, wagging it in the air from side to side. "Now, just hold on. I've had more than just beer, thank you very much. And I have to say that I am most impressed with the effects of all of it."

Ti laughed, glancing at his buddies or henchmen or whatever they were.

"Hey," one of them said in a whisper to Ti. "Let's see what he's got."

"Yeah," Ti agreed. "Hey, American."

"That's me!" Dak said, raising both fists to the sky as if he'd won some contest.

"Yes, that's you. If you think those drinks were good, wait until you taste the private stock." Ti lowered his blade as he approached Dak.

"Wow," Dak exclaimed, pointing at the weapon. "That is one long knife." He chuckled stupidly. "Remember that scene from the movie *Crocodile Dundee*? That's not a knife." He belly laughed. "I love that movie."

The three men approached him as they might a cornered badger.

"Never saw it," Ti said as he stopped close to Dak and put his hand on the American's shoulder to steady him. "But this is most definitely a knife. And now you're going to give us all your money."

Dak stuck out his lower lip and nodded. "Hey, if it's for the private stock or whatever you called it, I'm in."

Ti cast a glance over at his friend, unbelieving of how stupid this guy was.

Dak reached in his pocket then pulled out a fist. "Sorry, this is all I got." With a snap, and a pop, Dak drove his fist square into Ti's nose.

The leader stumbled back onto his rear, grabbing at his nose while dropping the knife. At first, his two associates glanced at each other in shock. Their surprise quickly vanished, and they attacked the interloper at the same time.

Dak stepped back, grabbed the two by the shoulders, and used their momentum to crash them into each other. Then Dak wrapped his fingers around the backs of their necks and smashed their heads together.

The two staggered and fell to the ground, dazed.

"You broke my nose, man!" Ti shouted. His fingers over his nose were covered in blood, and his eyes filled with fury. "You're gonna die, man." He added in a few obscenities with the threat.

"I don't want to kill you and your friends," Dak said, standing his ground. "I've done enough killing for one day, for one month. So, I'm going to make this easy for you. Give my friend his money back, and I'll settle his father's gambling debt. You three get to walk home with your money, and any shred of dignity you might have left."

He cast scathing glares at all three of the hoodlums, his green eyes flashing in the sunlight like some otherworldly being. "Or...we can do this the hard way. And I can't promise that none of you will die."

The three glanced at each other, as if considering the options.

Dak knew if he killed the three men, there would be trouble. Not for him, per se, but for Rith. It would only be a matter of time before Ti's father came looking for his son. The first place the father would look would be the last location Ti had visited. Which would lead him straight to Rith. After that, things would get messy.

That was something Dak couldn't allow to happen. Rith would be killed, along with his father, who, from the sound of it, maybe needed to get his butt kicked a few times to learn a lesson. That wasn't Dak's call to make. Then again, Dak would do what he had to do. It wasn't up to him.

Right now, the decision was in the hands of the three thugs. Dak hoped they would take his offer and walk. From the look in their eyes, though, he didn't think that was going to be their decision.

"I don't think you know who you're talking to," Ti said. "You're already dead. And your little friend here, too."

He motioned with a casual wave toward Rith, who cowered off to the side, still watching and wondering what was going to happen next.

"Don't be stupid," Dak said. "You're young. You have a lot of life to live. A lot of people to rip off. The three of you should just go about your day and let sleeping dogs lie. Take the easy way out, boys. Because the hard way is going to hurt."

Ti narrowed his eyes at the brazen American spitting threats at him and his two associates. Dak could already see in the man's eyes that the decision was already made. This was going to complicate things.

The leader held out the knife, turning his body at an angle. The other two retreated back a step and then also took up defensive stances.

Dak rolled his eyes and let out an exasperated sigh. "Looks like you want to do things the hard way. That's a shame. I've got places to be and I really don't have time for this."

"The only place you're going to be is dead," Ti replied.

"That's not really a place," Dak quipped. "More of a state of exis-
tence. Or the absence of it, rather."

"Shut up," one of the others said from Dak's right.

The men were closing in now, and he knew that the time for talk
was nearing an end. Dak stole a look at his friend behind the leader,
knowing that Rith would be no help in this scenario, unless the
gangly man somehow mustered the courage to step in and lend some
aid in the fight. That, Dak knew, was unlikely.

"Fine," Dak said. "Let's do this. I'll try to make sure none of you
die."

Ti snarled and surged forward, brandishing his blade. The other
two drew smaller knives and flashed them threateningly at the
American.

The leader's attack was sloppy, as Dak expected. These men were
untrained, save for a few random hours they might spend at the gym
each week. They weren't hardened by battle or expert trainers. They
were bullies, plain and simple. They preyed on the weak and felt
emboldened by their power. Now, they'd been smacked in the face.
And bullies didn't know how to react when they were punished.
Usually, it only made them angrier.

Ti stabbed with the tip of his knife, while the guy to Dak's left
stepped forward.

"Careful," Dak warned as he deflected the jab and turned his
body. "Those things are sharp." He twisted around while grabbing
Ti's wrist and used the man's momentum to shove him at the guy to
Dak's right. The knife tip sank deep into the man's gut, and he looked
up with fear in his eyes at the sudden realization that his friend had
probably just killed him.

Ti met his associate's terrified gaze with one of his own. He wasn't
sure if he should pull out the knife or keep it in.

Meanwhile, the other thug lurched forward clumsily. He swiped
and slashed his weapon at the American, but Dak easily dodged the
attacks. These men were no match for a seasoned, battle-hardened

soldier. Dak had seen worse than these three had to offer on his best days in the Middle East.

He sidestepped to the left and stuck out his right foot, tripping the attacker as he lunged forward. The goon stumbled facefirst onto the pavement, the knife in his hand flipping upward and stabbing him in the side as he tumbled over it.

The guy grunted in pain, then writhed on the ground, helpless.

"You think maybe you guys should give up?" Dak asked, his voice sincere with the question. "Or do you want me to go ahead and finish the job?" He looked at the knife sticking out of the leader's friend and pointed at it. "You might want to let the doctors remove that. He could bleed out if you don't."

"Shut up!" Ti shouted.

He turned and launched another attack, this time with his fists and feet. The flurry was fast, Dak had to give him that. Ti had at least paid a little attention in martial arts class, though his form still held much to be desired.

Dak blocked the punches, chops, kicks, and grapple attempts with relative ease. If it hadn't been for the humidity during this part of the rainy season, he wouldn't have even broken a sweat.

Ti, on the other hand, gasped for air. Dak detected the scent of tobacco on his breath and knew the man's smoking habit wasn't doing him any favors.

Then, when the attacks began to slow, Dak finally stopped messing with the group's leader.

Grabbing a fist out of the air, Dak twisted the man's forearm and jerked it down, cracking it over his knee in one swift move. Ti yelped in pain, but still thought it a good idea to throw another punch. Again, Dak snatched the fist, turned it over so the palm faced up, then paused to look at his opponent with a disparaging expression.

"You see," he said. "I would have thought you'd learn the first time. Why, when I just clearly broke your arm, would you be stupid enough to throw another dumb punch like that? Seriously?"

Water brimmed the edges of the enemy's eyes. Ti couldn't help it.

He didn't want to cry, but the anguish took over his impulses, his natural reactions, and squeezed his tear ducts like lemons.

Dak jerked him forward and snapped the elbow over his shoulder, then kicked the screaming man on the tailbone, sending him sprawling to the ground with both arms flopping limply around as if they were made of rubber.

The one with the knife in his gut clutched at the weapon, still unsure if he should remove it. He stared at the blood oozing from the wound, coating his fingers with the sticky substance. His face paled at the sight, and Dak knew the young man was going into shock.

"Leave that in," Dak said. "Call an ambulance. Let them deal with it. I wasn't joking when I said you might bleed out."

The guy looked up at the American, his eyes full of fear. He nodded weakly.

Then Dak walked over to where Ti writhed on the ground and flipped him over despite the wounded man's protests.

"Now, are you going to bother my friend over there and his father again? Or am I going to have to make things worse?" Dak only paused a second, not giving Ti a chance to respond. "Because if I have to come back here," Dak continued, "I am going to kill you, your family, and burn everything you own to the ground. I will erase you from the memory of Earth's history. And you know what? The people of Phnom Penh will thank me for it. You won't be missed. Sure, some other corrupt gang will rise up from the ashes and pick up your banner, but you won't see it because you'll be dead."

Dak straightened up and put his boot on Ti's neck. "You gonna say something or just lie there in agony?"

Ti shook his head rapidly.

"Does that mean you're going to leave Rith and his family alone?" Dak clarified.

A nod from under his boot confirmed the answer.

"Good. Now, what was it his father owed you, minus the vig?"

He didn't have to tell the goon what he meant by that. The terms vig, juice, and interest, were all interlinked in the underground. Loan sharks from all nationalities knew those words as part of their everyday vocabulary.

"Ten," Ti muttered, his lips trembling.

"That's what I thought." Dak reached into his left pocket and fished out a wad of cash. "This is your lucky day, other than the broken appendages." He indicated the leader's impotent arms lying limp on the blacktop next to him.

The American counted out ten thousand, then dropped the folded bills onto Ti's chest. "That's ten. Now, you and your friends go get some medical attention. Tell your dad you had an accident or something, but don't tell him you saw me or that you bothered Rith. Tell him you got what was owed to you, and that's it." He leaned down once more, locking eyes with his prey like a hawk pinning a rabbit with its talons. "And remember, if you disobey me, I will know. And your entire organization will die in such a way that it will make today seem like a trip to the candy store."

Dak took his foot off the man's throat, turned, and walked over to Rith, who no longer trembled but instead stood alone along the side of the alley, watching with rapt disbelief, and maybe a dash of horror at what he'd just seen.

"You okay?" Dak asked with an upward nod.

Rith stared beyond his friend at the three wounded assailants.

"Hey," Dak pressed. "Don't worry about them. They're not going to bother you anymore. Or your family. Your dad is probably going to have to find a new bookie, though."

The two walked out of the alley and onto the sidewalk. Rith repeatedly touched his lips to see if they were still bleeding and to test the tenderness where the bottom lip swelled.

"They didn't hurt you, like really hurt you?"

Rith shook his head. "Just a normal beating. Nothing too bad. I'll live."

"A normal beating?" Dak asked with a half laugh.

They turned left and kept walking away from the scene. For Dak, the movement was intentional. Rith merely followed along. In Dak's mind, his threats were mostly just that—threats. But he'd learned a long time ago that a threat, if good enough, could serve as powerful warning to bullies who thought they were stronger than they truly were.

Still, he meant what he said. "If they ever bother you again, Rith, you tell me, and I'll handle it. Okay?"

Rith looked over at his friend and nodded. "I will."

"Hopefully, that won't happen. Heaven knows I have enough to deal with. I don't need some local upstart loan shark on my tail. Until today, Cambodia was one of the few places I thought I could hide out. Looks like I need a new plan."

"Where will you go?" Rith asked.

Dak felt the phone in his pocket vibrate. The feeling startled him at first, probably more to do with the adrenaline still pulsing through his veins than actual surprise.

He looked at the device and noted the name on the screen, "BM."

Rith stole a glance at the screen. "Are you friends with Bill Murray?" His eyes widened at the possibility. "I've always been such a big fan of his."

Dak scowled at the insinuation, then the frown broke into a laugh-filled grin. "No, my friend. I have no connection to Bill Murray. This is someone else. And unless I miss my guess, I bet they have somewhere for me to go."

4

Priya stared at the thief through a chain-link fence dividing an old living room in two. The thief sat on the other side, on a bed, with a phone in his hand, pressed to his ear.

Her muscles ached, especially on the upper left of her back. She felt like she'd been beaten up, or in a car accident.

Sounds of the countryside filled the minuscule home. Birds chirped. A breeze blew across the eaves and windowsills with a gentle whistle. The smell of onions, tandoori spices, and roasting chicken wafted through the air.

She watched as the thief spoke on his phone, her eyes constantly probing, ears listening, aware of everything going on around her.

"I need to speak to the buyer," Gavin said. "I don't care if he's busy; just get him. Okay? The terms have changed. You hear me? You tell him I said the terms have changed."

He paused for a few seconds to listen to the response, then his face reddened. He ran fingers through his blond hair, shaking his head. "No, you don't understand, man. The terms have changed. Things are a little—" Gavin looked over at Priya, who still watched him with loathing in her eyes—"complicated," he finished.

She crossed her arms, flames burning in her eyes. Priya was

strong; she always had been. Growing up the youngest of six kids had taught her to fight for survival. And she'd succeeded, becoming a respected and successful member of the antiquities and historical communities before she turned thirty. Now, in her early thirties, she ran a highly respected museum in Mumbai. She held a great sense of pride in that.

Now she was here with this scumbag, and for the moment, there was no getting out of the situation.

"Look," Gavin blurted, "I don't care what he's doing. The terms of the agreement have changed. Got it? Just get him on the phone with me immediately."

Priya heard a muted voice coming through the earpiece, but she couldn't make out what the person was saying.

"Fine. You just make sure he calls me back as soon as he can." Gavin cast a fiery glare through the fence at the woman. "I don't want things to get messy here. You understand? And things are going to get messy if you don't get me on the phone with him as soon as possible."

He listened for ten seconds to a reply, and his face darkened. "You think I can't find another buyer for that thing? I can make three phone calls right now and have someone ready with cash in hand tonight. No, you know what? The price just went up. Let that sink in. Okay?" He swore before continuing. "You get me the buyer, or I am taking this item elsewhere. You hear me? I will do it."

More muted words escaped the device speaker.

"That's better. Get him to call me today before midnight, or I walk. I'm not even sure why I'm bothering with the likes of you. This is bush league he's even making me talk to one of his underlings. Do you have any idea who I am?"

Gavin held the phone in front of his face to finish the conversation. "If your boss wants this piece, he is going to pay the price I want. Not the one he wants. Got it?"

He pressed the red button on the screen and ended the call. He stewed for a minute, his chest rising and falling with rapid breaths. This situation was out of control, and there wasn't much he could do about it.

"Doesn't sound like the call went too well," Priya prodded. She inclined her head, letting the barb set.

Gavin flung an expletive at her.

She arched one eyebrow, unaffected by the word.

"Sooner or later, someone is going to come looking for me, thief. And when they do, you're going to be out of time." She crossed her arms and cocked her head to the side, peering down at him as she would a caged animal. "I don't think I have to tell you what they will do to you. The authorities here, they are...how should I say? Aggressive. Especially when it comes to dealing with known criminals, and even more so when it comes to thugs like you. They are particularly hard on kidnappers."

He narrowed his eyes, desperately wishing he could consume her with lasers or fireballs or bolts of lightning from them. All he could do was stare helplessly into her dark brown eyes and hope he could figure out how to handle this without getting arrested, or worse.

Gavin looked down at his phone again and thought hard, desperately trying to figure out another name he could call, another contact. But this was a burner phone. He'd only memorized the number of the one buyer. For all his bravado on the call, he didn't have another potential buyer he could hit up for a cool seven figures. This job had gone wrong in a number of ways, and it was getting worse.

The cops were looking for Priya Laghari by now, and if they weren't, they would be by morning. That much he knew. Most countries took their time with missing persons reports, often having a minimum numbers of hours they would wait before beginning a search. So, perhaps he had a little time on his hands, but he couldn't afford to count on that. He needed the buyer to make the pickup and take this problem off his hands.

Try as he might, Gavin couldn't think of a scenario where things worked out that way. He sighed and laid his head back on a couch pillow, then closed his eyes and tried to think. There had to be an answer. He simply needed to find it.

Dak stepped out of the cab as the bright rays of early morning sunlight sprayed onto his face.

It had been a while since he'd visited India, and that was during a vacation Nicole wanted to take. She had a thing for Indian food and culture, loved the saris the women wore, how lavish and beautiful so many of the weddings looked, and how friendly many of the people were.

Dak had opposed the idea, instead wanting to visit an island, or perhaps a place in the mountains somewhere, anywhere, so he could get away from people. Instead, she dragged him into visiting one of the most populous nations in the world.

He half smiled at the thought, the memories of that vacation rippling through his mind like the breeze from passing traffic through his hair.

The smell of exhaust filled his nostrils, mixing with a few other scents that he couldn't immediately identify. Food, one was definitely food of some kind, though it was difficult to tell what it was. One thing he knew for certain: there were onions and cumin involved.

He stood in front of the Mumbai Antiquities Museum, taking in the building's three-story façade.

The day before, Boston had called while Dak was still in Cambodia. The brief conversation gave Dak both another relic's disappearance to investigate and an excuse to get out of Phnom Penh. He was glad for both. Things had rapidly heated up while he was there, and the combination of Tucker's bounty hunters and Rith's father's gambling problem weren't going to make things any easier.

Not that *this* was easier.

He recalled the mission for the tenth time since taking the call from his young employer. A thief had broken into this museum, stolen a highly valuable idol from an exhibit, and somehow managed to kidnap the curator at the same time.

Dak wondered how the thief had done it, especially the part where they escaped with a hostage. From what Boston told him, the alarms didn't go off, and the security guard on duty had seen nothing suspicious until he checked the top floor and discovered one of the exhibit cases broken and empty.

Dak had argued that this wasn't really the kind of thing he'd signed on for, especially since the artifact in question had a legitimate, known owner. He understood Boston donated certain relics to charities, or to appropriate historical societies, but that didn't seem like a good use for the money he paid Dak, which was not insignificant per job.

Boston assured his employee that he would be compensated, perhaps even receive a reward from the Indian government for his assistance.

That, Dak knew, was a stretch. Despite assurances that the local authorities would assist him in any way possible, he remained dubious about the whole thing. Still, with pay or without, a woman had been kidnapped, and Dak felt like he might be able to help.

He walked inside through the center of three matching bronze doors, then a second, before entering the lobby.

Long, cube-shaped, orange fabric lanterns hung in a single row down the center of the high-ceilinged room. A young man in a navy blue vest and a maize tie stood behind a white marble information counter to the right.

Dak looked up at the three walkways visible from the ground floor. Each circled around the lobby, allowing visitors to look down at the entrance from the top floor.

The guy at the information desk cleared his throat. "May I help you, sir?" he asked in a distinct English accent.

Dak snapped out of his daze and walked over to the counter. "Yes. I'm here to see a Mr. Reddy?"

"You mean, Dr. Reddy?"

Resisting the urge to roll his eyes, Dak nodded instead. "Yes. Dr. Reddy. Is he here?"

"He's in his office at the end of the hallway on the left." The young man pointed his long, tanned finger in the prescribed direction. "Who should I tell him is here to visit?"

"Just tell him the American he was told about is here to help."

The receptionist's forehead wrinkled and his eyebrows drooped slightly. "Help with what?"

"He'll know. Just tell him. Or not. I'm going to his office either way."

Dak turned and started toward the corridor the worker had suggested. He imagined the guy was offended or bothered by his brutish encounter. No doubt, the man would go home and tell his friends about a rude American he'd met that day.

Dak didn't care. He was there to do a job, and he didn't have time for formalities or pleasantries.

When he was on the phone with Boston, Dak asked why the IAA wasn't getting involved with this matter. Boston explained that he'd called Tommy and Sean, but they were investigating something else in another part of the world, and Tara and Alex were likewise out in the field on what the boy could only describe as some sort of secret mission.

Dak wasn't sure what that meant, but he didn't spend any time worrying about it. The International Archaeological Agency and their Paranormal Archaeology Division often ended up in strange, and dangerous, situations. There was no telling where those people were in the world, but Dak was pretty sure there would be trouble involved.

He heard the desk worker speaking in hushed tones as he entered the hallway on the left of the lobby. Continuing down the passage, he passed two labs, a storage room, and eventually stopped at the door to a corner office.

A placard on the door proclaimed it to be the office of Dr. Amar Reddy, PhD, and Director of Antiquities Acquisition.

Dak raised a fist to knock on the door, but the knob turned and opened, leaving his arm up in an awkward position as a skinny man with receding black hair opened the door. He stood nearly as tall as Dak, perhaps only an inch shorter, and while Dak knew the man had to be his senior, typical signs of aging didn't wear on the man's face, particularly around his eyes. Dr. Reddy stared back at the visitor, taking only a second to figure out who it was. He lowered his glasses with his index finger, as if giving one last assessment of the American.

"Dak Harper?" Reddy asked.

Usually, Dak would respond with something like a "Who's asking" or "Depends on what you want," but in this case, he merely said, "I hear you have a problem."

"Yes. Very bad. Please. Come in. I've been expecting you."

Reddy stepped out of the way and allowed Dak to enter before closing the door behind him.

"Thank you for coming on such short notice," Reddy began. He made his way around an L-shaped, black, wooden desk and sat down in his matching chair.

"Not a problem. I was in the area."

"Oh?" Reddy steepled his fingers and crossed one leg over the other knee. "Where?"

"Couple of countries over. No big deal." Dak helped himself to a seat across from the man and ran a quick scan of the room. Bookshelves behind the guest seats displayed books on archaeology, ancient history, Indian religions, and wars. Pictures of Reddy with his wife and children also littered the desktop and walls. Three degrees hung in gilded frames on the wall next to the window.

"Which one?"

"Look, Dr. Reddy, I don't mean to come off as rude, but I'm not here to talk about where I was yesterday, or last week. I wasn't playing golf or sipping rum cacao on the beach. I'd prefer it if I keep my business to myself."

The host pursed his lips together and shook his head once. "No offense taken. I can understand a man of your skills and reputation would prefer to keep certain things out of public discussion."

"Thank you."

"You're welcome." Reddy turned to the computer and clicked on the mouse. The monitor bloomed to life and a picture of an attractive Indian woman popped up in the center. She smiled with bright white teeth, head tilted slightly at an angle, with long blackish-brown hair splashing over her shoulders.

"She's beautiful," Dak remarked. "Is she the one who went missing?"

"Yes. That is Dr. Priya Laghari. She disappeared last night. The police have been here all morning, asking questions, even trying to figure out if I had something to do with her disappearance. I assure you I did not."

"Okay."

"I saw her before she started her routine yesterday evening. She goes through the same process every day before locking up for the night. Very meticulous, that one. It's one of the reasons I brought her on. I could tell she would be an asset to this museum, and I haven't been proved wrong. Now, I fear by bringing her here I'm somewhat to blame for her kidnapping."

Dak breathed calmly, taking in the information as Dr. Reddy spoke. The host paused to take a drink from a bottle of water. It was easy to see the man was upset. Dak had seen people faking emotion before, but this guy was sincere. Nothing about his body language showed otherwise.

"It's not your fault, Dr. Reddy," Dak said, softening his tone. "You had no way of knowing something like this might happen. Perhaps, if you tell me exactly what went down, that could help me help you."

Reddy agreed with a nod and set the bottle down. "Yes, of course." He swiveled his chair around and pointed it at the monitor once more. With a click, the image on the screen changed, showing a glass display case with a golden idol inside. "This is the artifact that was taken last night. It's a thousand years old and comes from the Jain religion. It is one of their twenty-four deities."

Dak briefly considered asking if it should be in a temple instead of a museum, but he kept his lips sealed and let Reddy continue.

The image on the screen changed and displayed the broken exhibit case, minus the statue.

Leaning forward, Dak peered at the screen with eyelids narrowed. "Looks like a clean cut. Someone would have to use a diamond cutter, or maybe a laser for that kind of precision, and to cut through that particular glass."

"Yes, that is what we also assumed."

"How did they get into the museum in the first place?"

Reddy raised both eyebrows and shrugged. "We don't know. In a strange way, it's fortunate that this was a burglary on top of the abduction. Despite telling me that we needed to wait a little longer to make sure Priya wasn't simply passed out drunk in her home, or staying at a friend's, the police are on the hunt for both the idol and our beloved curator. Frankly, it's been emotional and frustrating."

"I can see why," Dak said, scooting the chair closer to the desk. The fact that Reddy led with the missing woman, and not the multi-million-dollar idol, went a long way in proving his innocence to the American, though Dak didn't voice that. If Reddy were feeding him information that could help, it was best to let him finish and not stir a pot that already had a lid on it. "Do you have any suspects in mind?"

Reddy shook his head, his lips frozen. "No. Not that I can think of. Sure, there are a few people who have access to this museum at all times, but no one I would believe to be capable of this. The police have already spoken to them. They're handling what they can."

"I'm not sure how I can help. I don't necessarily have jurisdiction here, or anywhere else. I'm not a cop."

"I am aware you aren't, Mr. Harper." Dak let the reference to his father slide. "I have also been told by Mr. Schultz and Mr. Wyatt that you are more than capable of assisting with a matter such as this. Not to mention, our young friend thinks very highly of you."

Dak pressed his lips together as he bobbed his head, feeling his cheeks burn ever so slightly.

"I appreciate the references, but I don't want to step on the cops' toes."

"You won't," Reddy reassured. "I have explained to the police that we have brought in someone who specializes in locating stolen artifacts."

Not exactly accurate, but sure, whatever.

Reddy went on. "They will not get in your way. Just as I assume you won't get in theirs."

"I'll do my best to stay clear," Dak said. "Usually, I'm not around too many cops. So, it shouldn't be a problem."

"Good. Is there anything else I can do for you?"

Dak tilted his head to the side. "I'd like to see inside the exhibit if that's okay. I figured the crime scene units would be out by now."

"Certainly. It's still taped off, but they've concluded their initial investigation."

Reddy and Dak took the stairs up to the third floor. Despite his conditioning, Dak felt himself breathing heavily at the top, while the older man seemed to experience no strain at all.

"If you don't mind me asking," Dak said as they walked from the stairs to the room with police tape surrounding it, "how old are you? You seem to be in great shape, but you've been at this job for a while now, based on the stuff I saw in your office."

Reddy smiled over his shoulder at his guest. "I'm seventy-two," he admitted. "Diet, exercise, and no stress. Those are the secrets to longevity and good health, my friend."

"Huh," Dak whispered. "Well, it seems to be working."

"Thank you." Reddy stopped short of the tape and lifted it so Dak could enter the exhibit room, then joined the American. "This is where the statue was kept." He pointed at the empty case in the center of the room. The glass hole in the front remained unpatched.

Dak drew close to the display case. He hinged his hips and leaned down, inspecting every inch of the cut in the glass. "Yeah, this is no ordinary thief," he said. "They knew exactly what they were doing." He straightened, rounding on the director. "You said no alarms went off?"

"That is correct," Reddy confirmed. He folded his hands in front of his waist, watching as Dak meticulously circled the room.

"I'm no investigator," Dak confessed, stopping next to a small golden statue in the corner. Its four hands and twisting body struck him as elegant and mysterious, almost mesmerizing. "But if your alarm didn't go off, and you don't have any footage of the heist"—he motioned to the cameras in the upper corners—"then it was an inside job." Reddy stiffened, ready to refute the claim, but Dak kept going before the man could speak. "That doesn't mean it was one of your people. It's possible that someone hacked the system."

Dak wandered over to the archway to his right. The opening led back into the hall where the visitors could continue their tour through the museum. He stopped and studied the laser panels where the beams fired across to the receivers on the opposite side of the entrance.

"Would have had to kill these, too, I guess," he added, indicating the panels. "That...or he had the ability to shrink himself."

Reddy arched an eyebrow at the comment.

"I'm kidding. Obviously, he had access to the security system. I'm not a thief—never really been involved in trying to catch them, either —but if I were planning a job this big, I would spend a long time working out the details. I mean all the little stuff. I wouldn't let anything go to chance."

"What kind of time frame are you thinking?"

Dak rolled his shoulders, his tone lifting slightly. "Not sure. Maybe weeks. Possibly even months. Whoever this thief is, he was good enough to slip by all of your security systems and kidnap your curator at the same time. If I didn't know better, I'd say it was more than one person. I don't see how a single thief could pull this off, not alone."

Reddy considered the theory silently, raising his thumb and forefinger to his chin. He rubbed his jaw for several seconds, staring at no particular part of the floor as he thought.

An idea emerged in Dak's head, though he wasn't sure he wanted to put that much time into this, only to fail. Chasing fruitless paths in a situation like this, where time was of the essence, could mean the difference between life and death. If it were just a robbery, he'd still want to work quickly, but in the end, it was a statue. An important part of spiritual culture, and history, but it wasn't a human life.

He scratched the back of his neck. "So, I have an idea. At first, I thought maybe it would take too long, but there's a chance we could cut down on the time."

"Time for what?" Reddy asked.

"Is there a chance I could have a look at your video footage?"

"Certainly," Reddy raised his palms for a second then let them drop. "Our records go back ninety days before they're transferred to an external server."

Ninety days was more than enough. "Perfect. Show me to the control room."

6

Dak sat down at the wide desk in the video surveillance room. He scanned the twelve monitors directly in front of him and then the additional four to the left. The center screens displayed every angle of the exhibit rooms throughout the museum, each divided into four squares.

He knew that looking through the footage would take more hours than he cared to spend merely watching with a bucket of popcorn and a Coke. Hardly must-see TV. There was, however, a better way to find what he was looking for.

"What is it you hope to find?" Reddy asked, standing close behind Dak's right shoulder.

Dak didn't like how close the man hovered, but he didn't want to be rude, so he kept it to himself. Personal space was one of those things Dak tried to respect, and wanted to others to respect as well—though in a country with around a billion people, it could be difficult to achieve.

"A thief this good would have visited the museum multiple times leading up to the heist. They would have known every nook, every corner of the building, like the back of a napkin with a gorgeous woman's number written on it."

Reddy's forehead wrinkled in confusion at the metaphor, but he said nothing.

"Anyway," Dak continued, "we need to export the footage from," he paused to think of a random number, "the last thirty to sixty days."

"That will take time. Where are you exporting it, or more importantly, to whom are you sending that footage?"

"I have a friend who is good with these kinds of things. He'll have access to facial recognition software. I'm going to assume that our thief was in a disguise. Even so, if he or she visited here multiple times, as I suspect, then they would have likely been seen by your cameras. From there, we might be able to get some details about their bone structure, hair color, skin tone, stuff like that. It's worth a shot. Plus, I'm sure Will isn't doing anything."

"Will?"

Dak smirked, still staring at the screens as people meandered through the exhibits, taking in the sights.

"My friend with the software."

"How long do you think that will take?" Reddy pressed.

"Hard to say," Dak admitted, crossing his arms. "But that's only one part of the puzzle."

He turned to the white-shirted security guard who'd been standing off to the side listening to the conversation.

"Can you tell me if there's a feed covering any maintenance access points, back doors, closets, supply rooms, that sort of thing?"

"Certainly," the guard said with a nod. "Right here."

The man stepped to the desk, rested his hand on the mouse, and shifted it around. He clicked a couple of times, and the screen in the center of the lowest row changed.

"These are all the ways in and out of the building," the guard clarified. His hand shifted again, and with another click, the screen to the right switched to a different view. "These are the closets and maintenance rooms you mentioned." After another quick few slides of the mouse, he clicked it again and brought up a new feed on the screen to the far left. "You'll find the other things here such as break room, bathrooms, the rest."

"All these feeds go back ninety days?" Dak asked, looking up at the man.

The guard sported a thin black mustache that matched his swept-over hair. "Yes. All the feeds are saved for ninety days before we archive them."

"How many people do you have working security here?"

"Only one per shift," Reddy answered. "We rely heavily on the advanced security system."

Dak decided not to point out that catastrophic failure.

"And," the security guard added, "we have a rotation of five guards working the shifts. It gives everyone a couple of days off each week. And it keeps us from being short if someone calls in sick."

"You sound like you enjoy working here," Dak said.

"It's good work in this business. Dr. Reddy and Dr. Laghari treat us well and pay us fairly. Normally, the job is pretty easy." Guilt fluttered in his voice.

"Were you the one here the night of the break-in?"

"No," the guard shook his head. "That was Devong. He's really good, sir. I don't think he had anything to do with it. I would stake my reputation on it."

"I never said he did," Dak reassured. "I'm just trying to figure out the setup here. With one guard on duty and the cameras watching everything, if our thief came in ahead of time, that would mean they must have hidden out in the building the day of the crime."

Reddy wondered at the statement. "What do you mean?"

Dak stood up and stretched, cracking his neck from side to side. "I'm saying that whoever did this came in during regular business hours then hid somewhere until operating hours ended." He whirled to face Reddy. "You said Dr. Laghari had a specific routine, one that she always used."

"Yes," the director's head bobbed once. "She never wavered from it, not that I know."

"She didn't," the guard confirmed. "I watched her go through that same routine every night I was on duty."

"That...sounded a little creepy, but let's keep moving." Dak ignored the guard shift uncomfortably. "If a thief knew about her routine, they could have monitored her every move, getting their timing down to the second. Did she start on the top floor?"

"Yes," the two men said at once.

"That's how I would do it, too. Start at the top and work your way down. Easier to go downhill. So, as soon as the thief knew she was done with the top floor, she would descend to the second, and the burglar could go into the exhibit room without detection."

"Yes, except for the lasers," the guard argued.

"The ones that didn't go off?"

The guard nodded. "Yes," he said, humiliation filling his tone.

"Right. Which tells us what, gentlemen?" Dak put his hands out wide, expecting an answer. Instead, the two merely glanced at each other as if hoping the other had something to add.

Dak sighed. "It tells us that the thief had control of the security system." The men silently mouthed a pair of "ohs." Dak inhaled and pressed on. "Now, I am going to guess that when Dr. Laghari finished her rounds on a floor, she switched on the alarm system. Or are all the floors synced to one security setup?"

"They all sync to one, but each floor has its own separate system," the guard answered. "If one of the alarms is triggered, then all of the exhibits on every floor will go into lockdown."

Dak recalled seeing the cages overhead, not-so-subtly concealed in the archways leading into the exhibit rooms.

So far, he'd been correct on all counts. But there was one more thing he needed to check before taking another step forward. He turned and spied a door on the left side of the room. "Is that where the servers, cables, all that stuff is kept?"

"Yes. Why?"

"Let's take a look and see."

The guard unlocked the door and held it open for Dak and Dr. Reddy to pass through. He followed them inside, allowing the door to close automatically behind him.

Inside, two racks of servers blinked with green and blue lights. Dozens of cables ran along the walls and ceiling, plugging into various devices—some of which Dak recognized and others he'd never seen.

"I assume you backup everything somewhere outside this building," Dak suggested.

"Yes. In case of a fire or something like that, we also have an off-site storage facility, but obviously everything that's hard-lined into the system is here, and it all runs through this room."

Dak nodded. Just as he'd suspected, this was the place a thief would need to go to fiddle with the surveillance setup.

He moved slowly through the room, inspecting the wall of gadgetry to his right until he came to the end of it, where the path allowed them to walk around to the other side. The wall on the other side contained stacks of similar equipment, including routers, Wi-Fi transmitters, and a relay from a satellite dish.

"This feeds it into the surveillance system?" Dak asked, pointing at a section on the wall where multiple video cables hung from black boxes.

"Yes," the guard said.

Dak stepped nearer to the wall, then reached out and placed his fingers on one of the boxes with blinking green lights.

"At what point did the video feed for the exhibit room come back online?" He grumbled the words while he concentrated on something near the back of the row of devices, close to the wall.

"What do you mean?" Reddy asked.

"I think," the guard ventured, "he's talking about how we didn't see anything, and then all of the sudden the feed was live again."

"Didn't see anything or you saw the room as it was before the theft?"

"Yes, that's the one," the guard confirmed. "Sorry, I didn't think to clarify the difference. We could see the room, just as it was after Dr. Laghari left it. The last footage we have of her is on the second floor, leaving one of the exhibit rooms. Then it's as if she just disappeared."

Dak nodded, his mind already way ahead of these two. He reached farther into the back of servers and wires and found the anomaly he'd been looking for. He winced as he twisted his body to get his fingers just a little deeper into the cavity. Then he relaxed and pulled his arm back out, a tiny black device with a network cable adapter jutting out of one end. It looked like an improvised flash drive.

"What is that?" Dr. Reddy asked, stepping close to get a better look.

"It's a receiver-transmitter," Dak explained. "To put it plainly, a thief can use one of these to alter what you see in your video feed. Usually, they take a small recording of, say, an empty exhibit room, then put it on loop. A device this small doesn't have the storage capacity for something like that, so the feed would be coming in remotely, probably from another transmitter the thief either carried with them or had positioned somewhere nearby. These things don't have a ton of range, so once they were, say, maybe a tenth of a mile from here, that's probably when your feed came back online."

The two men stared at the American. Their wide eyes expressed surprise, and their approval.

Dr. Reddy reached out and gently took the device from Dak's fingers. The director studied the tiny object and then nodded. "I should get this to the police," he said.

"Probably, and don't worry about getting your fingerprints on it," Dak added. Reddy immediately expressed the concern Dak warned against. "He would have used gloves every time he touched it, and I doubt they'd be able to pull any prints from it anyway. That's not as easy as they make it look on television."

The director nodded; his worry easily visible.

"If you go back and check the time when the display case first showed up broken, my guess is that is about the same moment the thief and their transmitter were out of range. You'll probably see a little fuzz, maybe some lines or blurring occur just before the image updated. By then, they were several blocks from here, making their escape."

Dr. Reddy nodded. "Most impressive, Mr. Harper. You said that this sort of thing wasn't your forte, but you seem to be a natural."

Dak shrugged. "We don't have the criminal yet, sir."

"What should we do next, aside from delivering this to the police?"

"We need you," Dak pointed at the guard, "to look back at all the feeds coming into this room, and any of the other closets, supply rooms, that sort of thing. Check the latter first. If our thief hid out in the museum until after closing, we should be able to spot where they went, and how they got in there. We might even be able to get a loose composite of them if we're lucky, though I doubt that."

"Then what?" Reddy asked.

"I suspect you'll find that part easier than the other," Dak continued. "There's no telling when the culprit managed to sneak into this security room, but I would assume it happened when one of you was on a break."

"We don't take many breaks," the guard lamented. "But when we do, this door is locked, and we have the system monitoring everything."

Again, a lot of good it did.

Then the guard's eyes lit up, as if he'd just found out he won the lottery. "Wait. There was a man, about three weeks ago. He came in to do a check on all our systems. He had all the credentials from the service company we use, and he was right on schedule."

"And he went in this room?" Dak motioned to the door.

"Yes."

"Do they always send the same person?"

"No," the guard shook his head. "It's usually one of the same three."

Dak tilted his head back. "Let me guess. You'd never met that guy before."

The guard met his gaze, slowing turning his head side to side.

"Okay." Dak paced to the other side of the room, staring at the floor as he thought.

"Why didn't you tell us that sooner?" Reddy pressed the guard.

The poor guy in uniform lifted his shoulders in defense, his face long with innocence. "I just now thought of it. They come in every month, sir. It's part of the routine. He had all the proper credentials."

"It's not his fault," Dak defended, stopping at the opposite wall to turn and walk back to the center. "Could have happened to anyone. And looking for someone to blame is never helpful. What is helpful," he said, speaking to the guard, "is if you can get in there and start looking for where this thief hid during the day until closing hours. Just watch the feeds until you see someone go in. When you do, simply check to make sure they are one of your usual workers, or if it's someone new."

The guard swallowed and then nodded his understanding.

"Now, do you remember what this technician looked like?"

"Sure. He was a little shorter than you. Darker skin than yours. Athletic build."

"Wait," Dak stopped the guard. "Did you say darker skin than mine? As in a tan?"

"Yes." The man looked confused.

"And his accent?"

"Similar to yours."

Dak took a deep breath in, and exhaled, flapping his lips in the process. "So," he said after several second of thought, "we're dealing with an American."

Dak walked out of the museum, fished the phone out of his pocket, and looked at the screen. He was about to dial a number when he sensed someone stepping out from the building's shadows. Dak froze, then rounded slowly to face the stalker.

"If you're going to sneak up on someone, it's much easier to do after dark," Dak offered.

A man approached him, fairly tall though a few inches shorter than Dak. He looked athletic, and slim, and he walked with the gait of someone who exercised regularly. The sharp jawline and nose made him look like a hawk. His short, thick hair on top was nearly as black as the windbreaker he wore, which must have been warm during the day.

Dak didn't need to see the man's identification to know this was a cop. He'd figured that out the second the man emerged from the pale shadows.

The man started to brandish his badge, but Dak waved it off. "I know you're a cop," he said. "So, you can just put that away."

"Just flew into town, Mr. Harper?"

Dak winced at the moniker. "Yep. Just got here."

"And what is it you're doing in Mumbai? Not causing any trouble, are you?"

"I'm sorry. I didn't catch your name."

"You told me not to bother. My name is Rhadi Naik. And yes, I'm a detective. *The* detective in charge of this case, actually."

Dak caught the way the guy emphasized that he was in charge. *Perfect.* He'd heard about jurisdiction stuff before, seen it in the movies more times than he could count and had no doubt that's where this little chat was going. But there was a huge difference to this scenario—Dak was no cop.

"Great," Dak said. "Looks like they got the right guy for the job. Nice to meet you, and best of luck." He gave a curt nod to the detective and started to turn, but the cop stopped him.

"I know why you're here, Mr. Harper."

Dak felt a surge of disappointment, and a touch of laziness, snake through his gut. He twisted back around and faced the detective.

"That right?"

"Yes," Naik said. "The museum director brought you here to help with the investigation. I assure you, your help is not wanted, nor needed. I would suggest you stay out of my way and leave this to the professionals."

Dak nodded. "Sure thing."

"We are doing everything in our power to make sure the woman is brought back safely," Naik went on. "And the statue as well."

"Don't want to forget the statue," Dak reminded, raising a finger like a schoolmarm from days long gone.

"Certainly not." The cop's Indian accent was as sharp as his nose. "This is a police matter, Mr. Harper. Please see to it that you stay—"

"Out of your way. Yes, I got the memo. Loud and clear. I'm just here on a personal errand for a friend, so don't worry about me."

"Good. See to it you keep it that way."

"I'll do my best. But I doubt we will run into each other again. Well, I mean, it's possible. Wouldn't rule it out entirely. Anyway, I have to run. Good luck catching...whoever it is you're after. I have errands to run. Pleasure to meet you."

Dak spun away from the man again and started toward his car.

He raised the phone to his ear, hoping he'd finally gotten away from the leachy detective. The sounds of the big city's traffic nearly drowned out the ringing from the speaker, but with every step, Dak grew more confident the cop had gone his separate way.

"Well, well, well," a man answered on the other end. "If it isn't my best and worst customer."

Dak chuckled in his mind, steering left on the sidewalk toward the side of the building where he'd been afforded an early morning parking spot.

"What makes me your best customer?" Dak wondered as he rounded the corner. In between the buildings, the street noise wasn't so overwhelming.

"You keep me busy," Will answered.

"And why the worst?"

"Because you're not a paying customer."

"Oh, come on. I let you be one of my friends. Isn't that payment enough?" Dak smirked, stopping at his rental car to fish the keys out of his pocket. He unlocked the car, slid inside the driver's seat, and started the engine, grateful to get into the relative peace and quiet the sedan's interior afforded.

"Where are you, anyway?" Will asked. "Sounds like you're in a pretty big city. I hope you're not being reckless. Big cities have cameras. Wouldn't want your old pal Tucker to spot you because some street cam recognized your face."

"I'm wearing sunglasses," Dak offered. "The cameras are actually why I was calling."

"Oh, no. You got spotted, didn't you? See? I told you to be careful. What do I always tell you? Keep a low profile. Stay out of the cities."

"Well, that's not much of a life, now is it?"

"Better than being dead, my friend."

"I'm not dead yet," Dak countered. "Besides, I have to go into the cities. That's where the nests are. I can't track down Tucker and his goons without going through the same channels they would."

"Still sounds reckless to me," Will admitted. "But I understand.

So, you mentioned something about cameras. What do you need me to do? Hack an underground database of targets who've been spotted out in the open?"

"I didn't know you knew about that database. Thought that was only available to the merc network. It's mostly kept offline." Dak peered through the windshield, watching cars and people go by at the end of the alley.

"That hurts, Dak. Seriously. You think I, of all people, wouldn't know about the database?" Will did his best to sound downtrodden.

"Well, it's a well-kept secret."

"Yeah, but if you know about it, then I guess it's not as well kept as once thought."

Dak snorted a laugh. "Back to the cameras. I'm hunting someone."

"What else is new. You're always hunting someone or something. And someone is always hunting you. Lot of hunting going on in your life."

"No doubt. I'm looking for a thief. It's for a job."

"For your little boss?" Will clarified.

"Yeah, sort of. Although I don't think he's going to get anything out of this. He doesn't even want the artifact that was taken. He just thought I could help out."

"Isn't that what the cops are for?" Will hedged.

"That's what I said," Dak said, "but I guess the kid thought they could use some help. Their director of antiquities seems to agree and was very helpful."

"Where do I come in?"

Dak switched the phone to the other ear and continued. "I have the security guards at the museum looking over some footage from the last few weeks. If I get you a clip, do you think you could run it through the database? It's possible he's on the network, although it's a long shot."

"Yeah, thieves like that don't usually end up on there, but I'll take a look for you. When do you think you'll have the footage?"

"Soon, I hope. Could be a known criminal we're looking at here.

They broke into that museum without setting off any of the alarms. So we're dealing with a pro. The way this thief went about the heist was extremely clean."

Will chuckled. "Sounds almost like you have a thing for this thief."

"I just know a pro when I see one. Whoever this is, they were meticulous. They did an override on the surveillance cameras, and the alarm system. Laser triggers were off when the thief went into the exhibit room."

"Wait," Will interrupted. "Did you say they overrode the surveillance cameras?"

"That's right."

"Then, how are we going to identify this person without any sort of image?"

A pigeon landed on the edge of the roof to the left. It looked out over the street below with an air of superiority.

"I believe we'll have footage from a previous feed," Dak explained. "The security guard said a technician came in at some point in the last few weeks to check on some things. They claimed that's a regular occurrence, and that the technician isn't always the same person. In this instance, it was someone they didn't recognize, but the guy had all the right credentials."

"So, the thief snuck in right under their noses, hacked the system while they were there, and then walked right out of the building without so much as a sneeze. Probably took them less than five minutes."

Will didn't have to consider the story long before he deduced what happened. "Let me guess. The culprit used an override transmitter-receiver."

"Yep. Found it a few minutes ago, tucked back behind some equipment in their server room. By the time the video feed resumed to live, the thief was already a few blocks away, maybe more."

"Well, if you can get me at least something with this person's face in it, I might be able to ID them. You said it was a guy?"

"Yeah," Dak confirmed. "The guards got a decent look at him, but

I'm sure he was in a disguise. This is a long shot sort of deal, but I'm covering all the bases."

"I'll see what I can do. Anything else?" Will asked.

"No. Not for now."

"What about you? What are you going to do?"

"That's the other thing I was going to ask you." Dak's suspicious tone invoked the next question from his friend.

"Ask me? Ask me what? Where are you, anyway?"

"Mumbai."

"Oh, I see. So, you want my contact in Mumbai." Will could see where this was going.

"Seems like you might have mentioned someone. Maybe you were drunk and just rambling on, bragging about how you know people everywhere in the underground. You specifically said Mumbai, right after a list of other cities."

"I wasn't drunk," Will defended. "Maybe a little buzzed. But I wasn't bragging. I do know someone in Mumbai. And he might just be able to help. He facilitates buyers for stolen artifacts, although he doesn't like to think of it that way. Thinks it gives a bad connotation. He swears he's not a criminal."

"Is he?"

"No more than you or me," Will quipped.

"That's not exactly what I was hoping you'd say."

"I'll call Chester and tell him you're looking for him. He's pretty well connected in that part of the world. He might be able to help you. Even if he didn't set up the buy, he's probably heard about it. He keeps his fingers on the pulse of that stuff. Just deal cautiously with him. Chester is a pretty stand-up guy, but you never know."

Dak chortled at the accusation. "Don't worry, pumpkin. You're still my first love."

"Yeah, don't you forget it."

"I won't."

"Cool. I'll call him and let him know to expect you. When I've arranged the meeting, I'll text you the address. He's there in the city. Runs a business of some kind. It's mostly legit. Mostly."

Dak grinned. "You sound jealous."

"Jealous? Ha! I'm just trying to take care of my boy. That's all. You be careful, though. Tucker is still after you. Keep your head down."

"Thanks, mom. I'll do my best. And I'll send you that footage if and when I get it."

"You wish I were your mom. If she knew what you were up to, I don't think she'd approve."

The statement sent Dak's mind spiraling. His parents had been through enough since the incident with the military in the Middle East. They'd been dragged into the sewage that is the mass media, questioned by every babbling talking head about their AWOL, traitor son. When the air cleared, and Dak was proved innocent, they didn't receive a public apology from any of the networks. And the damage had been done.

While Dak's parents had a loyal group of friends and family, they'd endured death threats from strangers, and the outpouring of hatred on social media would have been enough to break through a dam. Fortunately, at least for his parents, they weren't on any social media, so they missed much of that.

Now, they were withdrawn, retreated into their quiet lives once more. The events had taken a toll, though, and Dak worried about the long-term impacts on his parents' health.

He'd convinced himself it wasn't his fault. He couldn't change the course of how things went down when his entire team betrayed him and left him for dead. Sure, he could have gone along with them, taken the treasure, and never told a soul. He'd be sitting on a pile of money right now, and his parents would be fine, back home, having never endured any shame.

That wouldn't have been the right thing to do, though, and Dak knew it. He never regretted the decision he made to stand up to the men in his team, though he did regret the outcomes.

"You're probably right," Dak said after twenty seconds of thought. "Best she doesn't find out, I suppose."

"You think?" Will laughed.

"Thanks for your help. As always, I appreciate it."

"Don't thank me yet. I haven't done anything."

"Oh," Dak said, "I almost forgot. This isn't just a heist we're dealing with here."

"No?"

Dak shook his head once. "A woman was kidnapped, too. She's the curator of the museum. She was locking things up when the theft happened. Best we can figure is that the thief got caught and took the woman with him. The police don't have any leads yet."

"If they did, you wouldn't be on the phone with me. That's a big deal, man. Kidnapping on top of stealing a valuable artifact? If the cops catch this dude, he's going to be in for a long, uncomfortable vacation in prison."

"Yeah, it's messed up," Dak agreed.

"Not sure why you didn't lead with that," Will wondered. "Kidnapping is way more serious. Any idea if the woman is okay?"

"No clue. There's no footage suggesting she was hurt, but there's no footage of the exhibit room from the time the thief entered. The cameras must have still been offline when they made off with the curator."

"Then we'd better hurry. Dealing with a thief is one thing, but an abduction? We're against the clock. I'll get in touch with Chester. Expect to hear back from me within the hour."

"Thanks, Will."

The two ended the call, and Dak looked down at the screen for several seconds, mulling over whether or not he should call his mother. He calculated the time difference and realized she and his father were probably still in bed. They were early risers, but not that early. Plus, he didn't think adding additional stress to his parents' day was a good idea. Better they not know what he was up to.

Dak set the phone down in the passenger seat, shifted the car into gear, then drove out and onto the street.

8

"You look upset." Priya didn't offer the statement as some sort of consolation, or a way of showing sympathy to the man on the other side of the cage. She loathed him, and her eyes put that loathing on full display like two simmering volcanos.

He ignored her, staring at the phone as if willing it to ring. It didn't.

Gavin had been trying desperately to get in touch with his buyer, but the man wasn't returning his calls, nor were his underlings. He didn't understand why, though, and that was the root of Gavin's irritation.

He'd planned out everything, taken every possible precaution. Or so he thought.

How had the curator known to come back up to the third floor? It was a calculation he could not have anticipated, and the more he thought about it, the more it drove him crazy.

His imagination raced with all sorts of scenarios, some logical, others from the realm of fantasy bordering on hallucinogenic.

Try as he might, Gavin could come up with no rational explanation other than he'd failed to consider the woman might change up her routine. And it just so happened that the night he was pulling the job was the night she decided to throw a wrench in her otherwise flawless system.

He wondered if the buyer had caught wind of the situation, and if that's why the man's feet had abruptly turned frigid. The deal had been in place for more than six months. In fact, it was the buyer who'd approached Gavin about the job, promising him an extraordinary reward for the heist.

Gavin didn't usually do work for others. It often complicated things. This case was no different. The man had been like a ghost. They'd never even met in person, but there'd been an up-front retainer offered, which Gavin was happy to accept. One thing he'd learned about these kinds of gigs was to always get a deposit up front. That way, if things went south, he'd still get something out of it. Gavin didn't take risks without some potential of reward beyond the simple thrill of the job.

All of the communications between Gavin and the buyer had been by phone, and with new phones and SIM cards. They'd been careful, which Gavin appreciated, though he wasn't sure about some of the extremes of their cloak-and-dagger relationship.

The retainer appeared in his bank account the next morning, which told Gavin that this buyer was most definitely serious.

To his surprise, the buyer had also requested specifically to be as hands-off as possible. Usually, buyers setting up a for-hire heist like this wanted more involvement. They got in the way, thinking they knew how to do things better than the expert they'd hired. It got messy, which was one of the biggest reasons Gavin avoided those kinds of jobs.

"Didn't expect things to end up like this, huh?" Priya prodded, cutting into his train of thought. He still didn't look her in the eyes.

The frustration wouldn't allow it. The boiling cauldron of emotions in his head bubbled and steamed. *Why aren't they answering me?* The thought only stoked the fire.

"It's almost as if you didn't quite cover all the angles, isn't it?" Priya continued, pacing to the right, and then back to the left.

Gavin didn't know where this cocky attitude was coming from, but visions of choking the woman did not escape his imagination.

"How long were you watching me?" she asked, more curious than angry. "Two weeks? Four?" She paused her pacing and crossed her arms, then raised a finger to her chin, pretending to ponder the question.

Gavin sat with his elbows on his knees, his torso hunched over and his head hanging in his hands.

He loosened his fingers and turned his head toward her, questions brimming in his eyes. "Long enough," he said.

She laughed, sharp and sudden. "Apparently not," she argued. "Otherwise, I wouldn't have gotten the drop on you."

Gavin's jaw tightened. "You didn't get the drop on me."

"Are you sure? Because it certainly seems that way."

He put his head in his hands again and stared at the floor for a few seconds, then glanced over at the phone once more. *Why aren't they calling?*

"It almost seems like your buyer isn't interested in the product anymore. You know what that means? No payday for you."

He snorted. *Shows how much she knows.* He'd already been paid.

"Who was it that introduced you to this buyer? Huh? Perhaps you should give them a call and find out what's going on."

"Perhaps you should just sit down and shut up," he fired back.

She laughed at the retort. "You'd like that, wouldn't you?"

"Yes. Very much."

"Well, you should have thought of that before."

He sighed angrily and returned his gaze to the floor again. She wasn't entirely wrong, though, in her line of thinking. If he could get answers from someone, it didn't matter who was offering them.

Gavin remembered the man's name with ease. *Chester,* he thought. The guy ran an underground cryptocurrency mining operation and occasionally dealt in rare artifacts. Contrary to popular belief, the cryptocurrency wasn't one of the ways Chester scrubbed his money. Rather, it was a diversification strategy that added a level of legitimacy to his operation.

If Gavin could get in touch with Chester, perhaps he could find out what was going on with the buyer.

"What's the matter?" Priya poked. "You're sure not saying much. I thought you would be more of a talkative type. You're from California, yes? Hollywood? You look like Hollywood. If I didn't know better—"

"You don't. You don't know anything about me, or my life, or what I do. So just keep your mouth shut while I try to figure this out."

Gavin narrowed his eyes in determination and lifted the phone.

"Who you calling?" she insisted.

"Someone who might be able to tell me what's going on with the buyer."

9

Dak stood across from a long, skinny guy wearing red sneakers, blue jeans, and a gray zip-up hoodie.

The white office walls contained black bookshelves that burgeoned with tomes, some fiction, some non. Unlike in other offices Dak had visited, this one didn't feature pictures of spouses and children. It was all business, which didn't really take Dak by surprise.

Chester rested his feet on the edge of the desk, hands behind his head with fingers intertwined against his light brown curly hair. "I'm sorry, but I'm afraid I don't know what you're talking about. We run a telecommunications business here. We're a small operation, but we've been in business a long time now."

Dak didn't move. He simply stood across from the young business owner, studying his face, waiting for Chester to crack.

Seconds ticked by. Neither man said a thing.

Then, Chester stood up, put his hands out, and motioned to the door. "Now, if you'll excuse me, sir, I have a lot of work to do. I appreciate you stopping by."

Chester ushered Dak toward the door.

Dak looked up at the man like he was crazy.

Again, Chester urged him toward the door with a nod of the head.

Dak acquiesced and stepped back out into the hallway.

The place smelled sterile, like a hospital but with more paper. Open doors lined the corridor, and at the end, a huge room hosted a maze of empty cubicles.

Chester pointed in the other direction, just twenty feet away, to a closed door with a sign fixed to the center that read "High Voltage. Do not enter."

The two walked the short distance to the door and Chester shoved a key into the lock. He glanced back down the hallway and then unlocked the door, opened it, and stepped through. He waited on the other side until Dak was in, then closed and relocked the door.

"What is going on?" Dak asked, finally feeling like it was safe to do so.

"Sorry about that, Dak," Chester answered. "Been hearing stories about the authorities cracking down on local businesses that were fronting illegal operations."

"You mean like yours?"

"Very funny," Chester spat in a sharp, English accent. "No, we run a legitimate operation."

"Don't the others, too?" Dak raised both eyebrows to emphasize the question's legitimacy.

"That's beside the point. I have ethics. I figured our mutual acquaintance would have explained that to you. I'll have to have a talk with Will at some point."

Chester started down a metal staircase. Dak followed, noting that the bright lighting in the stairwell matched that of the previous hallway despite being older. The block walls in here were older, perhaps part of a building built long before the place that Chester's business called home.

"So, facilitating the purchase and sale of illegally acquired arti-facts—often stolen—isn't illegal?"

Chester rounded the first landing and kept going. "I guess that depends on who you ask. Look, Dak, I'm not stealing them. Okay? That's the illegal part. It might even be illegal for the buyers to possess those items. I concede that," he held up a palm as he descended. "But for what I do, it's pretty benign. I make good money, and now and then, what I do helps facilitate a little good on the back end."

"The back end?" Dak sounded suspicious.

"Yes, you know, if the cops or someone needs my help, it might turn out that one of the contacts is into some bad stuff. Could be a human trafficking thing. A drug thing. Weapons. Whatever. And who do they come to if they need information on those people? Me." He shoved two thumbs at his chest.

"Snitches get stitches, Chester. You better watch your back."

"Relax." Chester shrugged. "I only do that when it's someone who has it coming, especially those traffickers. I don't want anything to do with them."

Despite the ribbing Dak gave, Chester struck him as a stand-up guy—in a gray-area sort of way.

The two continued descending the stairs until they reached the bottom, where two brown metal doors blocked the way into another part of the building.

Chester entered a four-digit code into a key panel to the right of the doors, and after an electronic whir and a click, the door unlocked and opened automatically.

Dak followed his host through the doorway and into a room about the size of a basketball court. Shelves lined the walls, crammed with laptop computers tilted onto their edges, propped up in an upside-down V shape. Hundreds of cords ran along the walls and the edge of the floor to racks of servers at one end of the room. A collection of desks in the center of the room housed four computer workstations where graphics and numbers filled the screens, scrolling up with every passing second.

"What in the world is all this?" Dak asked.

Chester faced him with a curious expression on his face. "This is a cryptocurrency mine," he said, as if the answer should have been plainly apparent.

"Okay."

Chester walked into the center of the room and sat down at the nearest computer desk. Two large fans overhead pulled warm air out of the facility while four vents in the corners spilled cool air down into the room.

"Look," Chester said. "I run analytics for companies. That's the business you saw upstairs."

"So that explains the empty cubicle room, the empty offices, all that." Dak passed him a conspiratorial glance.

"It has to look official. And not all of those offices are empty. I have a few other workers."

"What did you tell them about all the space that wasn't being used?"

Chester pouted his lips and bobbed his head side to side as if he'd just received an underhanded compliment. "That we needed the space in case we expand going forward. The building was cheap enough; might as well get more than you need. Right?"

"Especially if you're going to turn a profit when you sell the place. Real estate is the only truly safe investment, after all," Dak drawled.

"Very true," Chester confessed. "And running this business is an easy cover for me. I'm good at what I do, and it pays the bills from a traceable, valid source. It's also a perfect cover for a nontaxable crypto mining operation. Now, if the government knew I had this setup down here, they would figure out a way to steal my money."

"You mean you'd have to render to Caesar," Dak countered.

"Precisely. And I'm no Roman." He shrugged and began pecking away at a keyboard while Dak remained standing off to the side of the workstation. "Look, we all want to pay as few taxes as possible. That's every person on the planet."

"Save your sermon about taxation," Dak said. "I'm not here to talk about that. I don't care. Hide your money, launder it, bury in the dirt for all I care. I'm here because you're connected in the underground. And I'm looking for someone."

"Ah," Chester said. The freckles on his nose danced as he twitched it. The fluorescent lights overhead made his pale skin look ashy. "Will mentioned he had a friend who needed a favor. And I'm always happy to oblige him. Diamond in the rough, that one."

"Yeah, he's good people." Dak looked around at the room full of computers. A dull hum filled the room, dampened slightly by two fabric mats that hung from the two end walls. "So, the whole charade upstairs. What was that about?"

Chester's fingers flew across the keys. He stopped when he was done entering in a line of what looked like code, though Dak wasn't as familiar with those kinds of things. And he didn't want to be. Learning that stuff was very much like acquiring another language. Speaking several different dialects already, he figured the real estate in his brain was pretty much all taken.

"I was being cautious upstairs," Chester said, spinning in his chair to face Dak again. "You never know if you have a wiretap somewhere, listening to everything you say."

"You think the government tapped your office?" Dak sounded dubious.

"Government. Rivals. Or worse. You never know. Better to be safe. You know? But hey, you're not here to talk to me about what I'm doing. You said you're looking for someone?"

"That's right."

Chester bobbed his head, pressing his lips together. "All right then. What are we talking 'bout? You need a buyer for an artifact? Or are you looking to buy? No offense, mate, but you don't look like the kind of bloke that's buying high-priced black-market artifacts."

"I'm not. And none taken."

"Oh." Confusion flooded Chester's face. "So, what is it I'm helping you do?"

"Last night, someone broke into the Mumbai Antiquities Museum. A valuable idol was taken from one of the exhibits. I need to know who took it."

The bewilderment in Chester's eyes only increased. "I'm sorry, you're not a cop, are you? Because last I checked...."

Dak took a threatening step forward. "Do I look like a cop?"

"If I'm honest...."

"I'm not a cop, Chester. I'm just a guy who finds things. And right now, I'm trying to find this idol." He held up his phone so Chester could see the golden statue on the screen. "Do you know who might have taken this?"

"Very pretty," Chester said, clearing his throat and shifting uncomfortably. "Looks like it could fetch a hefty sum. You know, if there were someone willing to pay for it."

"Who would be willing to pay for it?"

Chester rolled his shoulders, looking more and more uneasy by the second. "I'm not sure. I suppose I could put some feelers out there."

Dak lowered his phone and put it back into its pocket. He breathed slowly, deliberately, as he calculated what to say next. His host had already answered the first question with his body language. And now, Dak simply needed to pry the information from him.

"Will tells me that you're the go-to guy in Mumbai," Dak hedged, laying it on thick. He started pacing toward one of the shelves housing several laptops. "I suppose I could go to someone else. Would be a shame, though."

"Oh? Why is that?" Chester feigned interest, but it was obvious he only asked the question for appearance's sake.

"The reward they're offering for the recovery of that statue is one hundred thousand dollars. American."

Dak let the words set in and watched as Chester considered the information.

"And what's in it for me, mate?" Chester asked, the gap between disinterest and curiosity bridging by the second.

"All you have to do is help me find this thief. I return the statue to the museum. The curator is, hopefully, rescued, and you get half of that."

Chester's eyes blinked rapidly. His head snapped to the right, and he inspected something along the far wall. It was an intentional move, a way for him to take his focus off Dak and think clearly for a second about what he should do.

"What curator?"

Dak sighed, remembering he hadn't mentioned that yet. "The

museum curator was also taken by the thief. Word is, they still have her. Focus, Chester. You get half."

"That's a lot of money," Chester said finally, returning his gaze to the American. "I mean, for a finder's fee."

"It is," Dak agreed. "No strings attached."

"And what? You're going to just take the statue and the girl back, give me half the reward? What's Will get out of this?"

"He can have half of my cut. My employer doesn't want anything out of this. He just wants the statue returned."

"Employer, huh? What kind of boss has a guy like you running around trying to save damsels in distress and recovering stolen relics?" Chester arched his right eyebrow and clicked his tongue.

"I don't think my boss knows about the woman. And he's wealthy. He doesn't need the money."

Chester huffed. "I need a boss like that." He shifted in his seat. "Although I'm my own boss, so I'm good. Don't care much for working for the man."

Dak inched closer, his eyes full of determination. "Stay focused, Chester." Dak put his palm on the desk and leaned over, his face drawing closer to Chester's. "Do you know where to find the thief, or don't you? Who is the buyer?"

"Could be tricky," Chester said. "Like I said, I'll put out some feelers—"

"Fifty thousand dollars, Chester," Dak reminded. "Or, of course, we could do this the hard way."

"What?"

"You know about this thief. Your body language gives it away. I've come here, to your little fortress of solitude, to make you an offer. A very generous offer. Yet you're still playing hardball. Don't be coy with me, Chester." He spat the name.

Chester's eyes didn't move from Dak's. The younger man swallowed hard.

"So, here are your options" Dak continued. "You tell me where I can find this thief and you get half of the reward, or I beat the information out of you and you get nothing. Except maybe some broken bones, probably a concussion. You ever had a concussion, Chester?" He didn't wait for an answer. "Have you ever felt your arm break in multiple places? Or had both arms broken?"

Fear swept onto Chester's pale face. "Are you threatening me?"

"I'm trying not to."

The Englishman swallowed harder this time, pressing his hands into the armrests of the chair as if he could somehow retreat from the imposing visitor. "Take it easy, Dak. Okay? I was just messing about. No big deal."

"Where is the thief? Who is the buyer? You have to give me something."

"Okay. Relax, mate. I don't know who the thief is, but believe me, I want that reward money as much as anyone else. I hadn't even heard they announced that."

"Where?" Dak insisted.

"Yeah. Yeah. All right. But you have to understand my hesitance, mate. The people I deal with are dangerous."

"I'm dangerous."

"I'm getting that vibe from you," Chester confessed. "Look, the point is...I have to be careful. My clients, they come to me for connections because they know I keep secrets. I don't hand out information. They know I won't go to the cops."

"Maybe because your hands are as dirty as theirs?" Dak suggested. "Being an accomplice doesn't make you more or less innocent."

Chester rolled his eyes. "You're so high and mighty. Come in here, to see me in my place of business, making threats about broken bones and concussions and whatnot."

Dak merely stood there with arms crossed, his eyes boring through Chester's soul.

It only took a few seconds before Chester caved. "I don't know who they are. All right?" He threw up his hands. "This buyer, they were real cryptic. More than usual. And believe me, I deal with a ton of shady people. Some of them are direct. This buyer, though, they came to me through another connection. So, I don't know who they are. Okay? You have to believe me. This is all I have."

"What did you get out of it?"

Chester snorted, shrugging as if it was no big deal. "Few grand."

Dak stepped forward menacingly.

"Okay. Okay. Take it easy. Ten grand."

"Then take that off the fifty you were going to get from me. Your take is now forty."

"What?" Chester blurted, incensed. "You promised fifty."

"And you'll get it. With the ten you already made. The other ten will go to my employer."

"I thought you—"

"You're getting off track, Chester," Dak warned.

"Ugh," Chester gasped. "Fine. Like I was saying, I don't know who the buyer is. And I definitely don't know the thief. But I can give you my contact. They set everything up on my end. All I had to do was make the connection."

Dak circled the desk at a slow pace. Chester tracked him, spinning in his chair as Dak looped around, staring at him with suspicion.

"I don't mean to sound cynical," Dak groused, "but it seems to me like you're giving some conflicting information. You don't know who the thief is, or the buyer, but somehow you managed to set up their business interactions? And you said you keep secrets, but you also tell the cops what they want to know if it will save your skin. Sorry if I find all of this a bit...sketchy."

"Look, mate. We all do what we have to do to survive. Okay? No reason to get on edge. I said I would help you."

Chester spun around in his chair and faced the computer monitor. He typed in a few words, then the screen blinked, bringing up an image of an Indian woman with long, black hair dropping over her shoulders. Her dark eyes sucked Dak in, even through the photo, and he found himself mesmerized by her. The white blouse opened in a V several inches below the neckline.

"This looks like a surveillance photo," Dak said.

"Yeah, well, let's just say she's been watched for a while now. By a lot of people." Chester curled his lips. "She keeps the cops off her back with bribes. Runs an underground casino here in Mumbai. She asked if I knew someone who could get something for her. A real expensive artifact. I didn't know what relic she was talking about, and I honestly didn't care. She paid me in cash. Up front."

He flashed an accusatory glare at Dak, then continued. "She said she needed a thief. Said she needed the best for this buyer. Like I work with any scrubs. All the thieves I bring in are the best. It's not like there are a bunch of morons hovering about on the—"

"Get to the point, Chester."

"Right. So, I host a room on the dark web." He noticed Dak looking around the room and shook his head. "I only use one of these servers for that, mate. So don't think that's what this operation is. It's not. I already told you."

"Yeah. You're mining crypto." Dak leveled his gaze. "Keep going. I want to hear how you found this thief yet mysteriously don't know who they are."

"I was just getting to that if you'd stop interrupting." Chester sighed, exasperated. "I make the connections. That's it. I put the offer out there. I get a list of takers. No one was biting on this one. Usually, I get two or three willing to take the gig. In this instance, either the thieves that checked in weren't interested, thought it was too difficult, or didn't trust the buyer. That's all I know. I swear."

"And then what happened?"

Chester goosed his neck forward as if the answer should have been obvious. "I finally found someone crazy enough to do it. They pinged me. Then I sent the contact information to my buyer contact. They'll use a burner phone, so don't bother trying to track it through any of the networks or carriers. You won't find them that way. These aren't amateurs you're dealing with."

"So," Dak said, stretching his neck to both sides, "you sent the thief's information to this...woman who runs an underground casino?"

"Yeah, that's what I was getting at."

"Who is she?" Dak asked, his focus shifting to the exotic-looking woman on the screen.

"Name is Tamara. Word of warning, mate. Don't go in there all guns blazing. And don't threaten her. She doesn't take well to threats. So much as a flick of her wrist, and you'll have her entire entourage on you faster than you can say tandoori chicken."

"I'll keep it in mind."

"You better. Do us both a favor, and don't mention that I sent you. Okay?"

"I have more tact than to do something like that, Chester."

The Brit nodded, though he still didn't look certain. "Yeah, right. Well, you'll get a lot further with her if you're polite. Be nice, and maybe she'll work with you, though I doubt it."

"Why's that?"

"Are you dense?" Chester blurted. "You don't get how this works, do you?"

"The underground network? I think I have a firm grasp. You believe she won't tell me what I want to know because if she does, she could end up dead. And so could you. That's how it all works, isn't it? You guys all keep secrets, or else the big money you're working for comes in and takes you out, then goes and finds someone else who won't squeal. That sound about right?"

"Okay. Maybe you do understand it a bit."

"Don't worry, Ches. I won't blow your cover. Where do I find this Tamara?"

Dak sat outside the restaurant and stared at the front entrance. It looked like any number of places he'd seen that sold flatbread, rice, lentils, and potatoes. The façade read "Bogi's," but other than the unusual spelling of its name, there was nothing special about the eatery.

He hadn't even bothered looking up the online reviews. Dak wasn't there for the food, although the smells wafting out of the joint did their best to persuade him. He'd picked up a piece of flatbread from a street vendor, stuffed it with a creamy lentil base and potatoes, and hurried on his way. There was no time for sitting down to a nice meal, not when he was on the trail of a lead that could mean the difference between life and death.

Dak wadded up the parchment paper his to-go meal had been packed in and stood up from his little round table in the shade. He tossed the trash into a nearby waste bin, then waited for traffic to slow. This part of town didn't boast the same packed streets and sidewalks as some of the other locations he'd seen. Mumbai was a bustling city, pulsing with life on every corner. But here, a few miles outside the city center, it felt more like a busy small town instead of a metropolis of millions.

That wasn't to say the area didn't have a life of its own. People still hustled around on foot or in their cars, but to the tune of half what he'd seen earlier. Had Dak tried to get across the street to Chester's building without using a crosswalk, he might well have been run over. Probably a couple of times.

Looking down the street about thirty yards away, he saw Detective Naik sitting in his sedan, watching. Dak frowned at the cop and shook his head. He considered ignoring the guy and going across the street to his destination, but Dak felt like he should take this issue head on. So, he swiveled on his heels and sauntered over to the car.

Naik did his best to look like he was busy doing something else, but it was a feeble effort. Dak was surprised the man hadn't driven away the second he'd been made.

Dak stopped short of the black sedan and craned his neck to look in through a gap in the window. "Hey there, Officer Naik," Dak said in a childish, almost stupid-sounding voice. He waved his hand dramatically like a clown in a circus.

"Detective Naik," the man corrected.

"Fine, my bad. Thank you for that," Dak said, laying on the sarcasm so thick he thought he might choke to death in it. The amount of energy it took to keep a straight face could have powered most of the city.

"What are you doing here, Harper? Going to play some cards?" He peered through the gap in the window at Dak. Aviator sunglasses rested on the tip of the detective's nose. *Probably*, Dak figured, *because he'd seen it in some television show.*

"No," Dak said. "Just here—"

"Running errands?" Naik interrupted. "You sure seem to do a lot of that for a man in a strange country. I didn't know you had so many friends here."

"Well, I'm something of a renaissance man in that regard," Dak offered. "I make friends wherever I go."

The detective puzzled over the answer, taking it way too seriously.

"I don't like you, Harper," Naik said finally.

"Mr. Harper," Dak joked, though the guy didn't understand Dak's hatred for being called that.

"I don't care what you think I should call you. Just remember, I'm watching you. You got that, Harper?" He pointed a threatening finger at Dak, who did his best to look nervous or afraid, though he felt like the expression he came up with was more like confusion.

"You got it, Officer—I mean, Detective Naik." Dak put up his hands in surrender and crossed the street as the light thankfully switched to allow pedestrians to go.

He didn't look back until he reached the other side, and when he did, Naik's car was gone.

"Guess he'd seen enough," Dak muttered. "Interesting guy, though."

He trotted along the street and slowed down when he reached the curb in front of another eatery. There, the aromas of the food billowed out of the open doorway to the restaurant and begged Dak to reconsider his previous thoughts about not eating anything else.

His mouth watered and his stomach grumbled as he entered the building, ducking out of the hot sun and into the darkened restaurant interior.

A bar to the right offered an assortment of beers and twelve varieties of liquor, including one bottle of Jack Daniel's.

Dak grinned at the whiskey. He recalled reading that when Jackie Gleason introduced Frank Sinatra to Jack Daniel's, the stuff was extremely difficult to come by. The small distillery in Lynchburg, Tennessee, didn't yet have the global capacity that it now enjoyed. Back when Sinatra became a fan, the expansion of the brand almost seemed to happen overnight.

Now, the little whiskey that could was available in nearly every dive bar and, apparently, random eatery all over the world. Even in India.

Dak surveyed the rest of the room, noting the fifteen patrons idly talking or absently nibbling from their plates. He didn't see anything unusual that would tip off the presence of an underground casino.

Then again, it wouldn't be much of an underground casino if it were easy to spot.

He walked over to the bar and pulled up a stool. The bartender was a middle-aged gentleman in a white, button-up shirt with a black apron over matching black pants. His hair was nearly as black but had a slight tinge of brown that shimmered in the glow of the ceiling lights.

He smiled with a warm genuineness that you'd expect from a barkeep who treated you as a regular. Dak had been to those kinds of places back home. He'd gone there every Saturday night for a month after things with Nicole had fallen apart. Then he'd gone back to the Middle East, to Iraq, where this whole crazy life had taken its wild turn.

"What can I get for you, my friend?" the bartender asked, wiping down an already clean spot on the bar with a white rag.

Dak eased onto a stool and stole a sideways glance in both directions, making sure no one else was within earshot.

"I'm here to see Tamara," he said in an easy tone.

The bartender continued wiping the counter without looking up. "I see. So, you have business with her?"

"In a manner of speaking."

"Ah. Well, I'm sorry, my friend, but Tamara only does business by appointment. Do you have one?"

Dak took in a breath, sensing trouble over his shoulder. Both shoulders. The sound of a sitar played in the background through old speakers hanging in the corners.

"No, sir," Dak exhaled. "No appointment. It's just that I know she's going to want to talk to me."

"Oh? And why is that?" The bartender finished his phantom wipe job and finally looked up into Dak's eyes.

"Because," he said, "I'm someone she wants on her side."

The bartender tilted his head back an inch.

"And because I'm someone she doesn't want against her."

Dak noticed the earpiece in the bartender's ear. He'd correctly assumed the man was the gatekeeper to Tamara's operation. The guy had played it cool, too, not giving away any information while also not entirely turning away someone who could be a wealthy customer.

"If you know Tamara," the bartender said, "then you know that she doesn't take being threatened lightly."

"I don't give them lightly either," Dak sneered.

A tilted mirror behind the bartender showed the reflection of two men in zip-up hoodies and mismatched trousers.

"And look," Dak added, "if the two goons behind me are any indication of the talent she's going to throw my way, I have nothing to worry about. I'll take them down, and anyone else she's thinking about sending."

The bartender said nothing.

"You seem like a nice guy," Dak changed course. "You remind me of a man I knew back in Tennessee. Hard worker. Honest. Always liked talking to him. I would really hate to have to kill you just so I can have a conversation with her. These two?" He jerked his right thumb over his shoulder. "I haven't spoken to them, so killing them will be no big deal. I would prefer the rest of the good people in your establishment not have to see that. Would hurt business, too, which I assume is also Tamara's, but maybe she rents out the basement or the top floor from you. I don't care. I also don't care what your deal is in all of this. I'm not the cops. And I'm not here to cause trouble. But I will cause trouble, if provoked."

Dak leaned forward, balling one fist in the palm of the other hand. "So, don't provoke me. Okay? Neither of us wants police attention. Let's not give it to them." He stiffened his spine and waited for one of the two men behind him to make the first move. Dak had already planned out the defense, then the counterattack, based on five different scenarios. Each one ended with the two men unconscious on the floor.

He could tell the bartender was doing more than just considering what Dak said. He was listening. Through the tiny black radio piece in his ear, the bartender received instructions. Directly from Tamara, or from her head of security, someone was telling the man exactly what to do or say next.

"I remember being a puppet," Dak said, fully aware he was interrupting. "Being told what to do, and when to do it. Of course, when I was told what to do, people died."

The bartender shifted his feet, fear trickling through his vision.

He nodded, acknowledging what he heard on the radio, then started wiping the counter again. "The two men behind you will escort you to Lady Tamara. She has given you an appointment."

Dak creased his lips in a smile. "Thanks, barkeep. I appreciate it." He stood and turned, seeing the two bodyguards face to face for the first time. One was an inch shorter than Dak. The other about the same height. Both were Indian, locals Tamara had scooped out of a bouncing gig at a nightclub, or maybe out of a gym. The men's muscles bulged out of their hoodies, but Dak doubted there was much fight training behind the thick biceps.

"So, lead the way, boys. And I'm sorry about what I said earlier, you know, about killing you and all."

Both men merely turned away from him and started toward the rear of the building, where the main room narrowed into a hallway lit with a single lamp overhead.

Dak looked back at the bartender. "By the way, I think you missed a spot."

He walked away, following the two goons down the hall as the bartender stared after him, puzzled. Behind Dak, the man raised the rag and craned his neck, trying to see what spot he could have missed.

At the end of the corridor, the guards stopped and knocked three times on a gray metal door. A slide at the top opened, and two eyes set in a light brown face glared out. They flicked from the guards, to Dak, and then back to the guards. A few seconds passed, then the interior guard unlocked the door and pulled it open.

The smell of stale cigarettes blew out of the next room, mixed with a splash of cigar smoke that just barely made the aroma slightly palatable.

"Guess you guys aren't down with the new smoking laws, huh?"

Dak said as he stepped into the room behind the first guard, with the second right behind him.

The interior guard closed the door and locked the three dead-bolts, along with a stopper on the floor that would prevent someone busting through with a battering ram.

Dak took in the unremarkable room in seconds. There wasn't much to see, and the lights hanging from the ceiling didn't add any character to the place. It was gray and dark—save for the fluorescent lighting overhead—and it felt like he'd just walked into a morgue for the living—or the not yet dead.

A closed door on the other side of the room led to somewhere else. He assumed it was either the casino or a room where they'd try to murder him in. His mind lingered on the word *try*.

A miserable-looking man with a thin mustache and unbrushed black hair stood behind a counter in a makeshift cashier cage to the right. He wore a red polo and khakis. The shirt button flaps hung limp around the collar, and he perspired like he'd been running a half marathon in Charleston. In July.

Dak pulled back on the collar of his T-shirt. "It's definitely a tad warm in here." He waved a hand in front of his face to disperse the tobacco fog permeating the room. The act did nothing more than pave the way for more smoke.

The cashier leaned over his counter with a cigarette dangling between his fingers, the bluish gray tendrils twirled up into the rest of the haze, making the air denser by the second.

"And not very well ventilated. You guys know that secondhand smoke is just as dangerous to a nonsmoker like me as smoking direct."

A shove in the back nudged Dak closer to the cage.

"How much?" the cashier asked, his dark, vapid eyes probing Dak with a distant interest.

Dak looked over at the guy to his left then stuffed a hand in his pocket. He was surprised that neither of the security goons had bothered patting him down for weapons, though Dak had elected to leave his goodie bag in the rental car's trunk.

He hadn't planned on having to buy chips, but from the way the cashier looked at him, Dak figured changing out fiat for casino currency wasn't an option. It was required.

"What's the minimum?" Dak asked.

The cashier scowled disapprovingly at the question. "Ten thousand."

"Oof. High-roller room, huh? Lucky I brought a spare ten grand with me."

He pulled the wad of cash from his pocket, counted out ten big bills, and handed them to the cashier.

Unimpressed, the man counted out the money, then remarked, "Change for ten thousand."

He slid Dak twenty chips in a clear plastic chip rack, then took a drag of his cigarette. The long ash hung from the tip, and Dak wondered when the guy was going to knock it off into an ashtray. Not that he cared. It just always annoyed him when people ignored their cigarette ashes like that.

"Thanks," Dak said, unimpressed by the small amount of chips he received for the decent sum he'd traded.

Another shove in the back ushered him toward the next door. The first guard stopped ahead of him and spun around.

"Arms," the man said, motioning for Dak to raise his hands up to the side.

I knew I wasn't going to get away with no pat down, he thought with a smug grin.

The guard didn't know what to think of the expression but flashed a look of disgust as he ran his hands down Dak's side then along the inner and outer seams of his jeans.

"You're way better than the guys that usually do this," Dak said.

The man looked up at him when he was at Dak's ankles. Though he didn't say anything, the confusion melting into irritation was impossible to miss in the guard's eyes.

"He's clean," the man said to the other. Then he rapped twice on the door. "New player."

The door unlocked and opened wide. The security guard stepped in, and the one behind Dak reached out to nudge him forward. Dak took a step into the next room before the guy touched him.

Dak looked around the room as he walked in, taking in the scene. The sounds of Indian music filled the air. A bar with an impressive array of liquors and beers occupied half the length of the wall to the left. Two female bartenders in skimpy black corsets worked busily on drinks. To the right, a railing ran along the platform looking down into a recessed area where the table games occupied the floor.

Two craps tables, four poker tables, two blackjack tables, two roulette wheels, and several other casino staples filled the gaming area.

The casino, if it could be called that, wore an industrial look. The bare brick walls had been painted white, though the floors were left as unfinished concrete. Exposed air ducts hung from the ceiling, much as Dak had seen in modern home and commercial designs. Televisions hung from the walls, each one displaying a different live sport. Most screens featured cricket matches, though a few were showing soccer games.

More people than Dak would have expected sat or stood around the gaming tables, anxiously rolling dice or placing bets. By his rough, quick count, there appeared to be more than a hundred gamblers in the room.

Dak started toward the bar, but the guard behind him stuck out his arm, guiding him to the right, down a set of steps under a massive crystal chandelier. The gaudy lighting fixture couldn't have been more out of place in the casino. Its shimmering, sparkling crystals posed a stark contrast to the derelict décor, though Dak realized it was all intentional.

He followed the first guard, knowing the second was close behind, across the gaming floor to another set of steps that climbed back up to an elevated area where several booths lined the wall and stools sat under counters overlooking the railing above the game area.

Dak picked out Tamara the second he entered the room, though he didn't fully get a good look at her until he climbed the steps toward her deep blue chaise lounge wedged between two booths. A coffee table sat in front of a white, plush couch that occupied space next to the chaise.

There was no denying Tamara's outer beauty. The woman's long black hair was bound up in a high ponytail, and her dark chocolate eyes captured Dak before he could escape and pulled his gaze to her full, maroon lips.

She wore a dress the color of the ocean, a darker blue than the couch beneath her. To call the outfit a gown wouldn't have been entirely incorrect as its elegance would have fit almost any occasion. A long slit ran up the left leg she had crossed over the right as she sat back against the cushion. The high collar of the dress displayed swirls of gold fabric matching the collar's rim. The golden tendrils twisted and reached down to the low-cut, sharp-angled V below the neck.

Tamara stared at Dak with lazy, hungry eyes as he approached. Her right arm hung over the cushion to her right, with her left hand placed on her outer thigh.

Dak stopped short of her sitting area and waited as the guards moved to either side of him, both ready in case he tried anything stupid.

She raised her left hand and planted a finger against her temple, her eyes drifting from his eyes all the way down to his ankles, then back up again as she took in every inch of the American.

She breathed easily, casually, then motioned for the two guards to leave with a flick of her finger.

The men didn't question her. They simply obeyed, both turning instantly and walking back to the top of the stairs, where one remained on guard while the other returned across the gaming floor and out through the exit into the receiving room.

Dak watched them disperse over his shoulder, then returned his gaze to the beautiful Indian woman on the lounge chair.

"So," Tamara began in a smooth voice bordering on seductive, "what's your pleasure?"

He sighed at the way she said it. There were times when Dak

found it difficult to deny his masculine instincts, and this was one of those times.

"Chester said I should come see you," he confessed, doing exactly what the Brit told him not to do. Deep down, he had a laugh at Chester's expense, knowing he would freak out if he knew Dak said his name in her presence.

She raised her eyebrows at the statement. "Do you throw everyone you know under the bus?"

Dak allowed an easy smile. "No, ma'am. I just know it would get under his skin."

"I see. So you enjoy being an instigator." Her statement came with no menace.

"I don't follow the rules. Not anymore."

"As demonstrated by your interaction with my bartender."

"He seems like a nice guy," Dak said with a shrug. "But I don't have time for protocols or doing things by the book. No matter whose book it is."

"Ah." She reached over and took a martini glass from the table, raised it to her lips, and took a sip. After she swallowed, she let out a satisfied sigh. "Drink?"

"I'm working—but thank you."

"I'm working, too, love. Looks like you need to find another line of work. One that allows you to imbibe during hours." She grinned devilishly.

Dak looked around the room, partly to distract himself from the temptation lying before him, covered only by thin strips of blue fabric. "Nice place you got here," he said, changing the subject. His eyes played over the clientele. "Looks like you have some young money and some old money here. Foreigners, too."

"Yes, diversification is important in business. Perhaps you've heard."

He nodded. "Yep. So I've heard."

"We have startup business founders, oil tycoons, even the occasional celebrity. Although they're usually authors. Writers don't tend to stick out in a crowd as much as a movie star or musician."

"Interesting."

"Is it?"

"Not really," Dak admitted. "I was just being nice."

"Why start now, Mr. Harper? I much prefer your coarse honesty."

"Good," Dak said. "It was starting to get difficult. Although you do have something of a reputation. People are afraid of being honest with you. That must get old."

"Ah." She took another sip from the martini glass. "Chester must have told you that."

"He did." Again, Dak knew that the Brit would absolutely lose his mind if he'd been listening. "Actually, what he told me is that I should be nice, but he made it sound like I should kiss your feet. Or else."

She shifted forward, intrigued. "Or else what?"

Great, Dak thought. *Now she's flirting with me.* The way she stared at him gave it away too. Her perfume filling his nostrils begged him to return the favor. Dak considered it but thought better of it. There was a woman somewhere here in the city who needed his help.

"I guess that's up to the bards to decide when they're speaking of your legend around campfires. I personally don't care about your methods."

A man's voice shouted from one of the poker tables. He swore in English, but his accent was a distinctly Russian. He went on for several seconds, directing his anger at one of the other players.

Dak looked over his shoulder at the man. He was tall, probably a little taller than Dak, though from the angle it was difficult to tell. His buzzed hair looked like pepper on his pale scalp.

The dealer was doing his best to keep the man calm, but that only redirected new threats to him instead.

"What's his problem?" Dak asked, jerking his thumb at the poker player. His anger had simmered down, but it was easy to see the guy was a powder keg ready to blow again.

Tamara inhaled slowly and sighed. "He's the son of a Russian crime boss. He doesn't take losing well."

"Maybe he should try a different game."

"Yes, well, now he's become *my* problem," she said. "I lose some of my biggest players because they don't want to be at the table with him. And he's here at least two, sometimes three days a week."

Dak looked over at the guy again then back to her. "You have security here. Why let him in? Tell him he's no longer welcome. Seems like the rest of your patrons are...respectable."

She laughed. "Respectable isn't one of the criteria for being a member here. Every person you see here, whether they run a legitimate business or not, is a scoundrel in their own way. But there is a code, an unspoken agreement. No one talks about this place."

That's obviously not working, he thought.

"And," she went on, "everyone understands not to cause trouble."

"Everyone but the Russian kid," Dak finished.

"Yes," she hissed, elongating the word. Tamara peered into his green eyes, wishing to draw him in but finding a wall somewhere between them that she could not see or touch, but that blocked her from him just the same. Her attention jumped to the Russian, who was already talking loudly again. She returned her focus to Dak, tilting her head to the side as seductively as possible. "Tell me, Dak Harper, what is your game of choice?"

Dak wondered what she meant by that. From the way his host said it, there could have been any number of meanings behind the question.

"I'm not much of a gambler," Dak admitted. "I prefer to keep the odds in my favor."

"Yes," Tamara said. "I sense that about you." She took another sip of her drink. "You were in the American military. Something of a warrior, from what I've gathered. Although, I haven't dedicated much time to the matter."

"What have you heard?" Dak wondered, surprised she had heard of him at all. His senses tingled.

"Oh, not much. Just that you were left for dead in a cave in Iraq by your team. Delta Force, yes? After being accused of trying to murder your friends, your name was cleared." Another flirty smile crossed her lips, and she raised one eyebrow, holding the martini glass at her chin.

"Word travels fast, I guess."

"Your ordeal was well publicized in the more shadowy circles of the world. I'm sure you know of the mercs guilds."

"I've heard of them," Dak half admitted. No reason to tell her everything.

"Then you must know there's a bounty on your head."

He nodded. "Yeah. My old CO doesn't like me too much. I think he blames me for his downfall. Personally, he should have just let it go. The military gave him an easy way out. All he had to do was walk away quietly and everything would have been fine."

"You wouldn't have searched him out and killed him?" Her eyes twitched with interest.

"No," Dak said, with a twist of his head. "I wouldn't have. But I will now. I thought I had him a few days ago in Cambodia, but he got away." He didn't know for sure why he was telling this stranger, this dangerous woman, so many details, but he felt like it was the right move. It established a dark side for him in a world where that kind of thing was embraced, and where every creature in the shadows carried their own sinister burdens like badges of honor.

"I have no doubts you will succeed. You have a way with people, and if that way doesn't work, it sounds like you have other ways that are more...persuasive."

"I do what I can."

"Yes," she agreed. "I believe you do." She took another drink and then held the empty glass out over the coffee table.

An Indian man in a white shirt and black vest with matching bowtie appeared next to her and collected the glass. "Would you like another?" he asked.

"Why not?" Tamara asked. "And bring a drink for my new friend."

"Two martinis," the man said.

"No," she corrected. "He doesn't look like the martini sort. Get him a bourbon." She turned to Dak but only with her eyes, looking at him sideways. "Do you have a favorite? Or would you like me to choose?"

"I said before, I don't drink while I'm working," Dak reminded, keeping his gruff tone as polite as possible. "But thank you."

"Ah, but sometimes drinking is work." She returned her attention to the server. "Get him a Blade and Bow. Neat. He looks like a man who takes it neat."

Dak didn't protest further. There was no point to it. Whether he wanted it or not, he was getting a bourbon. At this point, it might be more trouble to turn it down.

"Please, Mr. Harper," Tamara motioned to the couch next to her. "Sit down. You look uncomfortable standing there."

The Russian poker player yelled again. This time, he was trash talking one of the other players, calling him a series of names that would have turned the filthiest sailor red with embarrassment.

Dak preferred to stand than sit next to the woman, but the sofa did offer a strategic advantage to where he stood. From the couch, he could look out over the entire room, keep an eye on the exit, and make sure no one could sneak up behind him. He'd displayed patience, and trust, by standing there as long as he had, though stealing a few looks over his shoulder afforded him a semblance of security.

He ambled over to the sofa and eased into it. The softness of the cushions surprised him at first, and he sank back lazily into the furniture's embrace.

"This is nice," he said, patting the cushions.

"It's one of the finest sofas money can buy," she explained, her right hand crawling toward his left shoulder, daring to brush it with her fingernails.

The man in the bowtie returned in record time with a tray carrying two drinks. He handed the lady her martini first then set the bourbon tumbler down on the coffee table in front of Dak.

"Thanks," Dak said.

"Of course, sir." The man bowed and disappeared to the corner, where he stood awaiting the next requirement from his boss.

Dak leaned forward and picked up the glass, raised it to Tamara, and gave a nod.

"To new friendships," she said.

"Sure," he groused.

They clinked glasses and each took a sip.

On the inside, Dak's impatience gnawed at him like a beaver chewing through a tree trunk. He didn't have time for this, sitting around, making friends with a woman who ran an illegal casino and who clearly had other things in mind for him. He knew what some of those ideas might be, but Dak also got the impression there was something else.

"So," he said, "you know how to find the buyer?"

She grinned, almost disappointedly. "What buyer?"

"We're going to play it like that, then? You pretend you don't what I'm talking about, then I have to beg, or maybe do you a favor. I scratch your back sort of thing?"

"You really are perceptive, she purred.

"So you know where the buyer is?"

"Of course I do. But it wouldn't be good for business if I betrayed clients left and right to every wanton vigilante that comes through these doors." She laughed. It was a low, sinister sound that put Dak on edge, but no threat approached from any part of the room.

"You see," she added, "The people who come to me aren't the kind to be passed off as currency. They are dangerous, and if I betray one, they'll all find out about it."

"And then you'll be dead." It was a statement, not a question.

"Perhaps," she mused. "Or I might lose everything. This casino does well for me. I make a lot of money, but it would be out of business if I betrayed my buyers. They need to know they can trust me."

Dak bobbed his head with a sigh. He looked into his drink, raised it to his lips, and downed the contents. He swallowed back the warm whiskey, placed the glass on the table, and stood up, ready to end his short visit.

"Well, I appreciate your time, but I really must be going. There's a woman's life at stake and sitting around here all day drinking isn't going to save her." He stared down at her for two seconds. "Thanks for the drink."

Dak started to leave, hoping she'd buy the bluff. She let him take three steps toward the stairs before she stopped him.

"Wait."

Dak froze and listened.

"Please," she urged. "Come back over and have a seat. I didn't say I wouldn't help you."

Dak kept his satisfaction buried deep as he returned to the sofa.

When he was back in his seat, he asked, "Where is the buyer, Tamara?"

"I will tell you," she said in a tone that obviously carried a catch with it. "But I need you to do something for me first."

Dak felt his spirits drop at the revelation. The curator's life depended on him locating her as quickly as possible, and now he had to do favors for the proprietor of an illegal gambling operation.

He had two choices at this point. Do whatever the woman said or go back to the drawing board and try to find another contact. If he chose the second option, it could take days just to locate someone who might have a clue as to the whereabouts of the thief—if he found the information at all. Dak knew that Tamara might be the only person with valid information. It wasn't as if a contact like her was easy to find.

If Dak wanted to get to Dr. Laghari as fast as possible, that route still passed through the woman to his left in the blue dress.

"What do you have in mind?" Dak asked reluctantly.

She lowered her head, peering into his eyes. "So many things I want to say to that question, but I'll stick to business. For now." Tamara drew her glass close, then took a long sip.

Dak knew she was messing with him, deliberately taking her time to test his patience—and his persistence.

She licked her lips after the drink and continued. "As you can see," she looked toward the poker tables, "I have something of a problem. That man is costing me money. Every day he comes in here, he sends more of my gamblers away. When players don't want to play, we take less money, we sell less booze, and they don't wander over to the other games to try their luck when they've had enough of cards. What's just as bad is when *he* is the one who makes his way over to the other tables. He's abusive to other players, and to the dealers."

"What's his name?" Dak asked.

"Dema Lebedev," she purred. "A spoiled brat, that one. From what I understand, he's also abusive to women. His last two girlfriends ended up in the emergency room with multiple injuries, but no charges were pressed and the girls ended up being strangely silent about the whole matter. He's a jealous one, doesn't like it when his women even look at someone the wrong way. I pity them, honestly. I truly do. I would never tolerate a man like that in my life."

"But you'll tolerate them in your casino," Dak quipped.

"Touché. The casino, however, is different. It's my business, and usually he is the type of person I want gambling here."

"You mean his money."

"Precisely. Impulsive, wealthy types are my favorite players. But not this one."

"And you can't simply cut him off the VIP list without consequences later on down the road," Dak realized.

"Yes."

Dak saw where this was going, and he didn't know if he liked it. "Let me guess. You want me to do something about it."

She nodded absently, without saying anything at first, as if weighing the repercussions of even insinuating what she was thinking.

"Accidents happen, Mr. Harper. Sometimes intentional acts of aggression happen, too."

"You mean murder."

Her shoulders lifted then drooped again. "I didn't say that. But if something were to cut Dema's life short, I wouldn't complain. Honestly, the world would be better off."

Dak sighed. "You sure are making a lot of justifications for killing this guy."

"I don't have to justify it for myself. I'm doing that for your benefit. You strike me as the type who doesn't want innocent blood on his hands. I can tell you with the utmost certainty that Dema is not innocent. Look for yourself at how he behaves. His actions betray the truth about his personal life, about how he treats people."

Dak wanted to ask if she was any better, if any of these people in the room were. But he didn't. Dak could already see that she was right about Lebedev. Just then, the man slammed his fists on the table and watched his chips get pulled over to one of the other players.

Lebedev swore and raged. Eventually, he hurled a few last insults at the player who'd beaten him: a bald, older man with black wire-frame glasses and skin that sagged off his cheeks like sandbags. The winner didn't look happy, but he was also holding back anything he might say to add fuel to the Russian's emotional inferno.

"So, you're certain about him beating up on women?" Dak glowered at the man, watching him storm over to the bar where he demanded a drink. The Russian made a lewd comment about the bartender and then turned around to sip on his cocktail as he surveyed the room, deciding which game he would play next, if any.

"Yes," Tamara confirmed.

"I'm going to need more than that if you want me to do something about this guy," Dak hedged. "Not to mention that if I do, it's going to bring his father's organization to your front door."

Her lips curled on the right side. "That's precisely why you're the perfect man for the job, Mr. Harper."

He cringed at hearing the name again but said nothing.

"There is no connection between us," she continued. "No one here knows who you are, except me."

"And Chester."

"He's harmless." She waved a hand. "Well, not entirely harmless. He has his uses. And he does work with some of the best thieves in the world."

"Like the one who nabbed the statue for your buyer," Dak said.

"Yes. The buyer, whose location you want." She looked into his eyes again, sucking him into hers. "Kill Dema Lebedev. And I will give you the buyer's location."

"Killing is a big deal."

"Lebedev has killed many for his father. Not all of them were rival targets, either. He's sloppy, allows too much collateral damage. Last year, he tracked a target into a restaurant and killed him in front of two families. Children should not see into our world, Mr. Harper."

"You know...." Dak interrupted. He'd finally had enough. "You can just call me Dak."

She looked surprised but acquiesced. "Very well, Dak. There have been innocent people killed by that man. His temper doesn't allow for precision, or tact. He shoots first and asks questions later. You won't have to look far before you find his trail of victims. A quick search on the internet or in the papers, and Lebedev's bloody handprints will be there."

"Sounds dangerous."

"He's a bully. I assure you; a man of your talents will have no trouble with him."

Dak considered the offer. It was his only chance. He could get online, try to find out what he could about Lebedev, perhaps connect the man to some of the things Tamara was talking about, but he didn't need to. He didn't fully trust Tamara, but she needed a problem solved, and from the sound of it, so did this part of the city.

The thought of getting into a turf war with a Russian mob didn't sound appealing, but he didn't have to get into the trenches. Take out Lebedev, get the intel he needed, and let the cards fall where they may with Tamara and her operation. If they came after her, that wasn't his problem. And he had no emotional attachment to her. No loyalties.

"Where does he live?"

Pleased with the question, she took another sip from her glass and then detailed where Dak could find the man.

"He has a flat about ten minutes from here. You won't have any trouble getting in, but Lebedev's family owns the entire tenth floor of the building. So, anyone who gets off on ten will face some resistance."

"Perhaps there's another way in?" Dak offered.

"There is. You could go in through the roof access stairs."

"But then I would have to get to the rooftop without using the stairs or elevator."

"True," she said it as if there was no consequence and took another drink. "That shouldn't be a problem for a man—"

"Of my talents. Yeah, thanks. I'm not that invested in this. I'm more of a Hail Mary."

Her sultry façade broke for the first time since he'd started talking with her, Tamara's expression changed to one of curiosity. "What did you say?"

"A Hail Mary." He realized not everyone used that kind of expression and added, "I'm like the last-chance guy."

"And who do you work for? You're no cop."

"No. That's true. I'm not."

"You're no criminal either," she added.

"Correct," Dak said with a single nod.

"Then what are you, Mr....I mean, Dak?"

"Just a guy, trying to make his way, I guess."

She rolled her eyes. "Oh, spare me, Monsieur Cliché. I didn't realize we were being so dramatic."

He laughed, genuinely, puzzling over her comment. "What do you mean?"

After a long pull from her glass nearly finished the drink off, she leveled her gaze at him, shaking her head. "You are more than just an ordinary man. Ordinary men don't sit next to me. They serve me, wait on me, do my bidding, but they do not sit next to me. Only extraordinary men may have that privilege."

Dak assessed her compliment, his pensive gaze locked in on a random place along the far wall behind his hostess. Tamara was a gambler, too, but was she trying to play him?

"All right then," he said after a minute. He stood up and bowed his head. "Thanks for the drink."

"I hope to see you later," she said, returning to her flirty tone.

"Likewise."

Dak spun and walked down the stairs, up the next set, and turned left toward the exit. He walked through Lebedev's field of vision, but he doubted the man saw him. Lebedev was focused on the cocktail runner, a young woman with a skimpy serving costume and a tray of Jell-O shots she was hawking to the gamblers.

From the look in the Russian's eye, Dak knew the man wasn't thirsting for sugary, alcohol-infused blue raspberry.

Dak wasn't going to pass judgement. Not yet. He reminded himself that everything Tamara said could be, and likely was, either a lie or a stretching of the truth. Even so, Dak couldn't deny the multiple outbursts he'd seen from the mark. Lebedev displayed all the makings of a spoiled brat, a bully, and someone who could snap at the slightest provocation. Dak wanted to know more about the girl-friends. He would have loved to see proof. Small chance of that happening.

Still, something told Dak he wouldn't have to wait long before he'd see everything he needed.

He walked back through the weigh station and exchanged his chips for cash. The man behind the cage looked confused. Probably because no one ever left with the same amount they brought.

Dak returned to the restaurant and nodded to the bartender. "Thank you," he said.

The bartender stared at him like he'd seen a ghost. Eventually, he nodded and waved. Dak wondered if the man had expected him to be chopped up and dumped in the alley out back.

Stepping out through the front door and onto the sidewalk, Dak surveyed the intersection. Time for the wolf to find a good place to hunt his prey.

Gavin sat on the mattress with his back against the wall. He peered through the fence at Priya, who glowered right back at him.

How is it she's always awake or asleep when I am, he wondered. It was creepy, and the superstitious side of him had started to believe that maybe this woman carried some kind of bad luck. As a baseball fan, he'd never really subscribed to curses, or rituals, that caused a team like the Cubs to go without a title for over a hundred years. Still, everything was falling apart now, and he couldn't help but think that it was due to her.

There was still a way out of this. He knew that. But without a buyer, it was only a matter of time until he was caught.

"I bet you can feel it," Priya sneered.

Gavin rolled his eyes and looked up from his phone. "Feel what, exactly?"

She snorted in derision and shook her head. "The pressure. It must feel like the walls are closing in on you."

"You don't know what you're talking about. And you can save the psychological stuff for someone else. Because it won't work on me."

She paced to her right with her hands on her hips, studying him as he gazed at the floor with his elbows on his knees.

"Maybe I don't," she conceded. "I don't know you, but I know what you people are like. You thieves."

"Oh? And how is it that you've come to know so much about us?" He made a mockingly shocked expression and then slumped back to a scowl. "Did you read stories? Watch a bunch of movies?"

"I've known criminals my entire life. I was friends with some of them." Priya's voice grew distant, drifting from her body. "You're all the same. And you feel the pressure. They all did. For a while, it was why they did it. They fell prey to the lure of excitement, to the thrill of nearly getting caught."

Gavin listened with disinterest in his eyes, but in his heart, he felt every word like the pounding of a hammer on his chest.

"Eventually, of course, all of them got caught. Now their lives aren't their own."

"I really hope this isn't some sort of weird, backhanded lecture about turning my life around. Because if it is," he wrinkled his nose in disgust, "I'll pass."

She made a humming noise.

Gavin had grown tired of the woman. He wished he could have just killed her in the museum, left her body there, and walked away. No one would have known. But he'd hesitated. And that hesitation led to the irritation he currently endured.

"I wonder," she mused, "what you think you're going to do when the buyer doesn't call you back. Because you said that you could get another buyer, that you had all these connections. But you know what? I don't think you have any connections at all. I think you're just a scared little boy who finally got caught with his hand in the cookie jar. You lived on the edge, believing you were immortal. And—"

"Shut up!" Gavin roared. "Why don't you ever shut up?"

Priya's head retreated an inch, and she peered at him through the cage with shock in her eyes. "Testy, testy, aren't we? I guess I must have hit a little too close to home on that one."

"I said shut up! What about that do you not understand?"

She shrugged and paced back toward the wall to her right. Priya paused, staring at nothing in particular on the bland wall. He was cracking, and she knew it, but what would that mean? She wondered if she should keep prodding him, keep pressing him on the same psychological path that she'd been doing since encountering the thief at the museum, or if she should try a different tack.

Priya stole a sideways glance at him.

The thief sat in the same spot on his mattress, legs hanging over the side with his feet planted on the floor. He was a pretty boy, or so she thought. He had that all-American look to him that she'd heard so much about, had seen in movies and on television. If he'd approached her at a bar and offered a drink, Priya wouldn't have refused. He was attractive, but also foolish. And of course, he was a career criminal. On a first-drink sort of encounter, though, there would be no way to know that.

She wondered how many women had fallen prey to his charms, though she'd yet to see anything even close to resembling charm out of him up to this point. All Priya had seen was a whiny brat who couldn't figure out how to handle a little curve ball thrown into his plans.

"What do you think is going to happen if the buyer bails?" she asked abruptly, her eyes remaining locked on the wall in front of her.

"I already told you, you crazy—"

"Watch your tongue," she warned.

"I have other buyers. I just have to get in touch with them, that's all."

She shook her head. "Like a broken record."

"You're no better," Gavin spat.

He stood up and walked over to a chair in the corner, spun around, and then walked back to his spot on the bed. He slumped down again, his mind racing with questions that had few answers.

Gavin was about to lie down on the bed when his phone buzzed in his hands. He looked down at the number, and a wave of hope crashed over him. He pressed the green button on the device and raised the phone to his ear.

Priya watched intently, listening carefully to see if she could hear what the person on the other end said.

"Hello," Gavin said. "I was starting to think you might have changed your mind."

"No," the man's voice said through the speaker. "I haven't changed my mind."

Gavin turned away from Priya, as if that would buy him some privacy. "Good. That's good to hear. When do you want to make the pickup?"

"We will be there in two hours. Make sure that everything is in order. No funny business. You know what that means."

"Of course."

Gavin did know. The buyer was referring to the presence of cops, hidden guards, anything that might smell like a trap. The buyer didn't have a clue what Gavin's situation was, not that it mattered. He'd always avoided settings that would spook a buyer. Dealing with those kinds of people in a personal, straight-up manner had always worked to his benefit. Repeat customers were commonplace for Gavin, and it was because he'd never acted fishy, never tried to swindle a buyer. Maximized profits, sure, but never cheated them. They, after all, held most of the cards. They had the money. All he had was an asset that could only be sold to a select group of people in the world.

"Good." The man clipped the word in his sharp German accent. "That is good to hear. Make sure it stays that way."

"I will. Definitely." Gavin did his best not to sound nervous, but he couldn't help feeling like the buyer could see right through the tremors in his tone. "You have our location, right?"

"Yes. I know where to find you."

The call went dead, and for a second, Gavin wasn't sure if the man hung up or if he'd lost cell service.

"Hello?" Gavin looked at the screen and saw the call had ended. "Okay, then." He slid the device into a pocket, relieved to be able to put it away after basically doing nothing but stare at it every waking second.

"Did your buyer bail?" Priya asked.

Gavin shook his head. "No. They will be here in a few hours."

"Wow," she said, genuinely impressed. "You know, I have to admit.

I had my doubts. I didn't think you were smart enough or organized enough to pull something like this off. But here you are." She clapped her hands together one time. "I guess everyone gets lucky now and then."

"I'm never lucky," he snarled.

"I guess we'll see."

Dak sat on a park bench around the corner from Lebedev's building. He'd taken a cab from the casino, though he wasn't entirely sure why. Every now and then, despite being exceedingly cautious, Dak got the feeling he was being followed. And whenever that sensation swept over him, he simply changed whatever routine could be traced. In this instance, he decided to leave the rental car where he'd parked it and hailed a taxi.

The phone in his hand displayed information about the Russian and the recent crime epidemic that came with more gangs moving into this part of Mumbai.

Organized crime, it seemed, operated much like the empires of old, always looking to expand and colonize new areas to grow their power and wealth.

Dema Lebedev had been linked to at least three killings, but was suspected to be involved with more, though the man never spent a single day in prison. Every charge that was thrown his way always ended up sliding off.

"The guy is Teflon," Dak muttered upon seeing how much evidence had been dismissed in every single case.

The mere fact that Lebedev had been caught so many times betrayed the man's true, careless nature. Dak had seen that kind of personality many times before. People like Lebedev believed they were above the law, that nothing could ever touch them.

He'd probably been brought up in a strange home. Dak doubted the kid ever had anything close to a normal family life. His father, based on what Dak could learn online, had been involved in organized crime since he was in his twenties, starting out with one of the smaller mobs in Moscow, then moving around the Eastern Bloc of Europe until deciding to head for greener pastures in a new country.

From there, the trail went cold, though it was easy to connect the dots to potential racketeering schemes, loan shark activity, and extortion. With so much poverty in many parts of India, the older Lebedev saw an enormous opportunity with people desperate to improve their lives with some extra cash.

Dak sighed, thinking about the people men like Lebedev had used to line their own pockets, selling their services as some sort of solution to their problems. With the money the father made off the backs of the poor, Dema Lebedev had grown up in a lavish lifestyle, where no one—probably not even his parents—had ever told him no.

That sort of upbringing almost never resulted in the creation of a kind, generous human being. It bred entitlement and a perpetual thirst for everything the individual believed they had coming to them.

There'd been a few people like that in Dak's high school. They were the ones who drove luxury cars to school while he and most of his friends were resigned to hand-me-down cars or old, beat up vehicles that their parents could afford—if they got a car at all. Many of his friends didn't get their first rides until college.

Not all of the kids in fancy cars were that way, Dak knew, but there were plenty of examples that ended up exactly like Dema Lebedev.

Growing up without restrictions led to a fully hedonistic life, and even that didn't satisfy the perpetual need for more—of everything.

And whenever a person like that met resistance, they almost always reverted to a childish response, just like a baby having their rattle taken away.

On top of the mound of "circumstantial" evidence that Tamara had provided him, Dak managed to find a newspaper article from Saint Lucia that made reference to the disappearance of a young woman in which Dema Lebedev was once a prime suspect but was later cleared.

From what Dak could gather, Lebedev had been there on vacation. He'd gone on another bender, gotten plastered, and then no one could piece together what happened next. Eyewitnesses testified that they'd seen the Russian with the girl, but the testimony was thrown out when the witnesses failed to accurately identify Lebedev in a lineup.

Dak knew that was a simple shell game to run. He figured the older Lebedev simply inserted several potential suspects who looked similar to Dema. He was surely no expert on police protocols, but Dak knew that enough money or power could bend the rules in nearly any country.

Peering up at the tenth floor of the gray contemporary building, Dak almost felt glad Tamara had asked him to do this. He would have been, in some ways, if a woman's life didn't hang in the balance, but that wasn't the only way to think of it. Other people's lives could also be weighing at this very second, lives that Lebedev and his cronies would snuff out as they would an ant under a magnifying glass. These animals didn't care about people or families or friends. Lives were expendable to them.

Especially to Dema.

Dak's phone vibrated and he checked the number.

"Hey, Will," he said, pressing the speaker to his ear while keeping his eyes on the building. "I trust you have some information for me. Because the guards at the museum don't have much. All they got was a guy wearing a Dodgers cap, but nothing else they could use to identify the thief. We did figure out where he hid, though."

"Probably a ventilation shaft in one of the storage rooms," Will offered.

Dak's forehead wrinkled with his frown. "Wait. How did you know that?"

"Lucky guess, but it's what I would do if I was trying to steal some multimillion-dollar idol out of a highly secure museum."

"Impressive," Dak said. "Because that's exactly what he did. Be sure not to tell the cops what you just told me, or they might start thinking you're an accomplice."

Will huffed. "You don't have to worry about me doing something like that. I keep most of my activities off the radar anyway."

"That you do, my friend. So, do you have something on the thief other than a really good guess?"

"Actually, I do. Didn't take long once I saw the hat. It's that guy's calling card. He wears it to every job he pulls. Kind of dumb if you ask me, but some people just want to be known for something. They get addicted to that odd kind of fame, I suppose."

Will cleared his throat and started again. "His name is Gavin Harris. He's suspected in a bunch of jobs, man. I'm talking all over the Eastern Hemisphere. Doesn't seem to have done much on the West side."

"If he's an antiquities thief," Dak said, "then that would make sense. We don't have a ton of ancient stuff in the States, although South America does. Central, too."

"True. Maybe he doesn't care to go back home."

"Home?"

"Yeah," Will sighed. "Grew up in LA. Wealthy parents. Not sure why he decided it was a good career move to go into theft of valuable artifacts, but he abandoned his family."

"Mommy and daddy were never there for him is what it sounds like," Dak theorized.

"Or maybe he just didn't like the way they did things, or the plan they had for him. I did a little more digging. Went to school in Redlands from kindergarten until college. Then he attended San

Diego State for a semester before dropping out. After that, he disappeared."

Disappeared, Dak thought. "Lot of that going around. At least he and I have that in common."

"That's where the common ground stops, my friend. He's suspected in seven high-profile heists, with four more linking him as a potential prime candidate. No one can seem to catch him, though."

"Hmm," Dak hummed. "Interesting that he wore his signature blue Dodgers cap to set up the transmitter receiver in the video link room. He must be getting bolder with every job."

"Probably," Will agreed. "A lot of times, these guys start feeling like they really are immortal, that nothing or no one will ever catch them. It's almost like a video game to them, where there are no real consequences."

"Sounds about right. Any idea where I can find him?"

Will laughed. "And that's the million-, or rather, multimillion-dollar question. No one knows where he lives. My guess is he doesn't have a permanent residence. Bounces around like a nomad from country to country, probably with a catalog of fake passports from multiple nations. Tracking him will be difficult. Despite his brazen move of wearing the Dodgers cap to the museum, I doubt he's so naïve to think he could continue getting away with that in airports or on the street."

"You never know," Dak said, voicing his thoughts. He knew that was a reach. Even the most careless of thieves weren't stupid enough to allow themselves to be caught simply by recognition. When Harris traveled, he most certainly used a disguise, and as Will suggested, multiple passports with a variety of identities. "You don't happen to know if he has an apartment around here somewhere, do you? Maybe the address? Passcode to get in?"

Another laugh burst through the speaker. "Nah, man. Nothing like that. Come on, now. I can't just put it all on a platter for you. You got to do some of the work, too."

Dak allowed a short huff. "I know, man. Thanks. I appreciate it."

"What are you doing, anyway? Sounds like you're kind of pensive about something."

"I am," Dak said. "I have to do a favor for someone, a person I would prefer not to do a favor for, but I don't have much choice in the matter."

"Heh. There's always a choice, man. No one can make you do anything."

"I know," Dak agreed. "Honestly, the favor is for humanity in general."

"Oh," Will realized. "One of those, huh?"

"Yeah. One of those."

"Too many scumbags like that out there in the world, making the place stink. Anyone I might have heard of?"

"I doubt it." Dak considered the question then reaffirmed the answer in his mind. "Small-time Russian-outfit guy. His daddy runs the organization here in Mumbai."

"Mumbai? I didn't even realize the Russian mob was moving in there."

"Me either. If the two of us didn't know about it, that means they must have figured their landing spot correctly. Off the radar." Dak paused. "He's hurt a lot of people. And even when he gets arrested, nothing sticks. Beats up on women, kills people, just a bad person. And you know me, I don't judge. I have plenty of blood on my hands."

"Yeah," Will half conceded, "but you were following orders."

"Does that make it right?" Dak wondered. "I don't know. I don't feel guilty about it. I did what I was supposed to do."

"And recently?"

"I did what I had to do. Always will. I keep thinking, though, that these situations, these moments in time keep being placed in front of my path, like it's my destiny or something."

"Okay," Will said, "let's just slow down a minute and not go quite that deep into the philosophical rabbit hole yet."

"I know. It sounds egotistical. I'm not saying I'm special. I'm only saying we all have a purpose, some sort of calling we're supposed to follow in life. Maybe mine is doing bad things to bad people."

"Does that make those things bad if you're doing them to the wicked?"

"I thought you said you didn't want to get in the rabbit hole." Dak chuckled.

"I don't, but if you're gonna keep digging, I might as well follow."

Dak looked around. The busy city street's constant flow of foot and vehicle traffic had slowed to a trickle. It was late in the evening, getting close to ten, and most of the locals were home for the night.

"I grew up in a home where I was taught that two wrongs don't make a right," Dak said after half a minute. "You probably heard something similar."

"I did."

"Yet we were part of a machine that preached the opposite, that wrongful force must be met with force. To the people we were up against, we were the bad guys, and they were the good."

"True," Will said. "I've thought about that many times. Just like every war ever fought on this soil or in our waters. Both sides believe they are on the right side of the line."

"There were times that sort of thing made me wonder if there was a right side at all. I believe there is. If you're standing on the side of those who can't fight for themselves, speak for themselves, and are hurt by aggressors, then you're doing what is right."

"Amen, brother."

Dak felt a calm wash over him. He wasn't in the murder-for-hire business, never even considered being some kind of assassin or hit man. Except for his own personal vendetta against those who betrayed him, he preferred to sit in the forest and embrace the quiet solace of nature. But there were bad people out there doing bad things. He thought he'd picked up a job as a relic runner for a rich kid out of Southeast Tennessee. What he'd really found was something deeper: new meaning.

"I gotta go, man," Dak said. "Thanks for the intel on Harris. I'm working on a lead to track him down. We'll see how far that gets me."

"No problem, man. Anytime. I'll let you know if I hear anything else."

"Thanks, Will. As always."

"You're welcome, Dak. As always."

Dak ended the call and slipped the phone into his left-front pocket. Then he stood up, glanced around at the empty street, secured his pistol under his jacket, and crossed the road to the front of Lebedev's building.

14

The interior of the building showed off multiple architectural personalities. Black columns supported a high ceiling in the lobby, with plain white walls and a black walnut floor. Those same walls served as an exhibit to random Indian artwork. Some paintings featured deities, Indian history, and a few with famous personalities from the past. The smell of jasmine filled the lobby with a subtle, yet intoxicating aroma.

A darkened leasing office to the left was partitioned off by a glass wall with black metal frames. There were no security guards on duty and no concierge working an information desk. This was, after all, a private residence, and getting in couldn't have been simpler.

Getting to Lebedev, on the other hand, would be a different matter.

Dak walked to the rear of the lobby, following signs to the elevators situated in an alcove to the left. He noted their location, then continued past the lifts. A placard on the wall displayed a rudimentary picture of stairs with an arrow, and Dak took the prescribed route down a corridor to the left.

He passed a series of closed doors, each with placards declaring Business Room or Exercise Center or Restrooms, until he reached the last one on the right with the stairs and stick figure going up next to it.

Dak looked back down the hall and then pulled on the lever to open the door.

The air inside the stairwell was hot and muggy and smelled of new construction, like fresh paint and concrete. Based on what he'd seen in the lobby and of the exterior, it probably was a brand new building, and Dak wondered how many of the units were occupied.

Not because he was interested in renting a place but because he preferred to keep witnesses to minimum, and collateral damage to zero. Fortunately, Tamara suggested that the top floor was owned entirely by Lebedev's organization. As Dak set foot on the first step going up, he silently prayed that the woman was right. At this point, he felt like it could go either way. She may well have intentionally sent him into a trap. Dak even considered the possibility that Tucker was behind all of this, and that she was working for him, throwing him into the fire so the former colonel could finally have his revenge.

Going up the stairs to the tenth floor was a leap of faith, but Dak had to take that chance. Fortunately, he had something in his pocket that would help.

Dak rounded the first landing and continued upward, checking around the railing at every stopping point for guards above. The slow, methodical progress dragged, but Dak's practice in patience over the years wouldn't let him move too quickly, or too recklessly. Prudence was one of the reasons he was still alive after all this time.

He safely reached the ninth floor and stopped to catch his breath. His legs burned from the climb, and he marveled at the strength and conditioning of firefighters who climbed two, three, or more times this many stairs for their jobs. Dak was in good shape, but he quickly realized he needed to add one more component to his regular workout routine: stairs.

After his breathing calmed, he reached out and pulled the handle on the door and poked his head inside. A quick check down the length of the corridor gave him what he expected—no sign of trouble. Up on the tenth, though, he knew it wouldn't be so clear. Which is why he needed a diversion.

Dak stepped out into the hallway and walked at a brisk pace toward the elevators, making sure his pistol remained hidden to any innocent tenants that happened to appear. The walk to the lifts felt dreadfully long, and the corridor almost seemed to stretch as he proceeded.

He heard a child crying in one of the apartments he passed. A television blared loudly in another a few doors down. Each sound brought Dak's attention spiking through the roof of his mind again, and he twitched, almost nervously at each noise.

Finally, after what seemed like minutes, he reached the elevators and pressed the up button.

Dak shuffled back and watched the numbers increasing from the third floor. He took a little cylinder out of his pocket and palmed it. The device was the diameter of a AAA battery, and half as long, with a single button on the side no bigger than the head of a pen.

When the elevator reached the ninth floor, Dak stepped off to the side and waited, just in case one of the Russian mob goons happened to be on board. Perhaps he was being a bit too careful. The Russians didn't know he was on his way there to take out their leader's son. If the doors had opened and one of the thugs had seen him standing there, Dak could have simply asked if this elevator was going down and then pretended to wait for the next one.

As it was, when the doors opened, no hulking armed figure loomed inside and the knots in his gut melted.

He leaned inside the elevator, pressed the button for 10, and then depressed the button on the device in his palm. Dak tossed the cylinder into the corner, and then took off at a sprint. He dashed down the corridor, silently praying no one stepped out of their apartment too rapidly.

Fortune led the way, and no one emerged in his path.

He barged through the doorway into the stairs and pumped his legs, climbing the steps two at a time until he rounded the top landing at the tenth floor.

Dak raised the thermal scanner and held it to the door. He wouldn't be able to detect all the guards on this floor through the surface, but he could get a reading from the closest ones, and that was a start.

Bright orange, red, and yellow filled the screen in the outline of a human form just on the other side of the doorway, a few feet to the left. As he suspected, one guard standing there.

The timer in Dak's head blared, anticipating that the elevator should have arrived by now.

Patience, he reminded himself, though his mind played tricks on him, telling him the device hadn't worked or that somehow the elevator went to the wrong floor.

Then the man by the door abruptly moved away from the wall, walking down the corridor.

Dak slid the scanner back into his pocket, drew his pistol, and attached the suppressor to the barrel with a twist. Then he carefully turned the door handle and pulled. Thankfully, the hinges didn't creak and he slipped through the narrow opening into the hallway.

White smoke billowed into the corridor, spilling in both directions from the elevator portal sixty feet away. Three guards armed with Heckler & Koch submachine guns stared at the bizarre cloud. One of them was saying something, motioning to the fog that continued to overflow out of the elevator's waiting area and into the hall.

The three men stepped back from it as the smoke encroached on their space. All the while Dak continued forward, padding toward the men on the balls of his feet with his pistol raised.

Fifty feet. Forty. Thirty.

At twenty feet from the nearest gunman, Dak couldn't see through the smoke to the other side where he knew more guards were likely standing, much like these three, trying to understand where the smoke was coming from and what the cause might be.

One of the men raised a radio and turned away from the diversion just as Dak closed the gap to fifteen feet.

The guard saw Dak and his eyes widened at the sight of the pistol.

The man got caught between pressing the button on the radio to alert everyone else to the trouble and raising his weapon to defend himself. His inaction led to a quick death.

Dak fired a single shot through the man's right cheek. The bullet exited through the back of his head and sprayed a pink mist on the other two guards.

The men reacted with bewilderment at first, looking down at their clothes and hands in wonder. Before they could turn and face the threat, Dak executed them both with a single headshot each at point-blank range.

Dak bent down and scooped up two of the guns from the dead men. Each weapon had been equipped with suppressors, which surprised Dak. From what he'd read and heard about Lebedev, he was a careless individual, perhaps with the exception of protecting his hearing, and that of his henchmen.

The smoke device had already drained all of its contents, but the thick haze lingered in the hall, still masking the other side of the corridor. That wouldn't last long. Dak strapped the H&Ks to his shoulders then took a deep breath and charged forward through the dying fog.

Dak burst through the smoke into the clear air on the other side and nearly collided with one of Lebedev's men. If he hadn't been holding his breath, Dak could have smelled the garish, overused cologne the guard wore.

The startled goon raised his eyebrows in alarm and tried to raise his weapon. Dak fired two shots into the man's abdomen, driving him back two staggering steps before finishing the job with a headshot above the nose.

The other two guards reacted faster than their comrades on the other side of the smoke spill. They stepped back and raised their guns, their trigger fingers itching for a kill.

Dak dove forward, dropping his pistol as he rolled between the men. He spun and twisted onto one knee, raising both submachine guns in one fluid, deadly motion. The men turned to defend themselves, but it was too late. Dak opened fire, his fingers flicking repeatedly on the triggers until each of the guards had received their share of bullets.

The peppered bodies stumbled backward into the thinning smoke and crumbled to the floor with their comrades.

Dak bent down and picked up his pistol. He looked over his shoulder at the door to Lebedev's penthouse, just two doors down from where he stood. He took a quick breath, then hurried over to the doorway. Pressing his left ear to the door, Dak listened.

The quiet hallway gave way to a flurry of activity inside. It didn't sound like Lebedev or anyone else inside had been alerted to what just happened in the corridor. Instead, what he heard was almost as chilling, if not more so.

"Please, Dema!" a woman screamed. "Please, stop."

"You don't tell me what to do!" The man's thick Russian accent brimmed with indignation. A loud smack came next and then loud sobbing. A new voice laughed, and Dak heard a third crack a foul joke in Russian about the girl.

She kept begging for mercy, which resulted in a thump, though Dak wasn't sure what that was. He hoped Lebedev wasn't bashing her head against the wall, but that's exactly what it sounded like. Dak felt a wave of pressure surge over him. He couldn't let the mad Russian keep beating this poor girl, whoever she was. But he needed a way in, and he doubted knocking would be the best answer.

An idea emerged in the swirling vortex of his mind. He looked back to the nearest guard and saw the radio on the man's collar.

Dak returned to the bloody body and started to pluck the radio from the dead man when he noticed a distinct outline in the guy's front-right pocket. It was a thin rectangle. Had the situation not been so dire, Dak might have grinned at the sight, but instead, he simply reached into the pocket and pulled out the room's card key.

Four seconds later, he was at the door again. He held the card to the magnetic disc over the handle and pressed it against the black circle.

A light blinked green, and the lock clicked.

Dak dropped the card, twisted the handle, and shoved the door open.

The first guard stood to the left, in a kitchen with white counter-tops and matching cabinetry. *Won't be white for long,* Dak thought.

The guard was laughing, watching through the opening in the kitchen to a living room where a tall, muscular man hovered over a young brunette girl. The young woman didn't look a day over nineteen, and couldn't have weighed more than 110 pounds. A cut on the side of her forehead trickled blood down her pale cheek, passing a black eye on its way to the edge of her jaw.

Lebedev's face burned red with anger and he fumed as he stared down at her, the hulking trapezius muscles between his shoulders rising and falling dramatically with every breath. He wore one of those tank-top undershirts, showing off multiple tattoos on his arms.

Beyond the fuming Russian, a wall of glass led out onto a balcony overlooking the city. The downtown skyline twinkled against the night on the horizon. Two more guards stood near the windows, each armed with H&Ks.

Four guards. One left. One right. Two straight ahead. And Lebedev.

Dak took in all that information in under two seconds, as he'd been trained. Speed in a situation like this was critical.

The guard to the left was munching on a bag of chips when Dak appeared. The man saw the intruder out of the corner of his eye, but by then it was too late.

Dak raised his pistol and fired a single bullet through the man's temple. He dropped to the floor beside the new crimson abstract art on the previously white cabinets. Even with the fall, the guard never let go of the chips.

Spinning to his right, Dak led with the pistol and squeezed the trigger, emptying the contents of the magazine into the second guard's torso. The gunman had reacted to the attack but never got off a shot as every bullet from the assailant's weapon ripped through his vital organs, driving him back against the wall, where he slumped down to his tailbone. Dak dropped his empty pistol and raised one of the Heckler & Kochs at his hip.

The guards on the far side of the room shouted a warning.

Lebedev turned his head in time to see the threat and dove for cover a split second before Dak took aim.

Dak fired, the rounds missing the target as the man disappeared behind a long, black leather couch. The bullets zipped through the windows in the center of the far wall, sending the two guards into an immediate counterattack.

They readied their weapons and returned fire, forcing Dak to duck and take cover behind the kitchen cabinet.

Dust and debris fell all around him as Lebedev's men continued their barrage, firing the semiautomatic weapons with reckless abandon. If they were trying to give suppressing fire for their boss to take cover, or perhaps escape, it was working. Though Dak wasn't sure if the men were actually deploying that tactic or merely shooting out of desperation, hoping against hope they might get lucky and clip the target.

Dak crawled to the right, just short of the cabinet's corner, and waited. Another flurry of bullets cracked by and burrowed into the wall behind him.

Then the gunmen's volley ceased. Dak knew they were either reloading or assessing whether or not they'd taken out the threat.

Dak peeked around the corner with his weapon, sweeping the sights to the first target on the right. The gunman stood behind a white leather chair with a high back and rounded armrests. The black base of the furniture matched the black tiles on the floor.

Dak squeezed the trigger, but the man ducked behind the chair a split second before and the bullet zipped through the air over his head, punching a hole in the glass.

The gunman remained under the chair, probably thinking himself safe for the moment, but Dak merely lowered his sights and took aim at the man's lower body. The legs, feet, and backside were all visible as the guard crouched. Dak saw the magazine drop from the enemy's gun and knew he had to seize the opportunity.

Lebedev was swearing in Russian, barking orders at the men in a panicked voice. The girl sobbed loudly, now panic-stricken by both Lebedev and the bullets flying around the room.

None of it distracted Dak. He heard everything, sensed every movement, every sound, every sight. The smell of burned powder filled his nostrils, a familiar scent that felt like an old companion he couldn't get rid of.

Dak paused for less than a second as the gunsights came to rest on the guard's knee. He fired a single shot. The round found its mark, smashing into the man's kneecap. The guard screamed, letting go of his weapon to grasp the mangled joint. He fell onto his side, clutching the knee and simultaneously exposing his back to the shooter.

Dak fired two more shots, straight into the man's upper spine. The agonized screams muted and the gunman's body stopped writhing on the floor, falling still into the cold embrace of death.

"Tell your other guard to drop his weapon, Dema," Dak ordered in English from behind the corner. He used the vocal distraction to eject the magazine and scoop up a full one from the dead guard behind him. He still had plenty in the second H&K, but it never hurt to have a little extra.

The response from Lebedev was a slurry of English profanity directed in Dak's direction.

"That wasn't very nice," Dak replied. "You could have just said no."

"You've made a big mistake coming here, American. Whoever you are."

The empty threat rolled off Dak's.

"I don't know," Dak said, looking over at the cabinets to his right as he kept his back pinned against the lower ones. Several black coffee mugs and matching saucers sat on the counter's surface, along with four teacups. "You might want to ask all your dead guards about that. They might have a different opinion."

Lebedev swore again, this time telling Dak where to go.

As the Russian offered his curt and unoriginal retort, Dak crawled over to the corner of the kitchen. He stood up and grabbed one of the coffee mugs, then hurled it around the corner at the window behind the second couch that sat in front of the glass, facing into the living room's center.

The mug flew through the air, tumbling toward the window, then crashed into the cracked glass, shattering it on the way through.

Broken shards rained down onto the hard floor close to the gunman. The diversion caused him to pop up and turn to defend himself—from what, he didn't know.

Dak aligned the sights on the gun and squeezed the trigger. He fired multiple shots at the target, winging the man on the shoulder with one and sending several through his side into his rib cage. The guard's lower back received two more as he turned instinctively from the barrage and staggered through the broken window and out onto the balcony, where he fell prostrate next to a metal patio chair.

Keeping his weapon ready, Dak crept around the counter and stopped, surveying the room for his quarry.

"It's just you and me now, Dema," Dak said in a haunting voice. "It's not too late for you to surrender."

Moving slowly, calculating every step, Dak eased his way into the living room and then froze.

There, on the floor, Dema Lebedev sat on a bright green rug with his back against a sofa, staring at Dak. In his lap sat the girl, with Lebedev's left arm wrapped around her throat—and a pistol to her temple.

"Perhaps it's time for you to surrender," Lebedev sneered.

Dak had no shot.

That wasn't entirely true. He could take the shot, but he risked the girl's life in two ways by doing so. The first was obvious. He could miss, take off a portion of her skull, and be left with the guilt for the rest of his life.

The other way, though also obvious, was more of a crapshoot. He could hit the target right between the eyes, but in the split second between him squeezing the trigger and the bullet striking Lebedev in the head, the villain might twitch his finger and kill the girl.

"Put the gun down," Lebedev ordered in slurred English. "Or I splatter her brains all over this apartment."

The man motioned with his head in the general direction of the splash zone toward the sofa nearest the window. A cool wind blew in through the destroyed window, filled with the smells of the city—a strange concoction of exhaust and Indian cuisine wafting up from the street below.

"Not going to happen," Dak warned, his eyes never wavering from the target. The sights on the gun rail aligned with the top of Lebedev's head. "Let her go, and we can settle this like men."

Lebedev didn't take Dak's offer seriously. In fact, he scoffed at

Dak's cliché statement, blowing air through his parted lips and squeezing the frightened young woman's neck tighter. Her face flushed red as she both wiggled to get air in her lungs and did her best not to move around too much lest she accidentally cause the pistol against her head to go off.

Tears streamed down her face, as if the Russian squeezed them from her like a lemon. Her chest shuddered intermittently from coughs.

The girl, under normal circumstances, would have probably been beautiful. She wore a black T-shirt with a low cut V in the neck and a pair of tight white jeans that might have been painted on her body if they were any tighter. But Dak didn't see her in that light. He only saw the latest in a long string of victims of this over-grown, drunken scumbag. He slowly exhaled and checked his sights again.

"You come in here to my place, talking about handling things like a man when you just killed all of my men with a sneak attack? Hardly an honorable way of doing battle."

Lebedev's words hit the wall behind Dak with no effect. "That's your defense, Dema? You're going to say I sucker punched your goons? I guess I shouldn't expect differently from a spoiled brat like you. But there's something you're going to have to square with, son. Daddy isn't here to bail you out this time. He's not coming to save you like he has so many other times."

Dak watched as the man's face flushed red with anger. He seemed to do that quickly, and often.

"You don't know anything about me," Lebedev countered. The statement seemed to cause an epiphany in the man's mind, and his eyes narrowed slightly. "You. Now I recognize you. I saw you at the casino. You spoke to Tamara. Yes, I remember you clearly now."

The accusation brought no reply from the American.

"Yes," Lebedev nodded. "It *is* you. I knew I had seen your face before. Did Tamara send you here to kill me? Is that it? I bring her business. Does she want me dead because I won last week? Those casino types don't like it when you take their money."

"From what I hear, all you do is lose, Dema. Just like you're going to lose now if you don't let that girl go."

Lebedev laughed hard, intentionally so.

"Didn't look like you did so hot yesterday," Dak added. "How much were you down when you left? Twenty? Forty? A hundred?" He saw the man's expression shift. It wasn't much. Just a flutter in the eyes, searching for the shameful truth. When Dak said "hundred," he noted Lebedev's eyes freeze for just a second.

Dak chuckled, even as he kept the weapon trained on Lebedev's head. "That's it, isn't it? You lost a hundred grand yesterday? Jeez, man. I have a number you can call that might be able to help."

"Shut up!" Lebedev roared, and for a split second, the pistol in his hand wavered a quarter of an inch—but not nearly enough room for Dak to take the shot.

An easy smile spread across Dak's lips. A gust of wind rolled into the penthouse, sending the long black curtains by the windows to whip around in a frenzy.

"Gambling is a tricky vice to deal with," Dak continued. "In the immortal words of Kenny, 'You gotta know when to hold 'em, know when to fold 'em.' And most importantly, like the Gambler himself warned us, 'Know when to walk away, and know when to run.' I feel like you failed to embrace that sage advice at every point."

"So, you're here to teach me a lesson? Is that it? Tamara sent you here to kill me. Good news, American pig. You just signed your death warrant. Even if you kill me, my father will find you. But not until after he kills Tamara and takes over her pitiful little casino."

Dak had him on the ropes; he just had to keep the guy talking. Sooner or later, he would crack, and Dak would seize the opening.

"Your father will do no such thing. Honestly, I would be surprised if he didn't send me a thank-you card for killing you. How much money has he lost because of your bad luck, Dema? Few hundred grand? A million?"

Sweat rolled down Lebedev's forehead and both temples.

"You know nothing!" Lebedev raged.

The girl's tears seemed permanently stained on her cheeks, but she'd ceased struggling against the man's strong grip. The fear in her eyes, however, remained constant.

"You say that," Dak mumbled, just loud enough for the enemy to hear, "but your body language tells me I'm spot on with that assessment." His eyes flicked to the lines of cocaine on the glass coffee table between the three sofas. "What is it with you guys and the cocaine?" He asked. "You know, if you're hitting that before you head to the casino, it's probably not helping your decision making. Sort of like it isn't helping right now."

Another mouthful of profanity spewed from Lebedev's mouth.

"It's all starting to come together now." Dak launched what he hoped would be the final assault in his psychological war with Lebedev. He was peeling back layers that the Russian didn't want to look at, didn't want to acknowledge. While Lebedev obviously worked out and was in prime physical condition—his addictions aside—he was weak-minded, and Dak's Jedi mind tricks were working. He just had to pry a little more before the Russian lost his cool and thought he could hit Dak before the American fired.

"Daddy never spent enough time with you, did he? Always working, building the family's illicit empire. And with all the women I hear he used to bring into the house, I bet it was difficult to know which one to call mom, huh?"

Lebedev's pain melted away, and for a second, Dak thought he'd pushed too far. The resignation in the Russian man's face was the look of someone who had lost hope—in everything. And when that happened, people did irrational things. Dak had inadvertently sent the enemy over the line, and now the girl was in greater danger than before.

"You think you know everything," Lebedev said in a much calmer, and more unnerving, voice. Dak knew he was going to have to take the shot before Lebedev executed the girl, and thus committed suicide by provocation.

"You Americans think you know everything," Lebedev went on, his voice dark and foreboding. "You all think you're the heroes, the cowboys riding in to save the day. You lack perspective, and you try to compensate by acting tough, or smart, or indestructible. But you're not indestructible. You're not always the hero. Sometimes you're the bad guy, and you don't even realize it."

"As much as I'd like to stand here and talk global affairs with you, Dema, I'm going to have to ask you one last time to put the gun down."

Dak didn't know how much longer he could keep it up. For a second, he believed the ordeal was nearly over and that he'd broken Lebedev's will. Instead, the man turned on a dime, lashing back out with his own barbs, his own—albeit feeble—attempts at psychological battle.

"No," Lebedev said. "I don't think so. You see, American pig, you've already lost."

"How long do you plan on sitting there like that?" Dak asked. "Because I can stand here all night if I have to." He hoped that wasn't going to be the case. Waiting it out until the coked-up drug lord's son passed out could be an endeavor in futility, and based on the residue on the coffee table, it looked like Lebedev was a couple of lines deep.

A sickly laugh escaped the man's lips, and his head rocked back a few inches, though the pistol remained firmly planted against the girl's head.

"Neither one of us is going to be here all night," Lebedev corrected. "You'll be dead soon enough."

"I don't think so."

Great, Dak thought. *A stalemate.* Now it was going to be a battle of staying power. Dak didn't have that kind of time. Somewhere in the city, or perhaps beyond its borders, a museum curator was being held prisoner by a thief, and Dak needed to find them before anything else happened.

"So," he groused, "what are we to do, Dema, wait here until Judgement Day?"

The enemy grinned fiendishly.

"Judgement Day is already here," a new voice grumbled from the doorway.

Dak clenched his jaw, pressing his lips together in anger. He'd been so focused on Lebedev, and getting him to flinch, that he'd ignored his six. Now, reinforcements were here, and Dak had no play.

"Put down the gun," the man's voice ordered.

For several seconds, Dak contemplated the demand, knowing that if he dropped his weapon, he would be a dead man. Then again, he was a dead man either way.

Inside, he fumed at himself for being so careless, especially when he was always so careful. *How could he let these thugs get the drop on him?*

"I will put the gun down if you let the girl go," Dak hedged. His attention never left the target, a spot just over Lebedev's nose.

"You are in no position to barter with me," the new man said.

The Russian accent, the gruff tone, and the years of experience that added gravel to the man's voice, all betrayed who had come to Dema's rescue.

"So," Dak said, "Daddy is here to save you again, huh?"

Lebedev fired another curse Dak's way.

Dak ignored it, the same way he'd done in the military, and in fights with his ex-girlfriend. "I will put my gun down if you let the girl go, Mr. Lebedev. She has no quarrel with you. This is between me and your son."

Silence from the doorway indicated the man was considering Dak's request, even though he held all the cards.

"Dema," the older Lebedev said, "let her go."

Dema scowled at the request. "What? You're taking his side?"

"Dema!" The father shouted the name as he would to a child who'd used their finger paints on the living room wall. "Let her go. This man has killed all of your guards. And based on the layout of the bodies, it was no challenge for him. He is a killer, Dema. I'm surprised he hasn't taken the shot yet."

Dak didn't like the situation he was in, a sort of Mexican standoff, but he had to admit he liked the father's moxie, even if he loathed the man for what he did as a career.

"Let her go, Son," the father's voice softened. "Then we will handle this together."

The drugs coursing through Dema's veins racked his brain with fanciful thoughts, flashes of daydreams where he sprang from the carpet and opened fire, blasting the interloping American to bloody pieces.

"Cocaine's a hell of a drug," Dak said, using a Rick James quote he'd seen in a television show once. "Not sure if your boy is listening to you or to the blow."

"You're a dead man," Dema said, his bloodshot eyes finally resting on the same level as Dak's. "I'm only doing this because my father said to, and my father runs this part of Mumbai."

For a split second, Dak considered saying something like "Yeah, always do what daddy tells you," but he thought better of it. The guy was going to surrender his weapon, which would allow the girl to go unharmed. He hoped.

Dak's mind swept him to a dark place where Dema let the girl go then shot her in the back of the head. Another one took the girl to the door, where the father shot her, then told his men to get rid of the body. There were a few dozen scenarios that blinked in and out of his mind, and Dak didn't like any of them. He kept his mouth shut, though doing so took considerable effort, and he watched as Dema lowered his weapon and removed his arm from the girl's throat. He set the pistol on the floor next to his hip and raised his hands in mock surrender, knowing that there was no way the American would take the shot now. To do so would be to sign the girl's execution.

The girl rolled over onto her side, coughing as she supported her weight with her hands. She hacked as if she might vomit, but she only continued to cough for another ten seconds before finally recovering enough to get control.

"Get out of here," the elder Lebedev commanded. "Before I change my mind."

On hands and knees, the girl looked over her shoulder at Dak, who merely gave an approving nod while keeping his weapon aimed at Dema.

She scrambled to her feet and stood by the broken window for a second, looking back toward the doorway.

"Don't make me tell you again," Dema's father warned.

The girl wiped her tears and scurried around the sofas. As she passed Dak, she flashed a grateful look at him, mouthing the words "Thank you."

Dak heard her leave the penthouse. Her expensive shoes clacked on the floor until she reached the thin carpet of the hallway, then her footsteps faded as she ran toward the exit.

"Now, your turn," the elder Lebedev said.

"Yes, pig," Dema agreed. "Put your gun down."

Dak was at a stage in life where childish insults bounced off him like rubber pellets. That didn't take away his desire to blast a cavity in the man's skull. With an exhale, Dak took his finger off the trigger, loosened his grip on the weapon, and lowered it to the floor.

He kicked the weapon a few inches away, anticipating that would be the next command, and raised his hands up to shoulder level.

"Good," the older man said. "Turn around. I want to see this monster who has killed so many of our men in one night."

Dak did as instructed and spun around slowly.

The man just to the right of the doorway wore a long, black wool trench coat, which Dak thought to be a tad too much in a warm country like India. Underneath it, a black tie went with a garish silver Armani suit. The man's black leather shoes gleamed. A ruddy nose stuck out from a plump, blushing face. The man's narrow eyes seemed to be squeezed by the skin below them and thick, dark gray eyebrows above. While not the epitome of fitness, the man was certainly someone who looked like a leader, a person who took charge and kept a firm grip on the reins.

Four gunmen stood at six-foot intervals, all of them holding pistols aimed in Dak's direction, each of them ready to kill when the order was given.

"I am Lesma Lebedev," the man said. "No need to tell me who you are."

Because you're going to kill me. Again, Dak kept his smart mouth shut.

"I'm going to kill you!" Dema shouted, mixing in some choice profanity with his threat. He stood up behind Dak and grabbed his pistol.

Dak knew that any second there would be a silenced report, followed by the pain of a bullet entering his body. Where the round entered determined how much pain Dak would feel, and all he could hope for was one to the head—quick, painless. He doubted that would be where the first bullet went, or others after it.

Lesma Lebedev motioned to the guard nearest him. "Take my son out for some fresh air," he ordered. "Help him calm down a bit."

"What?" Dema protested. "Father, you have to let me kill this man. He came into my home, killed my guards."

"Killed your guards?" Lesma corrected with the question. "Last I checked, these men were on my payroll." He indicated one of the dead men on the floor with an accusatory finger.

The guard Lesma spoke to stepped over his deceased comrade and passed Dak on his way into the living room.

He put out his hand as if to soothe Dema, who now held his pistol at arm's length, pointing it sideways at the side of Dak's face.

Dak turned his head just enough to lock eyes with the deranged man and wasn't sure what disgusted him more—the guy, or the stupid way he was holding the gun like a gangster from a rap video.

Dema resisted the guard's attention, his eyes blinking rapidly, the corners twitching every few seconds. "You're lucky for now, pig," Dema spat. "My father is going to make sure you get what you deserve."

Dak returned his gaze to the mob boss while the guard escorted Dema out onto the balcony to catch his breath and wind down from the hostage situation.

A sickening feeling crept into his gut, and Dak knew this wasn't going to turn out well for him.

"His whole life," Lesma began, "I have had trouble with this boy." He pointed at his son as he and the guard carefully navigated their way through the shattered glass door leading out onto the balcony. The older man hugged himself. "Windy night."

"Yes. Unfortunate there isn't much fresh air to be had in this part of town," Dak sidestepped.

"Indeed." Lesma sighed. "A shame, about my son. He never learned about consequences, about what it was like to be a man. Then I hear these things, how he beats women. This is no good, and it will tarnish my reputation. And then, there is the problem about the money."

"The casino?" Dak asked, keeping the man talking in case an opportunity for escape just happened to come knocking.

The man nodded, and his cheeks jiggled with the movement. A distant sadness filled the man's eyes. Dak puzzled at the look. He couldn't be sure, but his gut told him it was regret.

"He lost too much of our money," Lesma said. "I am a wealthy man. But I don't spend money so foolishly as he does." He jabbed a thick finger in the direction of the balcony. "He wastes our resources and tries my patience. And he makes me look weak to those who would challenge us for our territory."

"Can't have that," Dak said coolly, despite having three guns pointed at him by men who were paid to have zero inhibitions about killing.

"No. We certainly can't."

Dak knew what the man meant. It was just like the law of the jungle, or the savanna, or any other natural biome where the strongest animals survived and the weak often became dinner or were exiled to roam until their demise.

"My son," Lesma said, sadness filling his voice. "I remember when he was born. I was terrified. My wife, of course, was overjoyed. She thought that if I had a family to take care of, I would get out of the game, leave the organization." He shook his head, lowering his gaze to the floor. "That...never happened."

"Why not?" Dak asked, instead of remarking with something like an "obviously." The thought had crossed his mind.

"Because," Lesma replied, his voice distant and his eyes glazed, "I am a man. I know times have changed in many places, where being a man is no longer important. But I still believe in the old ways. I grew up in a world where a man takes care of his family, where he puts food on the table and a roof over the heads." He pointed up to the ceiling to emphasize his point.

Dak appreciated the way the man said "over the heads," sort of messing up the old saying, but in a way making it his own, Russian —authentic.

"You came from a hardworking family, yes?" Dak asked. He couldn't believe he was having this conversation and kept wondering when the bullets would fly.

"Yes," Lesma said. "My parents worked very hard to feed us. My mother raised six of us." He looked up again, and out to the balcony. "When my wife died, I thought it might bring my son closer to me. I started bringing him in on the family business, teaching him the right and wrong way to run things." He shook his head again. "I was wrong. My son never got close to me. I think it was partly because my wife filled his head with things, how I was a horrible person, how I did bad things. Perhaps that resentment," he looked at Dak. "Is that how you say it? Resentment?"

"Yes," Dak confirmed.

"Perhaps that resentment, combined with never being told no, turned my son into the creature he is now. It is unfortunate."

He twisted his head and met Dak's gaze.

"Being a parent is complicated," Dak said with a shrug.

Lesma snorted. Then he chuckled, his portly body jiggling with the laughter. "Yes. That is true. It is complicated." He laughed another thirty seconds, and then calmed down with a single sigh. "Do you have children...I am sorry. What is your name?"

Dak paused, hesitating to give his true identity. He could use any name he wanted. It wouldn't matter. He was about to die. "Dak Harper, sir. My name is Dak Harper."

"Ah. Dak Harper. An interesting name. Like the football player in America, yes?"

It was Dak's turn to sigh. "Yes. Although he's not on my team. Not yet."

"I like this football man, this Dak. He is fun to watch. Reminds me of you a little. You are like cowboy coming into this building, killing all my men."

"Sorry about that," Dak lied.

"They should have been more prepared. A man like you"—he raised a hand as if putting Dak on display at a charity auction—"you are a killer. A true killer. I would guess former military, yes?"

"Something like that."

The man clapped his hands together, sending a loud pop through the penthouse. Dema had his hands on the rail outside, and he swiveled his head around to see what caused the sound before sneering about something and returning his gaze to the railing. The guard stood just behind him and seemed unfazed by the clapping.

"I could use a man like you in my organization," Lesma said. "You would be well paid. And you could train my men to be real men." He puffed up his chest and bent his arms to flex muscles that were buried under years of personal disregard to fitness.

"I don't work for criminals," Dak refused.

Lesma pouted his lips while he bobbed his head. He looked to the guard to his left. "This man has three guns pointed at him. At the snap of my finger, he is dead. No one would ever know what happened to him." He leaned his body at an angle, returning his gaze to Dak. He studied the American for a few seconds, and then grinned. "But he stands his ground. You"—he pointed a finger at Dak —"are a real man. Unlike my son out there." He took in a breath, then set his jaw. "Moro!" Lesma shouted to the balcony.

The guard turned to the boss. Lesma issued a single nod. The guard acknowledged with the same then stepped closer to Dema. He patted the younger Lebedev on the back, then grabbed him by the belt and lifted him over the railing.

The man's screams filled the room for only a second, then faded rapidly until they were muted by the wind and the sounds of the street below.

Lesma Lebedev stared through the window where his son had stood. The guard carefully walked back through the open door and stood by the couch, waiting for his next orders.

For all the crazy things Dak had seen in his life, this was one of the most confusing, and it actually sent a twinge of fear through him to see this man have his own son murdered. Dak wondered if that was how this was all going to play out. Would Lesma claim his son had killed himself in a drug-induced craze? Or would there be another angle?

"How do you think I should handle my son's death?" Lebedev asked.

Surprised by the question, Dak raised his shoulders. "You're asking me?"

"Yes. The police will be here," he checked his watch, "in about five to ten minutes to investigate. Perhaps less. Perhaps more. What would you tell them?"

Dak had to think fast. *Was this guy really asking him this question?* Lesma watched him intently, and Dak knew he was on the clock.

"You have too many bodies out in the hallway and in here," Dak began. "No way they'll buy a suicide story. Not when it's obvious some kind of battle took place." He motioned to the walls, the windows, the upholstery, all damaged in the bullet storm. "Then there's the blood to consider. No time to get all that cleaned up in ten minutes, or even twenty if we had it." Dak wanted to tell the man if he'd just shot his son they wouldn't have to consider this issue. They'd have hours, perhaps longer to get rid of the bodies and clean up the place, even bring in a window repair person to handle the destroyed glass.

"So, what would you do?"

"Rival gang moving in," Dak said. "Play the victim. Or tell them that you don't know who it was. Either way, your son was murdered by someone, and you're not sure who. Maybe he owed money to another syndicate, or some other casino, maybe pick a place you don't like. Just do me a favor and leave Tamara out of it."

The man blushed, the way someone would when a secret crush was mentioned. "I have no intention of hurting her, or her business. She's a good woman."

"I see," Dak said. "Pardon me for being so bold, sir, but if you're going to get out of here, you need to move now. Like you said, the cops could be on their way any minute."

"Yes," Lesma agreed. He ordered his men back to the door. They filed through and into the corridor while their boss waited in the opening. "It has been good talking with you, Dak Harper. I hope to see you again sometime. If you ever need me, I'm sure you can find me."

Dak puzzled over the offer, and what just happened. *Is this guy going to let me walk out of here? Alive?* He tried to wrap his mind around it but couldn't bring himself to believe.

"You are lucky man," Lesma said. "And smart." He glanced around at the bodies. "And you are obviously a good warrior. You let me know if you change your mind, yes?"

"If I ever need the kind of work you need done, I'll let you know," Dak said, hoping his life never ended up in such desperate times.

"Good. It was nice to meet you, Dak Harper. I will see you again."

Lesma turned and walked down the hallway, leaving Dak in the apartment surrounded by carnage.

Dak took a second to look around the room and then stepped out into the hall and turned left toward the stairs at the other end. Lesma was correct. Dak *had* been lucky. Now, he needed a little more luck. He had no idea how much time Priya had left before the thief made their deal. After that, it was anyone's guess. Would Harris let her go free? Or had she seen too much? He shuddered at the thought of finding her body somewhere, just minutes too late.

The image pushed his feet to move faster as he descended the stairs toward the ground floor. He had to get back to the casino—and hope that Tamara could actually deliver on her end of the bargain.

Walking back into the casino, a thought flashed through Dak's mind —this was what it must have felt like for an opponent to step into the ring with Mohammed Ali. He had no idea what was going to happen, but he had a bad feeling it wasn't going to be fun. The difference between him and the men Ali beat in the ring was that Ali's opponents got paid.

If Tamara had been lying, or she had alternative plans, Dak would not only not get paid, he'd probably be killed.

He stopped in the holding room again, a room he'd affectionally come to know as "the weigh station,"—as the guards ran through their routine of checking him for weapons. He wondered if they could smell the spent gunpowder on his skin; they didn't make any mention of it, or seem to notice. Dak felt it on his skin, and his nostrils still burned with the scent. Or maybe it was just his imagination, a touch of paranoid worry concocted by his mind.

"Nice to see you guys again, too," Dak said as the guard from before frisked his legs. "Oooh!" Dak yelped in falsetto. "That tickles."

The bouncer grunted his disapproval, but Dak thought he caught a snicker from one of the other guards, or maybe the previously emotionless cashier.

When the guard was finished with his security check, he turned and knocked on the door. A second later, it opened and the smell of jasmine, cigars, and clove cigarettes washed over them.

Dak followed the guard into the next room, as before, and waited until the man stepped aside before he passed.

"Thanks," Dak said with a wink as he walked by. "Remind me to buy you a drink. It's the least I can do."

The Indian guy either didn't get the joke or didn't approve. He merely stood there, facing the far wall on the other side of the gaming hall, where Tamara lounged in her chaise as she had on their previous meeting.

Dak half wondered if the woman had even gotten up during his absence.

He walked, unaccompanied, across the game floor. The sounds of the dealers' voices filled the air, along with Indian pop music blasting from the overhead speakers.

She saw him before he even descended the stairs on the other side of the room. The American who'd come to her before seeking answers and had ended up doing her dirty work for her.

She watched him as he strode confidently, yet unassumingly, across the game floor, his eyes occasionally panning to the left or right. His long, powerful strides made him look like a lion walking among the weaker animals in the jungle. He carried an easy look about him, one that gave the appearance of not giving a care about what anyone else in the room thought. Tamara wondered if that carried over into the rest of the world, the rest of his life, or if it was just a front he put on to impress her.

She doubted that was the case. A man who cared so little about what others thought didn't put on a show for anyone. They were brave enough to be themselves at all times, and the consequences could fall where they may.

He climbed the steps to her platform and inclined his head.

"You didn't die," Tamara purred.

"No. Although I had my doubts about that for a few seconds."

"That you died?"

"No. Thought I was going to. You were right about Lebedev. That whole tenth floor was swarming with guards."

"Yes," she said, raising a bluish-green drink in a margarita glass to her lips. She took a sip, flicked her eyes appreciatively to the beverage, and then nodded.

"Good?" Dak asked, though he couldn't have cared less.

"Very." Tamara said the word with as much flirtation as humanly possible. "It's a tequila drink."

"Doesn't look like any margarita I've ever seen before."

"It's a hulk-a-rita. If you come by my place later, I'll give you the recipe."

Dak didn't smile, though she wore a look of disappointment as if the comment were supposed to have that effect. "Where's the buyer, Tamara?" Fatigue strained at Dak's brain and he found it difficult to remember who he was after: the buyer or the thief. It was definitely the buyer. *Wasn't it?*

She didn't correct him, so he assumed he'd spoken correctly.

"Darling," she drawled, doing her best to look offended. "So much business, not enough fun. You should set aside more time to play."

"I can play when I know the museum curator is safe and when the artifact is back in the proper hands." Dak leveled his head, staring into her eyes, pulling back the veil to her soul.

She couldn't pull herself from his eyes. They were greener than anything she'd ever seen. Mesmerizing, enticing, mysterious, the jade orbs would not be swayed from the man's purpose.

"Lebedev is dead," Tamara said. "It's not on the news. The local media is doing what they can to keep this quiet, but it's already spread around on social media. His body hit the sidewalk in front of his building, and only a short distance from a young couple walking home from a dinner date."

"That's..." Dak paused at the grisly visual, "unfortunate."

"I'm honestly not sure why you didn't just shoot him, or stab him, or break his neck. Why did you have to throw him from a balcony?"

"Well," Dak said, twisting his head to the side for a half second, "funny you should ask. I didn't throw him over."

She raised both eyebrows. The information caught her off guard. "What do you mean you didn't throw him over? Are you saying he killed himself?"

"I didn't say that either."

"Well?" She threw up both hands, demanding a further explanation.

"His father showed up."

"Lesma?" Tamara said the name as if it put a sour taste in her mouth. "What was he doing there?"

Dak was running out of patience, but he felt compelled to push through the conversation. "He came to check on his son, I guess."

"And then killed him? His own son?"

"That's right."

She tilted her head forward, looking at him under the edges of her eyebrows. "Did you kill Lesma?"

"No. We left with a mutual understanding. Actually, he offered me a job."

"What? A job? I hope you didn't take it."

"Look, lady, I don't know what kind of weirdo thing you two have going on, but I'm not interested. I just want to find out where the curator is, and get her and the idol back in one piece."

"Fine," she said, still daydreaming about other things. She reached into the top of her dress, making a show of it.

Dak had seen women keep phones, money, and identification in their bra. But Tamara wasn't wearing a bra, and she clearly wanted him to know it.

Finally, after extracting way more seconds out of the act than necessary, she pulled a folded sheet of paper out of her dress and held it out for him to take.

"The address is on this, darling," she said. "I don't know what kind of resistance you'll find there, if there are guards, all of that. So don't ask. I only have the location. If they're even still there."

Dak took the note and paused halfway back to standing up straight. "What's that supposed to mean?"

She rolled her shoulders and tossed her head to the left. Tamara looked absently out over the gaming room. The players made the usual noises gamblers made when they won or lost. The roars of joy came in spurts, followed by the inevitable "aww" of defeat. She surveyed the room, as she did every night from her perch. It was a boring life, but she didn't share that with anyone. This business paid the bills, kept the drinks flowing, and gave her something she'd always wanted—power, or at least a taste of it.

"From what I hear, the buyer is going to be leaving town tonight. I don't know much about it. Truly. I just found out a few minutes before you got here."

"What?" Dak fumed. "You could have told me."

"I just said I didn't know." She lowered her chin in warning. "You have the address. I suggest you hurry. And when you're finished, you're welcome to come back here and visit." She leaned forward, letting her gown droop enough to tease the view beneath. "Anytime."

"Thanks, Tamara."

He offered no flirty response. Dak didn't want to give the woman the pleasure. She was an attractive woman, but he didn't trust her, and there was no way he'd be caught with his guard down. Based on the way she'd been eyeing him like a steak, he was certain *down* was the operative word in whatever she had planned.

Dak tucked the paper into one of his pockets and walked out through the weigh station, then the restaurant. Before he was halfway to the exit, he saw the detective sitting by a window overlooking the sidewalk.

Rolling his eyes, Dak veered to the right and headed straight for the cop, waving gleefully like he was seeing an old high school friend for the first time in years.

"Roddy!" Dak nearly shouted. "It's me! Hey, man!"

He stopped at the table, where Detective Naik shifted uncomfortably.

"What a coincidence," Dak said. "You and me, here, at the same weird, late hour? Small world! Am I right?" He threw his hands up to the side and then pulled out a chair. Dak took a seat across from the cop and planted his elbows on the table.

"What are you having?" Dak asked. "I hear the naan bread here is amazing."

"What were you doing in there, Harper?" Naik said, unamused. His eyelids narrowed, and he stared at Dak through slits.

"In where?"

"Back there," Naik pointed at the hallway in the rear of the building.

"Oh," Dak turned and looked the prescribed direction. "Had to use the bathroom."

Naik tilted his head downward, feigning disappointment in the lie. "I followed you in there, Harper. You weren't in the bathroom for"—he checked his watch—"seventeen minutes."

"Can you do it in less time? Because that would be awesome. I would save hours every week."

The detective sighed, tossing his annoyed gaze out the window for a second. "I know you were in there, Harper. I know you were in the casino."

Dak leaned forward, putting on an expression that promised to keep every secret. "There's a casino here?" He pointed at the table. "In this building?"

"You know there is, Harper. What were you doing in there?"

"I don't see a casino," Dak said with a shrug. "But I would love to play some craps right about now. Or maybe a game of poker. Meh, maybe both."

Naik fumed. His nostrils swelled and shrank with every heated breath. "You can't hide the truth from me. I will find out what's going on here."

"Speaking of what's going on," Dak said, losing the act as he leaned forward, "I would like to know that, too. Because"—he twisted his head to the side and looked to his right at no one in particular —"you were supposed to be working on the case of the missing curator and the missing Jain idol. Yet every time I've bumped into you, you're following me."

Dak lifted his hands and turned the palms up. "Weird, right? I mean, a detective who is on the hunt for those things is following me? What was I doing before I got here?" Dak asked the question to get a read on Naik. The odds were substantially in Dak's favor that the detective didn't have a clue. Most likely, he'd been parked here in front of the casino most of the night, hoping he could milk some down-on-their-luck gambler to give up the goods about what Harper was doing for Tamara. That information, however, would remain strictly with Dak and Tamara, and neither of them was going to say a thing.

Detective Naik tilted his head up, lifting his chin to an almost snooty level. The man stared down the bridge of his nose at Dak, saying nothing for several uncomfortable seconds.

"What are you asking? Do you want to know if you're a suspect in all this?"

Dak's eyebrows pinched together. "What? No. A suspect? Wait. Unless I am a suspect. In that case, you have your own set of problems."

"You're not a suspect," Naik said, leaning forward as if about to share a great secret. "Not a good one, anyway. We already know when you flew in, so we know you didn't take the idol, or the woman."

"You said we," Dak interrupted, looking around for someone else. Only random customers occupied the restaurant. "Who's we?"

"The police."

"The police," Dak said loudly. "I was going to guess that."

"That doesn't mean, however, you don't have something to do with this. Usually, in these cases, there is a buyer who will come in. We have reason to believe that the buyer is going to come here, to Mumbai."

That was one of the first, if not the first, intelligent thing Dak had heard the guy say since they met. Although he wasn't sure how Naik knew the buyer was coming into Mumbai.

"Oh? That's good news, then. Isn't it? If you know the buyer is coming here, then you should be able to set up a trap to catch them."

"Indeed."

"Unless," Dak added, "you can't trust your source."

Confusion splashed onto Naik's face. "What?"

Dak leaned back in the chair, letting his left arm hang over the top of the seat next to him. "Your source. You said you have reason to believe that the buyer will be coming to Mumbai. You can't have intelligence without a source. Now," Dak said, raising a finger to make the point, "if you were the source, as in you'd seen the evidence of a buyer coming here, then you wouldn't have reason to believe anything. You'd just believe it, and you'd probably be on your way to wherever the buy was going down."

Naik's face twitched just below the right eye, either because he hadn't already considered what Dak just said prior to coming here, because he was bluffing, or because he had nothing.

"You make a good point, Harper," Naik allowed. "But you don't understand what's going on here. There is something bigger at play."

There it was.

Dak knew something felt off about this cop. His demeanor, the goofy, almost aloof way he went about his job, his conversations, or even his initial approach to Dak outside the museum. He was either the worst cop ever, or he was playing dumb. Either way, Dak still had every intention to continue antagonizing the guy, but not before he squeezed a little more information out of him.

"So," Dak said, leaning forward an inch closer toward the detective. "What do you mean, there's something bigger at play?"

Detective Naik put on a conspiratorial expression, eyes wide and alert as he scanned the room for at least the third or fourth time since Dak sat down. Whatever this guy was hiding, he was genuinely concerned, or doing a clip for an Academy Award nomination.

"We have reason to believe that the Rajan gang is involved with this heist. I can't say how I know. That stuff stays in the department."

"The Rajan gang?" Dak asked.

He'd heard of underworld criminal organizations here in India, and even Mumbai. That surface knowledge was one of the reasons he'd been surprised to hear the Russians were moving in, although based on his experience with those types, they seemed to gravitate toward areas where drug dealing, racketeering, and other forms of illicit income had already been proved by other entities. Like hobbyist stock traders who jumped in on high gains only to sell quickly after making a few bucks, Dak had heard of Russian mob groups acting similarly, like parasites of the criminal underworld.

"They've been one of the bigger organizations here in Mumbai for a few decades now," Naik explained. "A man named Khal Murteedi calls the shots. We've never been able to pin him for anything. We know what's going on, what they do, who they've killed, but we're—"

"Always a step behind?" Dak finished.

"I was going to say minutes late."

Same thing, Dak thought but kept it to himself.

"So, this Rajan group," Dak said, keeping on topic, "what is it you think they have to do with all this?"

"I'm not sure," Naik said. It was his turn to lean back and throw his hands up. "If we knew that, we might already have them in custody, as well as the curator and the idol back safely."

"Are you aware of other gangs who take interest in ancient artifacts?"

"Not really. They're usually involved in other enterprises, as you mentioned before."

Dak decided he'd spent enough time catching up with the detective. His initial reason for coming over to the table in the first place was to speed up the conversation so he could get to the address on the paper Tamara gave him. He'd thought it to be a waste of his time to spend more than a second with Naik, but now he wasn't so sure. If there was another gang involved, Dak needed to know about it, especially if they were going to be where he was heading. Any intel was better than none.

Unless the intel was entirely unreliable. He'd yet to decide on his position with the detective. Was the guy a moron? Or just playing one?

"I was wondering," Dak said, "because there's definitely a market for that sort of thing, but from what I hear, India is ripe for the picking in that arena."

"Yes," Naik agreed. "It's something we've had to deal with for a long time, though in most cases the stolen items are quickly taken out of the country. It's rare when the locals have any interest in buying them, probably because there's too much heat so close to home. Buyers from out of the country often feel like there are no consequences. They feel safe somewhere else, though many nations allow us to go in and recover stolen wares."

"Extradition. Can be a blessing and a curse, huh?"

"Indeed."

Dak stood abruptly. The metal chair made a grinding sound on the hard floor as his legs shoved it backward. "Well, thanks for the chat, but I really must be going, Detective. It's been a pleasure."

Naik stood as well. "More errands?"

There was no missing the cynicism in the cop's voice. He didn't trust Dak, though he'd given him information in such a way that perhaps the detective was warming to him, or had possibly started to consider Dak was on the same team. Just without the uniform.

"Something like that," Dak said.

"What are these errands you keep running?" Naik asked.

"There you go," Dak clapped once. "That's more like it, Detective. You keep asking questions like that; you'll eventually find your answers."

"So?" The cop put his hands on his hips and tilted his head sideways, as if willing the words to spill from Dak's lips.

"Do you know what it is I do?" Dak asked sincerely.

"I know what you did. You were Delta Force with the American military. Wrongly accused of attempted murder, among other charges, eventually acquitted on all counts. You were given an honorable discharge, and I imagine some form of compensation for your troubles."

"I get by," was all Dak revealed.

"You didn't sue the army for damages?" Naik sounded more than a little surprised.

"Not my style." Dak shook his head. "I'm not the suing type."

The detective didn't look convinced. He stood there for a second, pining over the statement. "Maybe you aren't. Seems like you could have gotten some good money out of something like that."

"And I'd trade any ounce of honor I had left."

"You haven't done so yet?" Naik asked.

Dak inhaled and shrugged. "Maybe I have. I'm no saint. But it wouldn't have been right to do it that way. They cleared my name, gave me my life back, or at least tried."

"But you don't have your life back. Do you, Dak?"

It was the first time the man had referred to him by his first name, and not Mr. Harper or just Harper.

Dak felt the night pulling him toward the door. He didn't have time to talk about all this, and he certainly couldn't keep answering questions from the cop all night long. Tamara had warned him he could well be against the clock.

"I'm sorry," Dak said. "Maybe we can talk later, and I'll explain more."

"But your errands are waiting."

"Right again."

Dak spun around and made for the door.

"There was a murder earlier tonight," Naik said. This time, Dak froze and didn't immediately turn around. He waited for a second, then turned to face the detective once more. "Several murders, actually," Naik added. "Russian mob guys. They all belonged to the Lebedev family. The younger Lebedev, the one who runs the organization here for his father—or who likes to think he runs it for his father—was thrown off his balcony."

"That's a tough way to go," Dak murmured.

"Yes. It is. Whoever killed him, and all his men, did it with ruthless efficiency."

Dak wondered where the detective was going with this and hoped it wasn't his direction. If he'd been a suspect in that crime, Naik would have already called in backup and had Dak arrested. That hadn't happened, so Dak held on to that frail strand of hope that the cops were looking somewhere else.

"We believe it's a rival gang, perhaps a group that's been here a while," Naik offered.

"Like the Rajan group you mentioned before."

"Yes. None of them take well to competitors coming into their territory and trying to stake a claim. Many of these Mumbai syndicates have been around for decades. They're entrenched in the city's underworld activities."

"Good to know," Dak said. Then he left through the exit.

Naik called out to him, "Be careful, Harper. It's a messy place in the underworld."

Dak didn't turn to thank him for the advice as he hurried through the door and out to his rental car.

He only looked back through the restaurant window when he drove by, just to see if the detective had moved to follow or simply hung back continuing his stakeout.

Naik was gone, and there was no trace of the man anywhere on the sidewalk or street.

Dak flashed a look in the rearview mirror to make sure he wasn't being followed, then cut the wheel to the left on the next street and sped away.

18

Gavin waited impatiently, rocking back and forth on the edge of the sofa against the wall. He'd been nervous before when meeting a buyer, but this one was different. Something about this entire operation felt off, and it wasn't just the company he'd picked up along the way. He raised his head enough to lay eyes on the woman. He glowered at her, wishing he could consume her with lasers from his eyes.

It would all be over soon. He had to keep telling himself that. She was just a pawn in all of this, and soon he wouldn't have to deal with it anymore. Priya would be someone else's problem. He wondered what they would do to her when they saw her. Knowing some of these types like he did, he wouldn't be surprised if they took her as one of their sex slaves, either for personal use or to sell on the black market. From what Gavin had heard, human trafficking was a booming business, though he'd never felt good about dipping his toes in that world.

It disgusted him, actually made him feel dirty in a way that no amount of soap and water could wash away. The fact that people were bought and sold in modern times was a sickening and mind-blowing thing to consider. Then again, it had been happening for thousands of years. Slavery had always been around. It never left. It merely put on a new mask and took a new name.

Gavin had never been extremely ethical. He'd done all the drugs, all the ones he could access, in high school. His sex life had started early, as it had with many of his peers, though Gavin ran through a series of young women in a short amount of time, doing more emotional damage to most of them than he could have realized. He justified that by telling himself they knew what they were doing just like he did. On top of all that, he'd cheated through most of school, copying the work of friends or mirroring answers on tests. It wasn't until later that he got into a life of crime, when he realized that college didn't have anything to offer a person like him, or rather, a personality such as his.

He craved excitement, thrills, high risk, and high reward.

It probably didn't help that he'd been the son of wealthy parents. Actual punitive actions against him for anything were never a real threat.

Still, despite all that, there were lines he never crossed.

Gavin never forced himself on a woman. He despised the men that did, even threatened to beat one of them up in high school purely based on a rumor that circulated around the student body. The other boy had acted defensively, much like abusers usually do, but the rumors stopped, and soon after the two split up and started dating other people. The boy eventually transferred to another school, perhaps because of the bad reputation he'd established, whether it was deserving or not.

Through the years, Gavin had heard more and more about the rise of the human sex slave trade. He'd heard stories from the underground about people who bought and sold other humans, sometimes children. Those tales were the nightmares that kept Gavin up at night. They were one of the few pieces of his new life that tugged on his strings to get out, to leave this kind of living behind and go back to the regular world, take his place, and maybe make a difference.

Deep down, though, he knew he could never go back. Besides, what difference could a guy like him make? He was just one man, not one of those types you see on television out there feeding all the hungry, housing all the homeless, and putting clothes on the backs of the naked.

Gavin was a thief. And nothing else. This was the life he'd been born to live, and while he realized that his sort of career was a short one that ended in either being caught or a lavish retirement, he was willing to roll the dice to get a few thrills. And to establish his own legacy of wealth away from the uncaring, tepid trust fund his parents built for him.

It had cost him family and friends along the way. His wondered if his parents ever thought about him, about their wayward son who'd vanished, never to return.

Gavin doubted his father stood on the rooftop for days and nights, watching the front gate for his prodigal son to come home. His father was too busy with watching bottom lines, making business deals, and living a lavish lifestyle of the rich and famous. It was all the man talked about.

As Gavin thought back over his life, he only carried two regrets, mistakes he'd made along the way that still haunted him so many years later.

The first was his sister. When he left home and burrowed into the hole of the thieves' underworld, he left his sister behind and hadn't spoken to her, or seen her, since. They'd been close growing up and had both talked about running away. Eventually, though, the life wrapped its deathly fingers around her and pulled her down into the dinner parties, the fundraisers, and all the other bull their family perpetuated.

Gavin remembered the day he left home. Both of his parents were out at one of those charity galas that seemed to happen on a weekly basis. He had looked at his sister as she stood in the doorway, he on the driveway with a backpack full of clothes and a few other things he needed to survive.

It was the one time he'd been happy to take his parents' money. Before hitting the road, Gavin had cleaned out all his savings and stuffed the cash in his backpack—hardly a safe place to keep that kind of dough, but if he lost it, he figured it was just destiny's way of telling him he didn't need it. After all, Gavin was forging his own path.

The second regret was the other half of his heart. While seeing his kid sister cry as he walked out of her life, Lisa was the other one.

She'd been the best of the girls he'd dated, and the only one who ever truly tugged at his heart. Her parents had immigrated to Southern California from Mexico when she was only three years old. She'd only been back to her family's homeland a few times since. Her parents were kind people and took to Gavin immediately.

Normally, Gavin would have figured it was because the parents knew about what his mother and father did or knew of them and their wealth. But after only a little prying, Gavin realized that Lisa's parents had no clue who he was, or his mom and dad.

They liked him for who he was and treated him like family.

Family, Gavin thought with a sigh.

"You okay over there?" Priya prodded from the other side of the fence. "You seem a little pensive."

He ignored her. His mind still lingered on the sweet smell of lavender and roses Lisa's perfume teased in the air. Her laugh made him smile. Even though he was only a young man, barely twenty-five now, the pain of letting her go still twisted like a dagger's point in his chest.

"Not talking?" Priya cut into his thoughts again.

"I just want to get this over with. To get this deal done and then go on my way. That's it." He twiddled his thumbs over and over, thinking the action might help him focus again on the dream of the girl he'd loved.

Losing her had been hard. And made worse by the fact that he'd allowed his father's idiotic and prejudiced ways to interfere.

"You can't date her," his dad had said. "She's beneath you. It's high time you started dating girls more in your...social circle."

Gavin knew what that meant. He understood the way the wealthy elites talked. His father never came out and said it was because she was from Mexico. Maybe that wasn't it. Her parents weren't poor.

They ran a bakery in Los Angeles. Gavin could still taste some of the pastries Lisa's father and mother made. He'd never forget the first time he set foot in that bakery. The smells were so good, they were unlike anything he'd ever had at home—though, to be fair, his mother never cooked, and they didn't have a nanny. Eating out had become a five-day-a-week norm for the Harris kids.

When Gavin's father threatened to take away everything—the car, the trust fund, his college money—Gavin stood his ground. He had held firm and told his father he didn't care about any of that, and that if he wanted to be with Lisa, he was free to do so.

In the end, it had been Lisa that backed away. She ended things because, as she put it, "She didn't want to be the cause of a rift in his family."

To her credit, family meant everything to her. It was part of her cultural upbringing. To lose one's family support system was a horrible fate, and a dishonor to an individual. He understood her reasoning, despite hating it to his core.

He did his best not to keep up with her, but every now and then he felt the call of the internet and would submit to the temptation that always renewed the pain in his heart. The mere sight of her with her husband and their two kids on her public profiles was enough to turn his stomach every single time. Just thinking about it caused it to tumble slightly, even now.

His phone vibrated in his hand and he checked the screen, though this time the nerves in his stomach didn't melt away. Instead, his gut stirred with anxious uncertainty.

"They're here," he said. "It's time."

Dak drove the car through a quiet suburban neighborhood. The trip took less than half an hour, and even though the area of Mankur was considered an extension of Mumbai, the place had a feel all its own, different from the busy, crowded city.

In most of India, a huge gap existed between extreme poverty and opulent wealth. The global middle-class index suggested that only a few years before, people earning between $10 and $20 a day fit into that middle-class category, but those earnings would fit them squarely into the top 3 percent in India.

For a couple of years, it seemed that was going to change, but now the momentum built up to widen the middle class in India had waned and the gap was starting to spread again. As home to some of the wealthiest, and some of the poorest people in the world, the nation had failed to create a manufacturing base that could grow the middle class.

As a result, neighborhoods like this were being swallowed up, either by the rich so they could build new homes or high-rise condominiums, or by the burgeoning slums that continued to sprawl outward from the big cities.

From the looks of it, everyone in the sleepy neighborhood was out for the night. Most of the homes' darkened windows offered no threat of a nosey witness. A few had lights on in kitchens or on porches, a form of security that only made the homeowners feel better at night but did little to deter thieves.

Dak peered through the windshield at the dying suburbs. He knew that the sprawl was coming, that constant population increases and the disparity of wealth would consume this place. It was only matter of time.

Most of the residents looked like they did their best to keep up appearances. The lawns were decent, not spectacular, and the cars fit the lifestyle the houses represented—moderate success.

Dak looked in the rearview mirror. No headlights behind him and no sign of someone tailing him with their lights off. He'd actually never seen that before, though he imagined such a tactic worked out well for the person attempting it. The thought made Dak smile on the inside with visions of some goon smashing into side mirrors or getting pulled over by a cop for not having their lights on.

He spotted the address up ahead and slowed down. Dak double-checked to make sure he was at the right place. The homes here were nice, and the rows on both sides of the street appeared to be newer construction, at least in the last five years or so. The houses were close together, only allowing narrow patches of grass between exterior walls. The two-story structures featured small, rectangular front yards with connected garages in the back that the homeowners accessed by way of small streets running behind the rows.

The only difference he could detect between the individual buildings were the colors. Some were painted white and some a light brown.

Dak passed the address, noting a single light on in an upstairs window, then sped up again lest someone happen to look out through the closed window blinds and see him driving by. He hadn't seen anyone out on the road since he pulled off the highway, except for a few cars near the exit. Once he'd ventured into the neighborhood, however, the place had turned into a ghost town.

At the next corner, Dak slowed down, looked both ways, then

turned left, drove to the next access street, then hung another left. This side of the row didn't offer as much to look at, with the backsides of the houses only featuring short driveways and minimal two-car garages.

Two small cars, Dak thought, the critical part of his mind noting the size and immediately wondering how the construction companies might have saved money by doing it that way.

He rolled by the house again, this time inspecting the rear for any signs of activity, but found nothing suspicious or even remotely interesting. The place was quiet. Too quiet.

Dak coasted to the end of the street then found a pull-off to the right where a dumpster sat next to the curb. He tucked the car in behind the metal bin, parking it between that and a row of cypress trees blocking the row of homes from the main road beyond.

Dak checked his pistol and stuffed it in his belt, pulling his T-shirt and windbreaker over it in case someone happened to look out a window while taking in a late night snack.

Head on a swivel, Dak scanned the area then stuffed his hands in his pockets and walked briskly toward the house. He didn't think for a second that someone would buy that he was simply out for a midnight stroll through the neighborhood, but he didn't want to run. Sudden movements were more suspicious than someone with insomnia who just needed to get outside for some air before bedtime. There were enough digital nomads living around Mumbai that they wouldn't think much of his physical appearance.

He ran through that list of things to ease his mind as he approached the house. Then, when he was at the neighbor's driveway, Dak checked down the street behind him, glanced into the home's windows, and then ducked down low. He crept around the row of shrubs separating the two driveways and into the narrow opening between the houses.

The space was barely wide enough for him to walk through facing squarely in either direction, reminding him of his first childhood experience at Rock City in Chattanooga. The so-called Fat Man's Squeeze and Needle's Eye had been fun for the kids on his school field trip to the world-renowned tourist spot, but as an adult he wondered how much fun it would really be.

Dak kept his right hand near his hip in case he had to draw his pistol, though in the narrow gap, he wouldn't have much room to move. He stopped at a window halfway down the wall. After a look back over his shoulder, he stood on his tiptoes and peered into the house through the glass.

Through the window, he saw the kitchen just on the other side. Modern and clean, the place looked immaculate, as if no one had ever set foot in there. To the right, an opening led into the foyer and the living room, beyond where residual light from a lamp, or possibly a fixture, seeped into the kitchen.

Dak watched for several seconds, listening, waiting for any sign of life within.

Nothing.

He lowered back down to his soles and thought for a few breaths. *This is the address Tamara gave me.* That nugget came with an asteroid-size caveat. He knew he couldn't trust her. This whole thing might be one big setup. Another thought drilled into his mind. He'd considered it before, but not seriously, only in passing. Now, he wasn't so sure.

Was Tamara working with Colonel Tucker?

Ten seconds of silence outside the address she'd given him didn't prove anything. And he knew he couldn't just stand out here in the dark peeping through a window. Dak had to get inside, but that could prove tricky. Any sound might alert whoever was inside. Then there was the issue of Gavin Harris.

According to Tamara, this was the location where the buy was supposed to go down. If that was the case, where were all the henchmen, the bodyguards, the paid muscle?

The kind of person willing to throw around millions for a stolen artifact wouldn't leave home without an entourage of personal security. They would have armed guards, and if they did it right, would send scouts ahead of the meeting to make sure the place was secure.

There was no sign of any of that. It would be risky, but Dak had to get inside. Maybe he was early. A plan birthed in his brain, and he started considering how he would play it when the thief arrived.

Dak recalled seeing a back door next to the garage door and decided that was the best way to go in.

He retreated to the driveway, gave another short look both directions, then crossed the concrete, passing the garage door. He stopped on the other side, where a walkway led up a single step to a white door. Dak looked up the brown wall to the window directly above the door. A light was on inside, but he'd already noted that before. Detecting no movement in the upstairs room, he walked up the step to the door and looked at the doorknob.

Before getting to the back entrance, Dak had taken out his lockpicking tool, barely wider than two credit cards stacked together. Now, as he stared at the doorframe, he realized that wouldn't be necessary. Instead, he was going to need another tool.

20

A chill crawled over Dak's skin, pebbling his forearms with goose-bumps. In a single motion, he slid the lockpick back into his pocket while drawing the pistol and ducking into a crouching position next to the doorstep.

The door was open.

Why is the door open?

There'd been no visible sign of forced entry, which meant either the buyer forgot to close the back door—*unlikely*—or they'd left and didn't care about locking up behind them. There was a third option, and Dak couldn't entirely rule it out.

The deal could have been hijacked. He'd heard of that happening before. One of his friends knew a drug dealer who told him he'd had a gun pointed at his head one night. The guy was dealing cocaine to some gang members in the city, and one of the gangsters had the idea to kill the supplier, keep the money, and walk away with the drugs, too.

Dak's friend said the guy saved his life by telling the gangster, "Yeah, you could do that. But then you'll have to find a new supplier you can trust. You can already trust me. You know how hard it is to get the quality I'm providing, at the price I'm providing it."

The gangster had lowered his weapon, putting on a satisfied smile in the process. Dak's friend said that later, his buddy almost soiled himself in the car on the drive home.

Could this be one of those scenarios? Dak wondered if the thief had showed up, taken the money, and left with his hostage, a boatload of cash, and an artifact he could sell to someone else. He might even run the same gig twice, though that was doubtful. Screw over too many people in any arena of life, and it came back to haunt you. In the criminal underworld, that was especially true. And the karma usually came in the form of bloody revenge.

Ruling out a trap set by Tucker or Tamara, Dak narrowed down the likely scenarios and made his decision. He had to go in, no matter what the case. A woman's life was on the line, and he'd delayed long enough.

He swept the immediate area but sensed no threat, no sign of trouble. The cypress trees on the other side of the access street tossed and swayed in the wind, but no gunman lurked in their shadows. The driveway two doors down had a red compact hatchback parked in it and was the only barrier to Dak seeing to the end of the street. Everyone else, it seemed, had room in their garages for their vehicles.

Dak pressed his left shoulder against the door, holding his pistol close to his cheek, and then swung around, and into the house.

He checked left, then right. He stood in a laundry room with a washer and dryer to his right. Through the door straight ahead, he could see the same glow from before coming from the living room. Between, a corridor connected the rest of the first floor in an L-shape.

Dak pulled the door shut behind him and locked the dead bolt in case someone tried to get in behind him. It wouldn't stop someone who knew what they were doing, but it could slow them down.

Through the laundry room, he stopped at the next doorway and looked to the right first, and then through the parallel doorway leading into what looked like an office. A desk with a chair sat near a window to the left. The wires of the desktop looked like they were all plugged in, but Dak continued to get the feeling that none of this was real, like one of those model homes that realtors stage to sway potential buyers into thinking, "Hey, this could be my place!"

He stepped across the hall into the corner, keeping everything in front of him except the small hallway window, which was behind him. He saw the kitchen at the other end of the corridor, and also had a view of the opposite side of the office. The place was empty. No trash cans, no other chairs, no television. The only other piece of furniture that took up space on the dark hardwood floor was an entertainment center—minus the gadgets that do the entertaining.

Whoever staged this place did a half-ass job.

Dak left the fleeting thought in the doorway and hurried down the hall, using the edges of his shoes as the main contact point to keep as quiet as possible. He did his best to keep his jeans from swishing, though he felt every fiber could be heard in the dead silence of the night.

He stopped at the kitchen door and poked his head inside, immediately sweeping the pistol around from right to left. From there, Dak pushed to the living room by way of the foyer. He looked up the stairs as he passed them but continued around the ground floor until he reached the opposite entry to the office.

A frown spread across his face. There was no sign of anyone, or anything, here. *Nothing except....*

Dak tensed, raising his pistol with arms extended. He swung the weapon around to the living room, back to the office, and around again. He suddenly felt exposed. Instincts took over and he rushed to the corner of the living room behind a gray upholstered chair. For an entire minute, Dak crouched behind the seat, waiting.

Nothing happened, but he wasn't about to let down his guard. He knew he smelled it, that familiar scent that only accompanied the lingering afterglow of a gunshot.

The second he detected that acrid smell in the air, he made for the corner and put his back against the wall in a defensive position. At least from here, he could see an attacker from any possible angle.

After ninety seconds in hiding, Dak slowed his breathing and looked over at the front door. He needed to check it.

With a quick breath, he steadied his nerves and broke for the door. He stopped in front of it only for a moment, rechecked the dead bolt and handle, then took two huge steps forward onto the stairs.

He checked left and right with his pistol then continued up the stairs to the top, where the hallway split to the left and right, with a shared bathroom at the end to the right.

Dak chose that direction first, recalling he'd seen the light on in this part of the house. Two bedrooms were at the end of the hall, one toward the front and one toward the rear near the garage. Dak took the illuminated room first, stabbing the bedroom air with his pistol as he surged in, moving steadily, deliberately, until he'd checked every corner. The pretend bed to the right by the window was made to perfection, again, like no one had ever touched it.

The set doors hung wide open, so visitors could see in and get an idea of how much space the room had for storage.

He faced the door, slid down to one knee, and checked under the bed. In one stride he was up again. Dak crossed the hall, checking the other direction, before entering the second room.

He ducked as he flipped on the light switch in case someone lurked in the shadows to take an easy pot shot.

The room, as the one before, was empty.

Dak clenched his jaw to fight back that familiar sickening feeling in his gut, the one that lingered on the possibility that Tamara had lied.

He returned to the corridor and moved like a ghost past the stairs to the other end. The scent he detected earlier grew stronger with every step, and Dak knew it hadn't been his imagination before. He'd smelled gun smoke.

The door to the right hung open and he stepped inside, careful not to touch any surfaces. He searched what looked to be a bonus room over the garage. The space was barren, and perfectly clean. Dak knew that only left one possibility.

The last door hung open, but just barely. A gap the size of Dak's fist opened between the door and the frame and gave view to darkness beyond.

If there was a threat in this house, it waited beyond that door.

Dak took in a breath and exhaled on his way across the hall. He counted to three in his head and then shoved the door open with his shoulder as he rolled across it to the far side of the frame. He snapped his weapon up and stabbed it into the room, rapidly sweeping from left to right. With a quick step, he flipped on the light with the back of his free hand and continued into the room. He froze, momentarily dumbfounded by what he saw.

A bed and bathroom blocked off by a chain-link fence stretching from floor to ceiling. A kitchenette on this side.

Dak didn't get the chance to ask himself why someone would build a room this way. It didn't matter now. It could have been a weigh station for human trafficking, or drug deals, or any other illicit thing criminals did. None of that amounted to anything.

He peered through the fence for what felt like twenty minutes. The body lay on its side, a blue Dodgers cap close to a bloody face. A hole in the side of the victim's temple continued to ooze and was the only movement in the room for several seconds.

Gavin Harris' body lay perfectly still, his eyes staring out through the fence, fixed on nothing. Dak searched the room for the killer, but he already knew the truth. They were gone. He'd gotten here too late.

21

The visions of how the buy went down played in the video of Dak's mind. The faceless buyer had set up Gavin Harris. They met here, in this room, and then the buyer killed Harris, taking both the money and the statue. And worst of all, there was no sign of Dr. Laghari.

The only solace Dak could take from that was that the woman hadn't been killed, at least not here. There were no signs of a struggle.

No, she was still alive. He didn't have to convince himself much over that. But his consolation melted as he considered fates far worse than death, especially for a woman. If she were indeed safe, it wouldn't be for long.

Dak paced on the hardwood, racking his brain. "How can I find her? How can I find her?" He found himself breathing heavily. Why? Why did he feel like this? He felt something in his chest. A tight, burning sensation radiated across his body from his center.

He knew what it was. It wasn't the first time he'd felt this kind of pain. It wasn't a heart attack. It was guilt.

He felt guilty for wasting time getting here, stopping to talk to the detective—though there really wasn't any getting around that. Either Dak went to the cop, or the cop would have called him over or stopped him on the street.

Working through that thought process eased the guilt a little. And then there was the fact that he was the first person on the scene. The cops were certainly not close to figuring out this mystery. They would have had to use underground connections or....

Dak spun and ran through the door. He flew down the stairs two, and three, at a time just as he caught sight of the first beams brushing over the houses up the street. At the bottom, he whipped around the stairs, hooking his elbow in the knoll, and then darted through the office and into the laundry room. He slowed at the back door, stuffing his pistol into his pants and covering it again with his shirt. With the top of the shirt in his hand, he unlocked the door, turned the knob, and stepped out. No one was there yet, but he had only seconds. He wiped off the doorknob and then sprinted from the back door, across the driveway, and into the cypress trees beyond the access street.

Dak dove under the lower branches and rolled to a stop in time to see the first squad car arrive. Another followed the first, and the two vehicles parked in the driveway. Dak saw more headlight beams beyond the gap between the houses and knew more cars were parking in front of the house. They were trying to surround the place.

Were they here for him? How would they know where he was going? Or what he was doing? The answer didn't take long to pop into Dak's mind.

Detective Naik.

It was the only explanation. *Wasn't it?*

Dak knew he hadn't been followed. Or had he?

He thought back over the events of the night, doing his best to keep away from Tamara's distracting imagery. When Dak left the casino, Naik had been there. He'd been there, too, when Dak left the museum, but that might have been the first encounter. Since then, Dak had seen the man two other times. Again, maybe Naik had been staking out the casino, hoping he might get lucky with one of the wealthy patrons who just happened to be the buyer. *Or....* Dak craned his neck and looked below the lowest cypress branches to his rental car at the end of the street.

They have been following me, he thought with disgust. *Naik has been following me ever since I left the museum that day. He must have planted the device while I was inside with the director.*

At least now he knew why the detective had been hanging around places Dak went. And why Naik didn't know about Dak's visit to Lebedev's place. Dak had originally thought of taking the taxi instead of the rental car to be a move born from irrational paranoia. Instead, he now felt thankful for that decision.

If Naik had been on his tail when Dak went to Lebedev's, his entire future would be in jeopardy. Russian mobsters or not, Dak didn't think the honorable Rhadi Naik would be amenable to Dak's brand of vigilante justice. Dak wouldn't have seen the outside of an Indian prison for the rest of his life, if that were the worst of it.

Fortunately, that wasn't one of Dak's problems right now. Immediately, he had to get away from a murder scene, and it would be mere minutes before these cops searched the house and discovered the victim on the second floor. They'd call it in. Then more cops would show up. They would flood the streets, cordon off everything, and then there would be no escape. Even getting away before all that wouldn't guarantee anything. Dak knew there was no possible way he could get far enough from the crime scene on foot with the net of roadblocks and search parties the police would deploy. Depending on the timing, it could be a mile, or five miles. He wasn't sure how their procedures worked in India, but figured basing theirs on what he knew back home would give a good indication of what to expect.

He needed a ride.

The thought of stealing a car sputtered for a second and then was gone. He wasn't going to steal someone's car. He wasn't even sure he could get away with it on most of the newer cars. If there was a cab around, he could take that to a bus station, or train station, and then vanish for a few hours. But at this hour, he didn't see any other cars on the road. Except one.

A garbage truck rumbled down the road, heading toward blinking red lights at the intersection near the entrance to the neighborhood. The cops were out of their cars now and had surrounded the back door, using their radios to coordinate with the rest of their unit on the other side of the house. Dak didn't see any sign of Detective Naik, but he was the last person Dak needed to see right now. A question snaked through Dak's head, and he couldn't come up with an answer.

If the cops had used a tracker to follow him here, how did they know which house to go into, unless someone already knew where he was going. But how?

He didn't have an immediate answer, but Dak knew he had to leave.

With the rental car close to the scene of a murder, if Dak hadn't been a suspect before—as Naik had suggested—he'd certainly move to the top of that list now.

The garbage truck squeaked and groaned as it stopped at the intersection at the other end of the neighborhood. The rental sat idle just behind the dumpster by the trees, just to the left of Dak's focus. The garbage truck lumbered forward again. Dak was only going to have one chance at this. He waited patiently, risking a look back at the house. The first cop opened the back door and entered with the second covering the rear. The flashlights on their guns shone around the laundry room inside and then disappeared as the men pushed deeper into the house.

The sounds of a diesel engine roared along with the rumble of heavy tires as the truck neared Dak's position.

No looking back now.

The second the truck passed by, Dak rolled out from under the lower branches, picking up bits of mulch that clung to his clothes. He reached the narrow strip of grass next to the sidewalk and sprang to his feet in a single motion.

He pumped his legs as fast as he could, the muscles twitching over and over, arms swinging hard back and forth to maintain balance and momentum. His feet pounded the concrete, faster with every step.

To his right, he caught flashes of light in the house through the tree branches but couldn't make out any details in his peripheral vision. He didn't need to. The cops were likely upstairs now, and it would be a matter of seconds before they found the body.

The garbage truck's brakes squealed, and the vehicle's frame shook violently in protest as the behemoth slowed at the next light.

Thirty yards and closing, Dak wasn't sure he'd make it. Then he'd be forced to try to escape on foot, and he didn't like the odds of that. Alone, in a strange city with few, if any, real connections, he didn't have much of a chance against the cops.

Twenty yards to go, the truck's brakes hissed and honked like a badly damaged brass instrument.

The balls of Dak's feet pushed harder with each strike against the concrete, and with ten yards left, he lowered his head to get every ounce of speed he could muster. The truck stopped then flipped on its blinker to turn right.

Dak could smell the foul stench emanating from the truck. It filled his nostrils with every deep, panting breath, and he felt a twist in his gut. The big vehicle's motor whined again and started moving forward.

Dak took four more long strides and reached for the back of the truck, where a metal handle hung from the rear quarter above a couple of metal steps hanging off the back bumper. Just as his fingers were about to grasp the handle, the truck swerved around the corner. Dak's fingers brushed against the smooth, round surface, wrapping around it for a second. The handle was wet, though. With what, Dak didn't want to know. It didn't matter. Whatever it was, his fingers slipped off as the truck accelerated forward.

A sliver of anxiety shot through Dak's chest and into his stomach. The truck picked up speed as Dak's stride fell out of rhythm, sending him stumbling forward behind the vehicle. He gasped for air but didn't dare stop to catch his breath.

He could catch it. He had to.

Against reason, Dak recovered his stride and kept pumping his legs, running against exhaustion now as he chased after the garbage truck in vain. The smelly truck was pulling away now, adding a couple of yards per second, then five, as it rumbled away.

Dak knew it was a lost cause and he was ready to give up. His heart pounded in his chest, and his feet started counting the steps on their own, knowing that they only had another fifty yards left in them at this speed. His leg muscles burned, then began to stiffen, demanding a pause from the work being forced on them.

Dak pushed through all of it, still chasing against hope that he might somehow be able to catch the truck.

Thirty yards. Thirty-five. Every passing second put him farther and farther out of reach.

Dak could feel his speed slowing. He couldn't keep up that pace. He'd already sprinted a hundred yards, or more. While he kept in great shape, there was only so far a person could push their limits.

His heart felt like a twenty-pound demolition hammer in his chest. His lungs felt like they were melting.

He tripped, catching the toe of his shoe on the asphalt as he veered onto the street to pursue the truck directly down the lane. His arms instinctively flew out and he managed to windmill his way back into stride, though the mistake cost him, and he knew it.

The truck was forty yards away when the brake lights abruptly glowed brightly. The huge vehicle groaned and shook as the driver stepped on the brakes, bringing it to a sudden stop.

Dak didn't know why, and he didn't care. He summoned the last scraps of strength in his core and pushed hard toward the back of the truck.

Thirty. Twenty-five. Twenty yards to go.

There were no garbage cans for the driver to pick up, and for a strange, fantasy-filled second, Dak imagined that the person had seen him, recognized his plight, and slowed down to give him a ride.

He knew that wasn't the case and didn't think for a second the driver had seen him. In fact, he hoped he hadn't been spotted. The driver might be suspicious of someone chasing after a garbage truck. Dak knew he would be if he were the one behind the wheel.

There was no stop sign, no traffic lights. Dak couldn't understand why the truck was still sitting there.

Then, with only fifteen yards to go, Dak saw the cause. Two adult brown-and-white runner ducks waddled across the street, followed by several ducklings.

The last of the baby ducks reached the other side of the street, and the truck driver stepped on the gas again. The red brake lights dimmed and the engine roared, spilling black exhaust from its smokestack.

Five yards. Dak was nearly there.

Three. *Only two more big steps*, he told himself.

He reached out his hand, struggling to keep his melting leg muscles moving. His fingertips were inches from the handle, but he could feel the truck was no longer getting closer. It was pulling away.

With one last desperate push, Dak leaped toward the back of the truck. The back of his fingers slapped the handle as they passed, and this time he squeezed hard while pulling his other hand up to assist. Gripping the wet metal bar with both hands, Dak hauled himself up as the truck rumbled down the street. He managed to land his right foot on one of the steps and then steadied himself, holding on tight.

Dak watched the entrance to the neighborhood until the truck made a left at the next intersection. He breathed hard, unwilling to loosen his grip on the handle, and turned to face forward, leaving the subdivision behind him in the night. The stench spilling out of the garbage truck tempted nausea to knock on Dak's abdomen, but relief was stronger. The air might have smelled of a thousand foul odors, but he was gaining precious mileage now.

As his heartbeat recovered to its usual rhythm, Dak watched the houses go by. The nice area where the homes of the middle class offered many of the creature comforts he'd grown accustomed to in the United States faded rapidly to shanties, lean-to structures, and dilapidated "homes" built from scraps.

Dak had seen extreme poverty before, many times when he was in the Middle East. He'd seen people living in a way that he couldn't imagine. He had his cabin on the Cumberland Plateau. It was a humble abode, a place where he could get away from everything and enjoy the simpler life. For these people, there was nothing simple about their lives. Every day was a constant struggle to survive, to get scraps of trash for food, or clean water to drink.

Poverty existed in many places, even in the United States. Every politician he'd ever seen vowed to help with that. He imagined it was the same here in India, and in every country. Empty promises given to the people at the bottom, the ones most desperate for something better in life. Billions of them all over the world lived on more hope than bread, and as yet there hadn't been a system invented that delivered.

Dak sighed, his breathing back to a steady pace again.

The truck sped up, and he clung to the handle as the asphalt blurred by under him.

The moment was gone. There was nothing he could do to help so many people. He was just a single person.

Right now, he needed to focus on helping one woman, Dr. Laghari.

Dak guided his thoughts away from the plight of the poor to how he could locate the buyer before they left the country.

Who would know where to find someone like that?

Chester came to mind. He could go see if the little worm might have some intel on the new situation.

It was worth a shot.

He calculated how far the truck had gone so far and decided to stick to the ride for another ten minutes. Then he would reassess and find another way back to Chester's.

No doubt, the skinny punk would be asleep.

Chester stood in the center of the clearing, a lush green forest wrapping around him like a mother's arms. Tall grass under his feet felt soft, softer than he ever recalled when he walked barefoot as a child.

The tree leaves glistened with morning dew, their ripened fruits dangling from every limb. Chester breathed in the clean air. It was fresh, and for a few breaths, he remembered what it was like to be out in the countryside, away from the city where he spent so many long days and nights. Soon, he hoped, he could be here again.

But why am I thinking that? I'm here now? Why not stay awhile?

He felt a tightness in his side and reached down to touch it.

The second his finger brushed his skin, he roused from his slumber and rolled over, adjusting the pillow in hopes to return to the meadow in the forest where life was peaceful and easy. He twitched his nose, realizing something wasn't right. It was a strange feeling, and one that came with a heavy dose of fear.

I'm not alone.

He reached over to the nightstand next to his bed, pulled open the drawer, and stuck his hand inside. The drawer was empty. All his fingers felt was the cold, empty bottom.

"You know," a sinister and familiar voice said from the shadows in the far corner, "I'm not sure about Indian gun laws, but I'm fairly certain you're not supposed to have this little number." Dak wagged the pistol from a gray leather club chair. "Last I checked, they have pretty strict gun legislation. Seems like I recall seeing it's not in their constitution to have the right to own one. That means either this one is illegal, or you're one of the privileged few allowed to make the purchase."

Chester nearly jumped out of his sheets at the sound of Dak's voice. He crawled backward, pushing his shoulder blades into the headboard as if he could somehow find a few more inches of safety during his retreat.

"What are you doing here?" Chester snapped.

"Oh, I'm sorry. I should have knocked. But I didn't want to be rude."

"So, you just broke into my house? I should call the cops."

"You do that, Chester," Dak wagered, eyeing the gun as if inspecting it for flaws. "I'm sure that will work out great for you. I'll just leave this lovely pistol here and be on my way." He stood and acted as if he was about to set the gun on the top of a dresser. "Please, tell Detective Naik I said hello."

Chester scowled, but curiosity wormed its way into his mind and he couldn't let it go. "What do you want?" he ventured.

Dak paused at the door then looked back at the man in the bed. "Your thief is dead," Dak said.

The frown on Chester's face mutated into one of concern. "What? You killed him?"

"No," Dak confessed. "I didn't kill him."

Chester's eyes pored over the sheets, the far wall, the window, any random item that might give him an answer. His mind constructed the only one that made sense. "The buyer?" He looked to Dak with eyes hoping for answers.

"That's what I figure. And they took Dr. Laghari, too."

"And the artifact, I assume."

"Yep. Trifecta."

Chester's imagination ran wild with new, more terrifying visions.

"You don't think they'll come for me, too, do you? I mean, I was the one who got the thief involved in the first place. But I'm just the handler."

"It's entirely possible they're on their way here right now," Dak hedged. "Good thing I got here before they did."

He had no clue if the buyer and their hit squad were on their way up the stairs to Chester's apartment or if they were on a plane en route to Buenos Aires. But at the moment, he had Chester in a spot where he'd do anything to avoid being the next corpse to turn up.

"What did you do?" Chester demanded. He looked around the room, for what, Dak didn't know. He searched the floor, nearly bumping his head into the wall near his bed. Then a belt rattled, and Chester picked up a pair of pants that had been discarded just before bedtime.

"I didn't do anything, Chester. Not in regard to the thief's death, anyway."

Chester slid one leg through the skinny black jeans and looked up, questioning Dak's statement with curious eyes. "What's that supposed to mean?"

"Nothing," Dak shrugged, looking innocent. "Just what I said. I didn't have anything to do with what happened to him."

"And how do you know he was murdered?" Chester pulled the left leg through his pants.

"I saw the body," Dak said.

"What?" Chester nearly shouted.

"Take it easy." Dak put his hands out, palms facing his host. "I already told you, I didn't kill him."

Panic set in, and Dak watched it happen.

Chester's head searched the room faster, and he looked directly at the door more than once, trying to figure a way past his uninvited guest.

"Chester?" Dak said in a soothing tone. "Relax. I wasn't followed."

"How do you know that? Huh? You don't. You don't know."

"I do know. I'm very careful about those kinds of things." He abstained from telling Chester about the issue with his rental car. No way that was going to help the situation.

"Yeah?" Doubt veiled the word.

"Yes, Chester. Now calm down. And thank you for putting on pants. Interesting choice with the boxer briefs, by the way."

"What?" He looked down at his legs then back up, puzzled.

"Never mind. But we do need to go somewhere else. Okay? Just as a precaution. I'm not saying someone is on their way here to find you, but I would rather be extra careful."

"Wait. A minute ago you said no one was coming here. Now you think someone is? Which is it? You know what? No. You're a liar." He pointed an accusatory finger at Dak.

"I'm not lying," Dak said, positioning himself in front of the door so Chester couldn't get by. "I said I wasn't followed. I can say that definitively. That doesn't mean the buyer hasn't figured out who hooked up the sale, or the thief. But you know what?" Dak paused, as if a thought just occurred to him. "Don't worry about it. You stay here." He looked at the gun in his hands, then tossed it on the bed. "That's a lot of gun for home defense. Not judging, just making an observation. Be careful with that thing. Don't want you to accidentally shoot yourself with it."

It *was* a lot of gun for someone who clearly didn't go shooting very often, or probably didn't know much about firearms. Dak figured Chester went to some underground arms guy and was sold the biggest, most fearsome-looking weapon on offer.

A .50-caliber Desert Eagle was hardly practical, but Chester wasn't buying it for practicality. He was buying it because he wanted to feel like Dirty Harry in case someone walked into his apartment unannounced. *Well, someone else.*

Dak didn't have the heart to tell Chester that Dirty Harry carried a .44 Magnum.

Chester looked down at the weapon, uncertainty dripping from his eyes. "You're...going to just let me have it?"

"I don't think you're stupid enough to shoot me with that thing," Dak said with a derisive snort. "You'd go deaf discharging that weapon in this room. Not to mention it would be messy." Dak let his eyes wander around the room. "You'd have to switch apartments, for sure. You never really get the blood and tissue out of the paint and carpet. You know?"

Chester stared at him with sheer terrorized confusion in his eyes. "What? Yes. I mean. No. No. What are you talking about? I've never killed anyone. And I don't want to start now."

"Then you better stick with me, kid. Because I'm your best chance to stay alive."

Dak watched Chester as he considered the warning, weighing the words in the balance. He'd just been in the middle of a lovely, peaceful dream, only to be thrown into a horrific reality. A gambit of emotions surged through his mind. He was angry at Dak for putting him in danger. He was mad at himself for even getting involved. His gut had told him to be careful with this guy. The second Dak walked in the room at their initial meeting, Chester had felt uneasy. Now, that foresight was bearing fruit.

But what choice did he have? Dak was right. If he stayed on his own, he might end up dead. Although if he went with Dak, it could be the same result.

He grunted in frustration, pacing back and forth.

"Better make up your mind, kid," Dak urged. "You stick with me; you'll be okay. We'll get you somewhere safe. But I need you to help me find the buyer before they leave the country."

"Pfft," Chester spat. "They're probably already out of the country."

"Maybe. But I can't do nothing. We have to try. A woman's life is at stake."

He peered into Chester's eyes, appealing to the human side of Chester that had been ignored for far too long. He'd been focused so much on getting ahead, building a name—and a fortune—that he'd become a recluse, nothing but a robot constantly striving. Dak didn't know any of that, but he risked the appeal anyway. He hoped he didn't have to use other methods to convince Chester to help. He liked the guy in a strange sort of way, the way a kid feels bad for another kid on the playground because no one else is playing with them. Pity. It was pity Dak felt, though he wasn't sure why.

"Fine," Chester said finally. "I know a place we can go. It's a safe house. No one else knows about it. And I bought it with one of my corporations."

"One of?"

"Yeah." Chester acted like the answer should have been obvious. "I have several under multiple umbrellas. Makes it harder to trace for a number of purposes."

"Like taxes?"

Chester snorted. "That's always the first thing people say. It's more about staying under the radar." He turned and shifted to the dresser, opened the top drawer, and pulled out a roll of cash bound by a rubber band.

"That's a nice stash," Dak commented.

"Emergency fund. Always have one of those. It's one of the first rules of growing personal wealth."

Dak raised his eyebrows. "Okay, Dave Ramsey. We should probably get going."

"One second," Chester protested.

He stuffed the money into a pocket, then plucked a pair of socks from the second drawer. As he sat down to put on his socks and shoes, Dak stepped over to the window and pulled back one of the blinds. He peered out through the narrow opening, searching the street around the block, then the buildings, the windows, the rooftops.

Despite the hour, people still strolled down the sidewalks, and cars trickled by on the street. Dak was about to let the blind lower when he spotted trouble parked on the opposite curb. A black Land Rover sat by the sidewalk, with another one only five cars up.

"You might want to make that half a second," Dak said.

Chester looked over as he finished tying a shoe. "What?"

"You're not exactly filling me with a lot of confidence, mate," Chester complained as the two men hurried down the stairs. "I thought you said you weren't followed."

"I wasn't," Dak answered as he rounded the corner on the next landing. "They already knew to come for you. That was part of the plan all along. And unless I miss my guess, they'll go after Tamara next. We need to get to her and warn her."

"What?" Chester panted the word in rhythm with his breathing. "I'm not going to see her."

"You know? I think it's time to get over this little fear you have of her. She's just a woman running a business."

"Is that what you think?"

Chester struggled to keep up with Dak, who appeared to be an expert at descending stairs quickly.

Dak stopped abruptly on the sixth-floor landing and held up a hand to halt Chester. The tall, skinny Brit nearly ran him over but managed to slow to a stop with the aid of his firm grip on the railing.

"What?" Chester asked.

Dak held a finger to his lips, signaling him to shut his yap. Leaning over the rail, Dak peered down through the shaft to the bottom of the stairs. He heard a door close, and footfalls pounding the steps in rapid succession.

Frustration spread across Dak's face. He pointed to the door with the number 6 next to it and quietly, carefully pulled it open.

"Inside," Dak mouthed.

He could tell Chester wanted to ask why or what they were doing going to the sixth floor or how they were going to get out when they were stuck in the middle of the building, but the Brit didn't ask any of those questions. Maybe he was too afraid the goons coming up the steps would hear him.

Instead, Chester simply obeyed and ducked into the hallway. Dak eased the door shut behind him and waited.

"I should have brought my gun," Chester whispered when they were both inside the corridor.

Dak snorted in derision, shaking his head. "No," he said simply and left it at that.

"What are we going to do? They'll find us here."

"Shut up," Dak ordered, pressing his ear to the door.

Chester blushed, either from embarrassment or anger. He didn't elaborate, which Dak was thankful for. Dak didn't want to have to slap his hand over the guy's lips.

Standing perfectly still, Dak listened at the door, patiently waiting for the footsteps he knew would come. After less than a minute of waiting, he wasn't disappointed. The sounds began as nothing more than a repetitive tapping, distant and nonthreatening. But the noise swelled with every approaching step, until Dak could hear the faint grunts of the men climbing the stairs; they were breathing hard from the exertion.

The footfalls pounded the stairs with every approaching step until Dak heard the men rush by, their cadence slipping from the climb but still pushing onward toward the top.

Dak waited, forcing himself to be calm and not make a rash decision. When the sounds faded to almost nothing, he eased the door open again and looked out, stabbing his pistol through the gap first.

The stairs were clear, though he could still hear the henchmen's steps from above as they echoed down through the shaft.

Dak reminded Chester to stay silent with a finger to his lips, then motioned for him to follow. Dak pushed the door open and stepped out into the stairwell.

He checked up and down once more then proceeded down the next section of stairs, keeping close to the wall instead of the rails in case one of the men above happened to look down through the opening.

The two hurried as fast as they could on their tiptoes, carefully navigating the steps, sometimes two at a time.

They reached the bottom without incident. A door to the right with an exit sign over it led outside to the back part of the building. Dak's ride was on the other side, nearly a full block away. Going that direction would lengthen their trip, but they might avoid trouble. Another door led into the lobby, where Dak figured the mysterious buyer's thugs probably had the all the exits blocked.

He opted for the rear exit and reached out to press the bar that unlocked it.

"What are you doing?" Chester asked.

"They probably have the main entrance covered," Dak said. "So we go out the back."

Chester didn't protest further, though the concern on his face showed his apprehension.

Dak pressed the bar and eased the door open. The alley behind the building looked clear to the left, and he could see the street at the end, where the occasional car drove by.

Dak pushed the door wide open, holding it for Chester to pass by. The tall Brit followed the unspoken order and walked out into the alley. Dak followed, but as he took a step over the threshold, a sudden movement from the right caught his eye. He couldn't react fast enough as a dark figure swooped into his vision and grabbed Chester with one arm while putting a gun to his back with the other hand.

Chester gasped, struggling to free himself.

"Easy now," another English accent ordered. The man holding

Chester was shorter than Dak, and therefore much shorter than the tall Brit, but he still managed to bend the lanky Chester backward far enough to make standing an awkward endeavor.

"You, stay there," the gunman ordered.

He wore a black, long-sleeve shirt and matching pants. While the man cowered behind his hostage, Dak could still see his face. He wasn't Indian, which meant he was either a local who'd picked up a gig for the buyer, or he worked solely for the buyer and came in with the rest of the crew to take care of all the loose ends.

"You shoot that gun, you'll have every cop in the area swarming on this alley within minutes," Dak warned.

"Shut it, Yank," the gunman said. His pale skin shone in the orange glow of a streetlight at the end of the alley. "Drop your gun. Do it slowly."

"Gun?"

"Don't play stupid with me. Do it, or I kill him now and tell the cops you did it."

"Drop the gun, Dak," Chester begged. "He's going to kill me."

"He's not going to kill anyone," Dak argued, even as he started to bend down and place his pistol on the wet pavement.

Dak watched the gunman's eyes as he set the pistol down, then slowly stood back up again. "There," Dak said. "I did what you asked. Now, let him go."

"Oh, no. He's the one we want. Not you, old boy. You're just collateral damage. Now, kick it away for me. Be a good lad, now."

Dak didn't appreciate the condescending way he was called "lad," but he was in no position to counter it. Yet.

"So, what's your plan?" Dak asked. "You going to just walk down the alley with your hostage, meet up with your crew on the street, throw him in the back of a windowless van, take him somewhere out of town to kill him, then dump the body?"

Chester's eyes widened at the horrific and callous way Dak guessed his fate. "Dak? What in the world, man?"

"Relax," Dak said. "This guy couldn't hurt a fly. You can see it in his eyes. He's scared. Too scared to even make the call."

The gunman's eyes did betray a touch of uncertainty but no sign of fear. Dak merely did what he could to wedge that little sliver of weakness into a gaping chasm, even though he didn't expect it to work. Still, he had to try.

Dak had already noted the radio in the guy's ear, but the gunman had made no move to call for backup or let the rest of his team know that he had the target.

"Shut up and kick the pistol over to me."

The man hadn't seen Dak reach into his pocket as he bent down to surrender his pistol. And he didn't see it when Dak retrieved the tiny cylinder—or palmed it while he spoke.

"Okay," Dak said. "Whatever you say." He reared back dramatically with his foot, making a show of it, and nudged the pistol forward a few inches.

"You think you're funny, don't you?" the gunman sneered.

"You didn't tell me how far."

"I said kick it *to* me, idiot."

"That's right," Dak agreed. "You did. My mistake. Here." He kicked it too hard this time and watched the pistol skitter across the wet asphalt, beyond the gunman by five feet. As the gunman turned his head to watch the gun, Dak flipped the cylinder at Chester's feet, where it stopped only a foot away.

"Better?" Dak asked.

"I should kill you just for being a pain," the thug spat, looking over his shoulder at the weapon on the ground behind him.

Chester wore panic on his face, worried that Dak had pushed the gunman too far. Then Dak winked at him, which only confused Chester further—until the device by his feet sparked. A burst of smoke spewed out of the cylinder, engulfing him and his captor in a cloud of gray within seconds.

The gunman swore and spun around. He coughed as his lungs filled with the acrid smoke. Chester coughed, too, doubling over at the hips, but realized that the gunman had loosed his grip with his own coughing fit.

The thug peered around, twisting his head back and forth to see, but all he could find was the foggy haze wrapping around him.

Then he felt strong fingers wrap around his wrist and a sudden jerk of his arm. The goon twitched his trigger finger. The pistol fired, but Dak had already turned the weapon away from Chester. The muzzle erupted in a short, loud pop, and the bullet zipped across the alley, smashing into a brick wall.

The gunman tried to regain control of his weapon, jerking his wrist back, but it was too late. Dak already had the upper hand—both literally and figuratively. He grasped the pistol, wrapping his fingers around the barrel, then in one swift move, he yanked the pistol backward and away from the assassin.

The man's trigger finger snapped at an awkward, gruesome angle. He screamed out in pain, but the sound cut off as Dak stepped around him and chopped the guy in the neck with the bridge of his hand.

The yelling turned to gurgling, and the would-be killer became the victim as he clutched his throat with his one good hand, the right dangling limp to the side with a broken index finger.

Dak ejected the magazine from the pistol, pulled the slide to send the chambered round to the ground, and then stuffed the pistol in his belt. The choking man fell to his knees amid the cloud of smoke. Dak stepped around behind him and wrapped one arm around the guy's neck, placing the opposite hand on the man's temple. He jerked the gunman's head to the side with an audible crack, then added a twist.

The body instantly tripled in weight as the dead man's muscular control ceased with his life. Dak let go and allowed the corpse to fall to the ground, where it twitched in death's embrace.

Dak stepped out from the fog and found Chester standing a few feet away, still trying to clear his lungs of smoke.

"What the—"

"Don't say it," Dak cautioned. "We need to move."

"You just—" Another cough racked Chester's body. "You just killed that guy." The wonder and horror in his voice were impossible to miss.

"Yes. We have to move." Dak grabbed his charge by the arm and started pulling him toward the street.

"But...he's dead."

"It was him or us," Dak clarified. "Would you prefer the other way around?"

Chester quickly shook his head. "No. No, you definitely made the right choice. I've just—"

"Never seen someone's neck broken before? First time for everything, kid. We gotta move."

Dak practically dragged Chester down the alley until they reached the sidewalk. Then Dak spotted a nearby trash can, walked over to it, and smoothly took the pistol from his belt and tossed it into the bin.

"They'll be around the building, most likely," Dak said. "So we'll have to move fast—and hope we don't run into trouble."

"What kind of trouble?" Chester asked.

"That kind." Dak jerked his thumb back toward the smoke-filled alley. The artificial fog shrouded the body, for the most part, but that wouldn't last long.

"Oh. Right."

Dak led the way to the right, away from the main entrance. When they were halfway to the next intersection, Chester leaned close as they walked briskly.

"What are we doing? I thought you said your car was on the other side." Chester spoke in a conspiratorial tone, despite no pedestrians being in their immediate personal space.

"It is," Dak said. "Oh, and it's not a car."

"What?"

Dak didn't answer, instead leaving some room for mystery in Chester's mind.

They rounded the next corner, and when Chester's building was out of sight, Dak checked behind them again, then took off at a trot.

"So, running now, are we?" Chester asked, kicking his long legs out to catch up.

Dak still remained oddly silent.

"Do you mind terribly telling me where your car is? If someone is here to kill us, getting off the street seems like it would be a good idea."

"It's right around the next corner, half a block up to the right." Dak said, barely breaking his breathing pattern from the light jog. "And it's not a car."

Chester looked over at him with suspicion in his eyes, along with a dash of confusion. "Why do you keep saying that? What did you bring here? A rickshaw?"

"Nope."

The two reached the next corner, and Dak again glanced over his shoulder to make sure they weren't being followed. Then he broke down the sidewalk to the right and continued until they came to a black-and-red motorcycle parked along the curb.

Dak slowed down and fished a key out of his pocket, then unlocked the helmet dangling from the back seat and a second one hanging from the seat strap.

"What is this?" Chester asked, confused.

"It's a Suzuki GSX-R 1000. It replaced the 1100 back in the early 2000s. I think 2001." Dak gave the answer in the most matter-of-fact voice possible, but he could still see the confusion on Chester's face. "It's a motorcycle, Ches. Get on." He shoved the helmet into the tall man's hands then fit his own over his head and climbed onto the bike.

With the push of a button, the motorcycle roared to life. Chester still stood on the sidewalk with the helmet in his hands, and the same dumbfounded look on his face.

Dak flipped up his tinted visor and stared at the lanky Brit. "Chester, get on the bike. Now."

"I'm not getting on that thing." Chester wore a disgusted expression on his face, as if the motorcycle were made from some vile material.

"Any second now, they're going to realize you're not home. My guess is they already know and are on their way back down the stairs. Meanwhile, the other goons they brought with them, who stayed on the ground floor, are now searching the perimeter. I'd say it's give or take thirty seconds before they find their dead comrade back there in the alley. Then it will be all hands on deck. They will scour the city for us. And when they do, it's important we're somewhere they can't find us. So, your best option is to get on the bike and hold on tight. Or...you can stay here and die. Up to you, Ches."

Dak turned the handlebars toward the street and shifted the Suzuki into first gear with a quick push down of his right toes.

Chester stared at the helmet for too many heartbeats before resigning himself to his fate and shoving it down onto his head.

At first, the thing was tight, and uncomfortable, but the cushions within helped, and he found it wasn't so bad once he got it all the way down on his skull.

"Why do I have to ride on the back?" Chester complained as he saddled his right leg over the seat.

"Because I don't know if you know how to ride. And second, it's not your bike."

"Where did you get this thing, anyway?"

"Don't worry about it. Just hang on."

Chester awkwardly looped his arms around Dak's torso, which received a slap on the hand from the driver. "Don't hold on to me, weirdo. There are pegs on the side you can use."

"Oh," Chester said, blushing with his voice. "I knew that."

"Sure you did. You want that kind of action, you're gonna have to buy me a few drinks first."

"I could use a drink right about now."

Dak revved the engine with a twist of his right hand, and slowly let out on the clutch with his left, careful not to accelerate too fast and send his rider flying off the back.

Glancing down into the right mirror, Dak saw the black SUV whip around the corner, tires squealing as the vehicle lumbered through the hairpin turn, leaning heavily to one side.

"On second thought," Dak said, "you might have to hold on to me."

"What?"

"I said hold on!" Dak yelled and twisted the throttle hard.

Dak gunned the engine, giving it all it could handle with the burden of the two men on the back. He was glad he'd opted for the 1000 instead of the 600 or 750. While both of those engine blocks could handle two riders, the 1000 could do it without breaking much of a sweat.

He slowed down at the next intersection then cut in between cars despite having a red light. There was no time to stop right now. The buyer's men were on their tail, though Dak had a significant advantage.

He weaved between the cars, cutting through narrow spaces with a daredevil's grace. He made the maneuvers look simple, gliding in and out of gaps that could barely fit a grocery cart.

Every few seconds, Dak glanced down at one of the side mirrors to see how far back the Land Rover was, but he couldn't spot it.

He kept going straight, heading for the highway out of town, when another SUV screamed into view only a few cars back.

"I think we lost them!" Chester shouted over the howling wind.

Dak shook his head and pointed at the side mirror. Chester angled his neck so he could see and then patted his driver on the back. "Go faster. Must go faster."

Traffic was thin, which was both good and bad. Because of the late hour, few people were out on the town going to clubs or bars or whatever else people did at that time of night. With fewer cars on the road, Dak had more room to maneuver. But with a giraffe on the back of the seat, Dak wasn't able to shift the bike as quickly.

"Where are we going?" Chester shouted over the sounds of wind and the roaring engine.

"Highway," Dak said, pointing at a sign on the side of the street. The arrow pointed toward an on-ramp.

Dak started to cut left, but he saw movement there. He reacted instantly and twisted the throttle, veering hard to the right, swerving past a transport truck, bypassing the street leading to the highway.

Chester was about to ask what Dak was doing when he saw the two black Land Rovers blocking the lanes to the left.

"How do they know where we are?" Chester shouted over the swirl of sounds around them.

Dak didn't answer. He didn't have time to respond to pointless questions right now. That, and he didn't know. The buyer had come after Chester. It was a surprise, but not completely unexpected. Dak had considered that might be their next move. And now he wondered if they would target Tamara next—if they didn't already have someone over there. On the plus side, if Detective Naik were still hanging around the casino's secret entrance, maybe he could prevent these thugs from getting in.

A white luxury sedan slowed down ahead and Dak swerved around it, crossing the center line in front of a truck barreling straight for them. A quick shift, and Dak had the motorcycle farther on the wrong side of the road, skirting along between a row of parked cars and oncoming traffic. The thumping sounds of the vehicles passing on both sides filled the riders' ears, and the wind from the passing trucks and cars swooshed over them, shaking the motorcycle with every pass. Dak tightened his legs against the seat and fairing as they shot through the narrow gap between the cars.

Then they were through and back onto an open lane.

He risked a look back in the side mirror and saw three of the black SUVs barreling through traffic, weaving in and out around other cars. One of them followed the hard way that Dak had taken. The SUV didn't have enough room on the road, though, and the driver nearly hit an oncoming truck. Fortunately for the other driver, the Land Rover's driver jerked the wheel to the right and smashed into a tree growing in a planter on the sidewalk. The violent crash sent the back end of the vehicle launching upward and then back down to the pavement, where the tires slammed down hard.

Dak was too busy navigating the road to check if the occupants survived, but that wasn't his concern. They couldn't follow anymore, and that was good enough for now.

Up ahead, a red light glowed its warning. Traffic going through the intersection was sparse, but it was still there.

"Hold on!" Dak shouted back to his rider.

"What?"

The sounds of the engine and the wind combined to a deafening roar as Dak twisted the throttle. The bike surged forward, speeding toward the busy intersection like a missile. Merging back into the correct lane, Dak watched the SUVs behind him. The drivers somehow managed to keep up, though still a good distance back, around a hundred yards. Maybe less.

I can lose them here, Dak thought.

"Daaak?" Chester said, elongating the word to emphasize his concern over their speed and trajectory. "Are you going to slow down? That light is red!"

The only response he received was Dak leaning forward over the gas tank, getting into a more aerodynamic position.

"Dak?" Chester pressed, leaning forward a little himself to brace for what he was certain would be an awful and dramatic crash.

The Suzuki screamed down the street, kicking up droplets of water from the wet street in its wake.

They'd been lucky so far, Dak knew. Driving a bike like this on wet roads had proved difficult in most of his limited experience on motorcycles. You had to baby them a little, and he'd not been able to do that, instead pushing the machine to its limits.

A red car sat at the stop light just ahead, while the lane for opposite traffic remained empty, with two cars on the other side of the intersection waiting for the light to change.

"You're not actually going to—" Chester couldn't finish his sentence as Dak yanked the throttle to its max.

The bike shot forward.

At the last second, Dak leaned right, blowing by the car at the stop light and into the busy interchange.

He dipped left to avoid a produce delivery truck, then back to the right, narrowly skirting by an old gray hatchback. The front-left mirror nearly grazed the car as the motorcycle zipped by. The air whooshed over the two riders as they missed the vehicle by mere inches.

Then they were through, except that now they were facing oncoming traffic with no way to get back to the other lane in time.

Dak improvised, letting up on the throttle and gently applying the front and rear brakes. Chester surged forward from the abrupt slow-down, then eased back as Dak let up on the brakes and steered the bike to the right, onto the sidewalk.

The few late-night pedestrians walking by the shops and cafés panicked at the sight of the speeding motorcycle, though to be fair, Dak had slowed down significantly by the time he hit the concrete. Some of the people dove out of the way. Others screamed or shouted. A few younger men, drunk from the looks of their staggering gait and lack of balance, laughed and pointed at the motorcycle as it sped by. Two or three offered rude hand gestures and some profanity that Dak couldn't hear as they shot down the sidewalk.

Just past a fruit cart, Dak turned the handlebars and dove the motorcycle back onto the street, where it belonged, then cut hard left to avoid an oncoming van.

He merged back into the correct lane and looked back in the mirrors to see the SUVs trying to navigate their way through the busy intersection.

At the next street, he slowed down and cut to the left, putting their tails out of sight for the moment. Dak shifted gears fluidly through the transmission, accelerating through the top end of the gearbox. Then, at the next intersection, he let off on the gas, gently applied the brakes, and decelerated, shifting back down through the gears to make a safe but quick turn to the right after a rolling pause at a stop sign.

He continued snaking through side streets, making multiple turns, until he was certain they'd lost the buyer's goons. Then Dak made for the highway again, taking an alternate route by way of three turns that looped them around to the on-ramp for the expressway.

With the ramp in sight, Dak glanced in the mirrors one more time to make certain the Land Rovers hadn't miraculously found them. No one was behind them, and he felt a wave of relief as he turned the throttle and accelerated onto the highway.

"Did we lose them?" Chester shouted, twisting his head around to check for himself.

"For now," Dak answered back.

He knew they wouldn't stop, though, and that the buyer would do whatever in their power they could to rein in the two men.

There was a positive side to all of this, and Dak locked his focus on that thought as he merged onto the expressway. If the buyer's henchmen were still cleaning up loose ends, that meant there was a chance the buyer was still in town. And if that were the case, a chance remained that Dak could save Priya—and get the statue back.

Dak drove up the road, keeping the bike at a steady speed under the limit, his eyes constantly checking the mirrors for trouble behind them. After they passed four exit ramps, he abruptly switched on the blinker and steered to the right, getting off the expressway. He followed the lane around to the left, under the bridge, and into an area rife with high-end retail shops, luxury car dealerships, and expensive restaurants.

There weren't many people on the streets or sidewalks here, as they sought the more exciting nightlife in other sectors of the city.

Dak found a hotel less than two minutes off the expressway and turned into the parking lot. He guided the motorcycle around to the side of the building, where it would be out of sight from the road, then killed the engine and used his left foot to push out the kickstand.

"What are we doing here?" Chester asked.

Dak removed his helmet and surveyed the lot. It was half full, some cars parked in groups, and a few parked on their own along the far reaches of the asphalt where they wouldn't be damaged by other vehicle doors opening.

"You're going to call Tamara," Dak said.

"What?"

"You say that word a lot. Did anyone ever tell you that?"

"What?"

"Yes. That's the word. You say it frequently."

Chester puzzled over the statement, while Dak felt like he was in a bad Abbot and Costello skit.

"Oh," Chester finally realized. "Sorry. But I don't understand. You want me to call Tamara?"

"Yes," Dak confirmed. "I need you to call her for me."

"I don't want to talk to her."

"I'm aware of that," Dak said.

Both their heads snapped around as a car with a loud tailpipe roared by on the road. Dak caught a glimpse of the blue paint and the angled body, immediately recognizing the Aston Martin Vanquish.

He brought his focus back to the problem at hand and stared with deadly intensity into Chester's eyes.

"Listen, son. I know you have something going on with that woman. I don't know why you're afraid of her. Maybe you like her. Maybe she likes you. Maybe the two of you should just run off and get married. I have no idea. But what I do know is that you need to call her...because if you don't, she's going to be up to her elbows in those thugs from the hotel back there. If she's not already." Dak's voice escalated until he finished his rant. Then he took a deep breath and sighed. "I don't have her number. You call her. I'll talk. Okay?"

Chester looked as though he'd been told there was no Santa. He nodded and retrieved a phone from his pocket.

"She and I," Chester said, "she intimidates me. That's all."

"And you have a crush on her. I get it. Look, kid. Make the call. I'll talk. You just make sure she answers."

"At this hour?" Chester asked. "I don't think that's a good idea."

"She'll be awake," Dak said. "She sleeps in the morning. Probably gets out of bed around ten or eleven."

"How do you know that?"

Dak rolled his eyes. "Because she runs an underground casino,

Ches. She's a woman who keeps late hours. But she has to sleep sometime. Please, just make the call."

"Okay. Okay. Hold on."

Chester found the woman's number and pressed the green Call button, then handed the device to Dak.

"Hello?" Tamara answered wearily.

Dak noted the absence of the loud music from the casino, and he knew she'd probably gone home for the night.

"Hey," Dak said. "It's me. Dak."

"Oh," her voice brightened, as if she'd just been splashed with a bucket of cold water. "Now, what can I do for you at this late hour, Mr. Harper? Are you going to tell me, or do you want me to use my imagination?"

Dak blushed a little at the insinuation, but Chester didn't seem to notice. "Unfortunately, it's something you need to do for yourself." He didn't wait for her to respond. "There are men coming for you right now. The buyer killed the thief, took the statue and the curator."

"That is unfortunate," Tamara said, without a trace of insincerity. "Why are they coming for me? And how do you know this?"

"Because they just tried to get to Chester."

He waited as she considered the statement. A warm breeze flowed over him and he spun around, again surveying the parking area for any sign of trouble. It was easy to think they'd lost the buyer's hit squad back near the apartment building, but after all he'd seen, Dak wasn't about to take anything for granted.

Chester swiveled his head around at the sound of his name.

"What do you mean?" Concern bubbled in her voice.

"He's fine. But I had to extract him from his flat. The buyer sent a hit squad there to take him out. He's safe with me for now. You need to get somewhere, though. Is there a safe place you can hide out until this is over?"

"A safe place?" She thought for a second. "I have an aunt with a house in the country. I could go stay with her, I suppose."

"Go there now."

The woman exhaled audibly. "I'm sorry, Dak, but what makes you think this mysterious buyer is going to send their people after me? I'm the one that set up the deal!" She emphasized the last sentence.

"Because you're a loose end, Tamara. I know that these deals usually go down without a hitch and everyone walks away, happy to do business again sometime down the road. Believe me when I say this time isn't like the others. There's something strange going on here, and I don't fully understand what it is yet."

"So, you're asking me to take your warning on nothing but pure faith," she said.

"Yes, I am. And I'm asking you for one more thing."

"Oh, two for one?"

"I need you to take Chester with you," Dak said.

The look on Chester's face would have fit perfectly on a cowboy trying to ride a bull for the first time. "What? No!" He mouthed the words silently, but his exaggerated expressions did all the yelling.

Dak held up a finger, instructing Chester to wait.

"That's an interesting caveat," Tamara said. "What does he have to say about it?"

"He's completely comfortable with it," Dak lied, ignoring the Brit's silent begging, shaking his head and whispered complaints. Chester did everything but get down on his knees. "Look, you two obviously have some things to discuss. I don't know what, but you need to just get it all out on the table and probably start dating or something. I honestly don't care. I just know I need to leave him with you while I figure out what's going on, who this buyer is, and stop them before they leave the country with Dr. Laghari."

"Such a noble hero," she cooed. "Fine. Bring him to my aunt's house. I'll send the address to this number."

"Thank you. I appreciate it."

"Don't mention it. Besides, you should save your thanks for when we're all out of this alive, I would think." She paused. Then said, "What makes you think the buyer is still in the country?"

"I wouldn't have thought that. I'm still not a hundred percent certain, but if their security team or thug squad, whatever you want to call it, is still here, then there's a good bet the one pulling the strings is, too. Then again, they could be long gone. But I have to find out where they are and get Dr. Laghari back to safety."

"And the artifact, I'm sure."

"If I can, yes, but that's not the priority."

She hummed at the response. "So honorable. Not many men like you around now, Dak Harper. Pity."

"I hope you're putting your shoes on and getting your keys while you talk to me," he diverted.

"Yes, yes. Fine. I'm getting ready."

"Good." Dak turned his head and took a few paces away from Chester, who had finally stopped acting as if his life were about to end. When Dak spoke again, he kept his voice hushed, just above a whisper. "You don't happen to know where the buyer might be, do you?"

Tamara barked a laugh that nearly hurt Dak's ear. "My dear, if I knew where they were, then this call would be a touch superfluous, wouldn't it?"

"It would, but it was worth a shot," Dak confessed.

"Where will you go?" she wondered. "I may know who could locate the buyer. I could put out some feelers, though there are no guarantees."

"No guarantees in life, either. Put out your feelers, but be careful. Right now, I don't know who you can trust, who any of us can trust."

"I'll be careful. What are you going to do? Where will you go?"

Dak didn't like the idea simmering in the back of his head. The plan had about as many chances of going wrong as it did right, maybe more. He knew it was going to take some work to even locate the guy, and when he did, Dak wasn't sure he would even be allowed an audience.

"I'm going to pay a visit to a new friend here in town and see if they can help me out."

"New friend?" Tamara asked. "You're making all kinds of friends here in Mumbai. A regular social butterfly."

"Not quite," Dak said. "I'll rendezvous with you where you tell me, although I would prefer to keep the drive under thirty minutes, if possible. The longer I'm on the road, the less time I have to locate the buyer."

"Understood. I assume meeting at the restaurant is out of the question."

"Not only that," Dak chuffed, "but the police have been hanging around there lately. They might even be outside your house right now." He wondered if the statement unnerved her, but she didn't reveal it if it did.

"Let them sit," she said. "I know the perfect place to meet. Then I'll take Chester from there."

Dak looked over his shoulder at the nervous Brit.

"Sounds good."

"And your friend?" Tamara pressed.

Dak exhaled, exasperated. He was tired and could see there would be no sleep while the sun was down.

"The enemy of my enemy is my friend," Dak demurred. "Let's just say it's a good thing I speak Russian."

Lesma Lebedev rubbed his eyes with pudgy fingers. He stared at Dak from a deep, black leather chair in his study. Two cups sat on a round, wooden-top end table supported by wrought iron legs and base. One glass contained three fingers of vodka. The other was a brown coffee mug brimming with steaming, fresh coffee.

"Mr. Harper, when I said if you ever needed anything, I didn't think you were going to show up at three o'clock in the morning. And less than twenty-four hours after the invitation was extended." He struggled with the English but had a firm enough grasp on the language to carry on a conversation.

Dak eased the man's pain by speaking in Lesma's native tongue. "Russian, please," Dak requested. "I am in your home."

And what a home it was. After dropping off Chester with Tamara, which turned out to be a funny exchange—watching the tall, slender man squirm at the sight of the woman he clearly had a thing for—the two of them were safe, at least for now. Dak had done all he could do. The rest was out of his hands.

He considered the thought and momentarily lingered on it, distracting himself with the bizarre string of events. Here he was, in a Russian mobster's study, after just meeting up with two other underworld figures to help make sure they were safe. Protecting shady characters wasn't something he'd expected when he took this gig a few days prior.

A fire burned in a hearth between the two angled chairs. If Dak was honest with himself, he wouldn't have minded having a place like this to sit and sip bourbon by the fire on a cold night, maybe have a cigar every now and then. He noted the humidor in the corner but didn't let his eyes stay fixed on it for long. He didn't have time for that right now.

"Thank you," Lebedev said. "You have a sense of honor. I can appreciate this. In my world, there is little honor."

A vision of Lebedev's business passed through Dak's mind, though he decided not to bring up the problem of honor with pilfering money from local businesses for "protection", or selling drugs to a ravenous and seething base of addicts. He could see that the man had been through an emotional night. After all, he'd just murdered his own son. Dak couldn't imagine how that would feel, and he didn't want to.

"I learned a long time ago," Dak said, "to be respectful to people. You can be on top, but you had to climb the ladder to get there, and the ladder goes both directions. You never know who you'll pass on the way down if things go south, and that's when you know who your real friends are."

Lebedev puckered his lips and nodded in approval, rubbing his chin with a thumb as he considered the statement. "Wise words. Is a shame you won't come work for me."

"I agree. You could use a man like me in your ranks."

The big Russian burst into a bellowing laugh that nearly shook the end table next to him. When he finally calmed down again, he reached over, picked up the vodka, and took a drink. He shook his head, placing the glass back where he got it, and released a satisfied exhale.

"Are you sure you don't want vodka?" He motioned to the bar in the corner where several bottles of the finest vodka in the world lined the shelf, along with a few cognacs and a single bottle of Jack

Daniel's.

The last one made Dak smile inside. *It really is everywhere,* he thought.

"I'm sure; but thank you. I have to keep a clear head, and I'm running out of time."

Lebedev nodded. "Yes. You mentioned you have to find someone before they leave town."

"There was a theft at a museum here in town," Dak began. "A very expensive artifact was stolen. I'm trying to get it back."

The Russian listened but said nothing, knowing that Dak had more to add.

"The curator was also kidnapped. I'm afraid her life is in danger, at the very least."

"She is young? Attractive, this curator?" Lebedev released the thumb from his chin and held up his hand in a questioning gesture.

"Yes to both."

Lebedev nodded. "I see. In that case, your assumption is correct about her life being in danger, as well as the insinuation about things getting worse. She might be a prime target for the sex slave trade. Many young girls are taken every day here, and everywhere from what I hear. Sold in the black market." Disgust rotted his words, and he made no qualms about how he felt regarding the underground human trafficking network. "They are vile, those people; the ones who trade human beings. Sure, I kill people, and some say the things I do are bad, but I provide services. Do I charge high rates? Of course. But so do the governments of the world."

Dak wasn't sure he agreed entirely with the justification, although the part about the governments was both funny, and true. He was, however, glad to hear his host didn't care for the darker side of the criminal underworld.

A murderer with ethics. Interesting. For a second, though, Dak wondered how he was any different. He killed people, more by the day it seemed in some weeks. Usually, it was in self-defense, except for taking out Lebedev's son. He'd not liked the idea, but after seeing the mountain of evidence against the man, Dak had decided that, for once, he would play judge, jury, and executioner. As it turned out, he didn't have to be any of those things.

But he couldn't think about that now. Dak took a deep breath, refocused, and relayed what he knew about the museum theft up to this point. "Earlier tonight, the thief who stole the artifact, and abducted the curator, was murdered in a house about thirty minutes outside the city."

Lebedev hummed quietly at the information. "And how do you know about this thief's death? Who killed him?"

"Because I went there shortly after he was killed."

The weight of the statement sucked the air out of the room for a second, but only for a second. The men within the confines of the study were hardened, accustomed to dealing in murders the way an ice cream shop dealt in chocolate chip.

"I didn't kill him," Dak added, "if that's what you were thinking."

"No. I wasn't."

Dak went on. "He was supposed to meet a buyer there. I believe he'd been waiting for the meeting. Not sure how the curator fits into his plans, but I'd guess leverage."

"For extra money?" Lebedev wondered.

"Maybe," Dak hedged. "Or it could be that he simply wanted to have a little insurance on hand in case things got out of control. If the cops caught up to him, he probably figured it would be the smart play to have a bargaining chip. Either way, the cage he constructed in there probably took some time. Couple of days at the very least. Or one long day. This guy had been in town a while, too. He probably scoped out the museum for a few months and visited several times in person, as well."

"Sounds brave. Stupid, perhaps, but brave."

"He went in disguise, I'm sure. No one would have any way to know it was him, or what he was truly doing there to begin with."

"Yes," Lebedev agreed. "I know that the security systems in such places are usually very good. But the personnel they use is only so-so." He held out his hand, palm down, and twisted it back and forth.

"Their crew is okay," Dak sided, "but they never saw this one coming. The thief hid out in one of the maintenance closets, in a ventilation shaft. Then he came out after the place closed down."

Lebedev visibly puzzled over the statement. "The cameras did not detect him? None of the guards saw him?"

Dak shook his head. "No. This was the real genius to his plan. Prior to taking his place in the maintenance closet, he visited the security room, accessed the servers and video system, and hijacked it with a receiver that would keep the entire feed on a passive loop for as long as his mobile transmitter was nearby. The feed only returned to normal once his transmitter was out of range, probably a few minutes after he escaped."

"So," Lebedev tried to understand, "he was able to control what the security guards in the video room were seeing with this device?"

"Correct. All they saw was a view of every room in the building as it was before he stepped out of that closet. He could run around waving his arms like a madman and no one would have noticed, unless one of the guards happened to physically come across the guy."

Lebedev huffed a laugh at the visual.

"So, now this thief is dead," Dak continued. "I believe the buyer killed him and took the statue and the curator."

"Hmm, yes," the Russian agreed. "Sometimes I have heard of people doing things that way. Drug dealers, mostly. They think they will make more money if they take the drugs, hostage, and the money with a deal. This is foolish. No one will work with you if you kill those you do business with. Short-minded thinking, that."

"I agree. Now, I have to figure out where this buyer is before they leave the country. If they haven't already."

"What makes you think they're still here?"

"Because," Dak said, "they just sent their goons to take out an acquaintance of mine. We barely escaped. He's safe now, but if their assassins are still here, then there's a chance the buyer is, too. I need to find them before it's too late."

Lebedev flashed a look over at the two guards by the closed door. The two men looked like they could be brothers, both sporting close-shaved heads, clean-cut pale faces, and strong, broad jawlines that went with their muscular physiques. One look at them told Dak that these two spent all of their off time at the gym.

Dak interpreted the glance at the guards. "I wasn't followed. I'm certain of that."

The Russian's eyes fell to the motorcycle helmet at Dak's feet. "Yes, I'm sure you are a difficult man to keep up with, Mr. Harper."

Dak didn't feel the need to give any sort of confirmation. He hoped he wasn't beginning to like the guy, but felt like it might already be too late. Dak did his best to keep perspective. *This guy ruins lives for money. Right now, he's only a means to an end.*

"I try. Anyway," Dak steered back on course, "I need someone with connections, someone like you, to help me locate this buyer."

Lebedev stole a long breath, sucking in air through his nostrils and mouth. "And you know nothing of this buyer?"

"Not a thing. The only piece I can figure is they came in from out of town, most likely another country. It may not even be the actual buyer. Possibly a representative the buyer sent to do the deal."

"But if you can find this representative, they can get you to the buyer."

"I would think so. I'm hoping I don't have to take that extra step."

"Yes. Understandable," Lebedev grumbled. "Time is of the essence, hmm?"

Dak only nodded. He was worn out and felt his eyelids dragging downward in a losing battle against fatigue. He needed sleep but knew that wasn't coming anytime soon.

"Sergei," Lebedev blurted, snapping a finger.

The guard nearest Dak snapped to attention.

"Get our guest something to eat with his coffee."

"That's not necessary," Dak insisted.

"Oh, really? You come into my home and refuse my vodka, and now you refuse my generosity?" He really sold it, laying on the guilt extra thick.

"Fine," Dak said, turning his head just enough to acknowledge the bodyguard. "Smells great, by the way."

He couldn't tell if Sergei appreciated the compliment or not, but the man walked over to the bar in the corner behind his boss, took a pot from the coffee machine, and poured another mug. He brought the white cup over to Dak and set it on the end table next to his chair, before returning to the door and resuming his post.

Dak thanked his host, raising the mug in a toast. "I wasn't aware to turn down a drink was an offense in Russian culture."

"It's not. Well, not for most. In certain circles, they might consider it rude to turn down a drink. Now, we will certainly make fun of you if you don't finish it. Although, since you're not Russian, you might be given a pass."

"Good to know," Dak said with a wink. He took a sip of the hot coffee. It was just a taste, since he knew the brew would be too hot to consume at a normal rate.

"Yes," Lebedev said, his voice as distant as the look in his eyes. He stared down at the lavish rug beneath them, his mind deep in thought. "I believe I might know of someone who can help with this matter. I haven't heard about anything regarding the stolen item, or the woman, but I network with people who know about such things."

Dak felt a flutter of hope in his chest.

"His name is Pavel. He dabbles with many things, art being one of them."

"This isn't necessarily art," Dak reminded.

"Yes, I know this. But Pavel knows people who deal in the black market of such things...." He waved his hand around, trying to think of the word.

"Antiquities," Dak said, the word rolling off his tongue.

"Yes. Antiquities. If this buyer is still in Mumbai, then there is a chance Pavel knows something."

"Will this Pavel be awake right now?"

Lebedev snorted. "That didn't stop you from coming into my home."

"Good point."

"Pavel keeps strange hours, as do many in our world. He usually stays awake most of the night, spending time on the internet. I have no idea what he does for so long on his computers, I suppose looking for clients, or perhaps searching for valuable items he can buy and then flip for profit."

Dak flaked up his eyebrows in surprise at the last one. "I wasn't aware arbitrage like that could work on the black market."

"Ha! The black market is all arbitrage. People stealing from one another, sometimes with money, sometimes by simply taking what they want, as was the case with the thief from the museum."

"Apparently. Can you get me in touch with Pavel?"

"Of course. I will take you there myself."

"That's not necessary," Dak protested.

"No," Lebedev shook his head sternly. "You will follow me over to Pavel's. I will introduce you. This is the way it must be. He might not react well to a stranger showing up at his door."

Dak could understand that, though he didn't like it. As much as he wanted to accept the Russian's generosity, Dak also knew that men like Lebedev could be volatile. They were usually consumed by ego and an unquenchable thirst for power. In this instance, though, Dak didn't appear to have much choice, and while it hadn't offended his host to turn down the offer of a beverage, things might well take a bad turn if he tried to reject Lebedev's plan.

"How far is it?" Dak asked.

"Not far," Lebedev said. "Ten-minute drive."

Dak nodded. "Okay, then. Let's do it."

"Good." Lebedev looked over at the guards. "Get the car ready. We're going to Pavel's."

Deep down, Dak had a bad feeling about all of this, like everything could come off the rails at any second. Then he reminded himself that the tracks were long gone, and that he—and a very dangerous, slightly drunk Russian mobster—were plowing through uncharted territory.

Pavel's home looked more like an abandoned shop than a residence. The old building was situated in the middle of a series of defunct shops, cafés, and businesses that had either gone out of business or were teetering on the edge.

The dingy white paint on the exterior flaked in places. One of the black window shutters hung crooked next to a second-floor balcony that looked like it might collapse at any time, crushing the modern patio furniture sitting on the platform below.

A black metal door blocked the entrance.

No cars passed by on the quiet street. That didn't surprise Dak. He kept his head on a swivel, constantly looking for signs of trouble. And the signs were everywhere.

Apparently, Pavel had chosen to live in a place where crime was higher than average, and where few of the elites traveled.

"You must understand," Lebedev said upon arriving at Pavel's home, "that Pavel is an eccentric sort. The man might even have more money than me."

"And he lives in a place like this?" Dak said, failing to hide his disapproval.

Lebedev laughed hard. "That's what I say to him whenever I see him. I say, 'Pavel, you need to have a nice home, a luxury car, eat at fancy restaurants. You have the money. You might as well live a little.'" The Russian shrugged. "It's his life. He can do what he wants with it."

One of the guards knocked for the second time, then stepped back and assumed a professional stance with his hands crossed over his belt. The other stood in the exact same way, just behind Lebedev.

"All right, take it easy," a muted voice shouted from inside. "Not sure what you're doing here at this hour of the morning."

Dak looked up at the camera over the door. The thing was old, or at least it was made to look that way. Upon closer inspection, Dak realized that the camera had been painted meticulously to appear worn and aged. It lacked the red recording light, though the port for it was still intact, as if someone had intentionally removed the LED. A black cord hung limp from the back of the camera, but Dak knew that the real cord went in through the mount, at least that's how he'd have done it if this were his place.

Several locks clicked, then the door opened with a cacophony of loud squeaks as rusty hinges protested the movement.

A five-foot six-inch skinny guy with brown hair tucked under a New York Yankees cap stood in the doorway. His black Affliction T-shirt hung over a distressed-leather belt buckled around dark blue jeans.

"Good morning, my young friend," Lebedev said, greeting Pavel with a smile and opening his arms for an embrace.

Pavel looked at him with skepticism. "Again, do you have any idea what time it is?"

"Of course. It's not like you're ever in bed at this hour. Everyone knows you sleep until noon."

"Eleven-thirty," Pavel corrected. "And I'm not talking about me. I'm talking about you. Aren't you usually in bed by seven in the evening, old man?"

The jovial look on Lebedev's face tightened into a fierce how-dare-you scowl. He took a menacing step toward the smaller, younger man and stopped when they were less than a foot apart. "You think that's funny?"

For a couple of seconds, Pavel looked as if he might soil himself. He stared up into the mobster's eyes with both fear and confusion. Dak watched, hoping the Russian crime boss wouldn't kill the only person who could help them locate the buyer, and the curator, but he was in no position to prevent it. He had a feeling, though, it was going to play out just fine.

His theory proved correct when Lebedev's grim expression cracked, first to a smile then to a full belly laugh. He clapped Pavel on the shoulder, shaking his head. "Seven o'clock!" he erupted. "That's a good one, my friend."

Pavel visibly released his tension. His shoulders sagged and he took a breath of relief.

"Come, my friend," Lebedev said, motioning inside the open door. "We should get off the street. Would hate for one of our competitors to think they could get an easy shot at us while we're out here laughing like a couple of hyenas."

Pavel stepped aside, allowing everyone into the building. As Dak passed, the mousey Russian eyed him suspiciously but didn't address the newcomer until the last bodyguard was inside and the door was closed.

Dak swept the room with his eyes, taking in the extraordinary contrast between the interior and exterior.

The windows were covered with black fabric to keep out light, and probably to keep anyone from seeing inside at what was akin to stepping into some kind of futuristic cyberpunk world. Dak found himself standing in the living room where a deep, black leather couch sat off to the right, cornered by two gray leather chairs on each end. A black wooden coffee table sat in the midst of the furniture with blue LED lights glowing around its base. More LEDs lined the walls, illuminating the white ceiling and the edges of the bare concrete floor. A huge computer station occupied the left corner, featuring three widescreen monitors, three desktop computers on the floor under the black L-shaped desk, and a white gaming chair.

The square room narrowed into a hallway in the back, where Dak presumed there must be a bedroom and bathroom. A set of metal stairs climbed up to the second floor to the left, crisscrossing halfway up to the next level. The kitchen took up the back-right corner, featuring modern white cabinetry with brushed steel appliances.

"Who's this guy?" Pavel asked, motioning casually at Dak.

Dak didn't answer since the question was directed at Lebedev, though he wondered what the man was going to tell him.

"This is a friend of mine. His name is Dak. That's all you need to know."

Pavel didn't seem to accept the answer. "How do you know what I need to know?"

The corner of Lebedev's mouth curled slightly. "Because I said so."

"He looks like an American."

Dak resisted the urge to laugh.

"That's because he is," Lebedev confirmed. "Dak," he turned to introduce the two, "this is Pavel. Pavel, this is Dak."

"Why did you bring a stupid American here?" Pavel said with chagrin.

"Because I need your help locating someone," Dak answered in Russian. "And he says you know people."

Pavel blushed, which in the blue light made his face take on a faint purple color. "So, you speak Russian. What other secrets are you keeping?"

"I'll tell you whatever you want to know, kid. But I don't have a lot of time for sharing war stories, so if it's just the same to you, I'd like to get to the part where I ask you if you can help or not."

Pavel's right eyebrow raised slightly. He appraised the newcomer, studying Dak's face for several seconds.

Dak looked around again, making a show of it. "Nice place, by the way. For a second, I thought our friend here had brought me to some kind of opium den or something."

Pavel's forehead tightened at the comment, clearly not under-standing the reference.

"It's a nineteenth-century thing. Don't worry about it."

"Ah," Pavel said, still not getting the joke. "Who is this person you're looking for? I know a lot of people, as I'm sure our esteemed Mr. Lebedev has probably mentioned."

Pavel turned and walked back toward the desk in the corner, motioning for his visitors to follow. Dak hesitated then walked behind Lebedev over to the corner while the two guards stayed at the door with their arms crossed like bouncers trying to keep people from leaving the club instead of keeping them out.

At the desk, Pavel sat down in his seat and swiveled around to face the monitors. He clicked on the mouse and the center screen blinked as he pulled up his desktop.

"So, who are we looking for tonight?"

I hope we didn't come here just to watch some guy do a web search. Dak kept the thought to himself, though it was a real concern.

"There was a theft at a local museum. A valuable statue was taken."

"Statue?" Pavel asked. "What kind of statue?"

"An ancient idol from the Jain religion. It's made of pure gold."

Dak watched his host's eyelids dilate.

"Did you say pure gold?"

"Yep."

"There was a woman taken as well," Lebedev added. "The museum curator was abducted by the thief." He left out the part about the thief being dead, which Dak was glad for. With the body still probably in the house, he thought it best that as few people as possible know about his knowledge of the murder, until it had become official public information.

Dak had no intention of being used as a pawn for blackmail, or leverage, to get Pavel or anyone else out of a legal jam.

Pavel absorbed the information before he spoke, his mind stuck on a single piece. "You said it's valuable? Like, how valuable?"

"A few million," Dak offered, though he didn't want the guy to get distracted by the artifact's value. "There's a buyer in town, and we believe that buyer has already acquired the statue, and the woman. We need to locate them before they can leave town."

Lebedev took over. "Have you heard anything about someone like this buyer? They would have to be wealthy, and aren't locals, at least we don't think so."

"Sure," Pavel said, as if it were no big deal. "I hear about those types coming and going all the time here in Mumbai."

Dak waited patiently, guessing that his host was holding back information, either for dramatic effect or because he wanted something in exchange.

Pavel didn't let him down.

"I just have to ask," Pavel said, twisting his chair so he could face his guests, "what this information is worth to you?"

Lebedev's pleasant expression darkened. "What do you mean, what is it worth to us? You owe me, Pavel. In fact, you owe me several favors."

"That's true," Pavel admitted. "I do. It's just that, well, I know for a fact that a particularly big fish jumped into the water here just yesterday, and from what I hear, they're not the kind of fish you want to try to catch."

"What's that supposed to mean?" Lebedev asked, the irritation in his voice beginning to simmer to the point of boiling.

"Look, Lesma, you have to understand, I appreciate everything you've done for me, truly, but these people, they're international players."

"Sounds like you're afraid of them," Dak said easily.

"I am," Pavel confessed. "And you should be, too." He looked back to Lebedev. "Trust me, Lesma, these are not the kinds of people you want to mess with."

"I'm not the kind of person you want to mess with either, Pavel. Who are we talking about?" His voice escalated again.

"Take it easy, my friend." Pavel held up a hand and reached over for an energy drink can sitting to the left of his keyboard. "No need to get angry. I will help you. I only wanted you to know that it's risky. Okay? Relax."

"Don't tell me to relax," the older man growled.

Dak decided it was time to step in before things escalated more than they already had. The last thing he needed was for Pavel to decide it wasn't worth his while to help them out, which would put Dak back to ground zero, and the buyer out of his reach—probably for good.

"Does a thousand dollars change your mind?" Dak asked, knowing full well he was lowballing.

Pavel turned to him, scoffing at the paltry offer. Lebedev seemingly forgot about his irritation and also looked to the American.

"A thousand? That's nothing. You don't understand who we're dealing with here. These are international criminals."

Dak ignored the obvious elephant in the room and continued with the negotiation. "Two?"

Pavel's eyelids narrowed to slits. "Risking my life is worth more than two." He looked at Lebedev with derision.

"That's debatable," Lebedev groused.

Dak shifted his feet, stuffed his right hand into a pocket, and produced a roll of hundreds. He counted out $2,500 and set it down on the desk. "I'll give you twenty-five hundred. The rest I have to keep. It's all I've got on me. If that's not enough, I can be generous in other ways." He took a step closer to Pavel, hovering over him like a thundercloud ready to burst. He peered into Pavel's eyes with a lifeless gaze that could have chilled the fires of Hades. "But I'm going to tell you right now, if you don't like the cash way, you're definitely not going to like the other way."

28

At first, Pavel almost couldn't believe what the American was saying. He looked to Lebedev, then back to Dak, and again to Lebedev. "Did you hear that?" Pavel held out his hand toward Dak, who briefly considered snatching it and twisting it to the point of breaking. "He just threatened me. Is this the kind of person you bring here, Lesma?"

Dak had taken a risk with his threat, but he had a feeling the older man was also growing tired of the negotiation.

Lebedev took on a somber look, his face ashy, pensive. "He killed many of my men this night. And he did so without getting a scratch."

Dak heard what the man said and briefly considered the statement for the first time. He hadn't gotten a scratch. How that was possible, he wasn't sure, but gratitude would have to come later. And besides, the night wasn't over. Not by a long stretch.

"What?" Pavel blurted. It came out sounding like a laugh, but when he realized Lebedev wasn't joking, the humor left his eyes, replaced by bewildered fear. "You said he killed your men?"

"Many of them," Lebedev clarified. "This man is not one you should annoy. I have offered him a job to come work for me, but he turned it down."

"Did you just say you offered him a job, the man who killed a bunch of your men?"

"Yes."

"And he turned it down?"

Dak decided to interrupt. This was taking too long. He inched closer to Pavel, hovering like a hawk over a rabbit. "I would prefer to pay you in cash, instead of extracting the information I need by using pain."

Pavel swallowed nervously. His head started bobbing involuntarily and then grew more emphatic. "Twenty-five, did you say?"

"Twenty-five," Dak repeated.

Pressing his lips together, Pavel's head nodded in several directions, uncomfortable with the exchange, but happy he just made a few grand and didn't get tortured.

"Right," he said. "The buyer you're looking for is a German. He flew in from Frankfurt several hours ago."

"What's his name?" Dak asked.

"I don't know," Pavel confessed with a shrug. "No one seems to know his name. But everyone knows what he's into."

Lebedev offered a disbelieving laugh. "How could no one know his name? Everyone has a name!"

"Some people prefer to keep their identities a secret. It's possible he does this because he has a legitimate life, perhaps even a public persona. Many of the people who deal in black market goods and services work regular jobs, usually in high positions. They are very wealthy, most of the time."

Dak's patience wore thin. A woman's life was on the line. "Where can I find this German?" he pressed.

Pavel flashed a look over at Lebedev, then rested his eyes on Dak. When he spoke, his tone stayed low, just above a whisper, as if the two bodyguards shouldn't hear what he had to say.

"I'm...." He hesitated for a second, his voice catching in his throat, but another look at the American beast convinced him the more immediate threat stood less than two feet away. "I'm not supposed to tell anyone about this. And if the people who run it find out—"

"Whatever your secret is, Pavel," Dak urged, "I don't know a single person who might be interested in knowing. Just spit it out."

"You might be surprised," Pavel said dryly. Then he let out a long exhale, planting his hands on his knees to calm his nerves. "There is a hotel here in Mumbai. Most major cities have them."

Dak scowled at the information. "Yes. Most cities have hotels. Which one?"

"No, you don't understand. I'm not talking about a Marriot or a Hyatt or a Hilton. This is no ordinary hotel, man. This place is by invitation only. It's run, they're all run, by underground operations, usually big crime syndicates."

Lebedev frowned, crossing his arms. He looked insulted. "Why have I never heard of this *hotel*?" He emphasized the last word with skepticism.

Pavel looked him in the eyes without affect. "Because you weren't invited."

The older man puffed a derisive snort. "How is this? I am a powerful man in this city."

"That's true, but you're small time compared to these guys." Pavel noted the irritation flicker in Lebedev's eyes and quickly added, "But only because you haven't expanded to an international level yet. When you do, I'm sure they'll extend an invitation."

"Let's focus, please," Dak cut in, rubbing his eyes. "Where is this hotel?"

"It's in the middle of the city, in a bank."

"A bank?"

"Yes," Pavel nodded.

"Convenient." The idea of disguising a hotel where international underworld buyers and sellers could keep a low profile was a new concept to Dak, though he'd heard of similar places for assassins and mercenaries. But putting it in a bank? That was just outright mocking the establishment. Dak could see the multitudinous benefits for such an operation, and his mind rapidly unfurled the possibilities. The ultra-wealthy patrons of the seedy black market could own their own bank, essentially moving money around with ease, exchanging and cleaning it with every transaction, and right there in the same building where they slept.

"It is pretty smart, and since most of those types would be expected to be at a bank at some point in their business travels, it truly is the ultimate cover."

"Which bank am I looking for?" Dak asked. He was ready to put an end to this.

Pavel spun his chair around, pushed the mouse around, and after a click and a few swift keystrokes, a new image appeared on the screen. The Paladin Banc building stood out in the downtown like a sparkling jewel amid a pile of charcoal. The gleaming structure's glass exterior reflected the lights from buildings all around it. The main downstairs floor's windows were clear, while from the second floor all the way up to the top of the thirty-story building, the glass mirrored light, providing privacy beyond the walls for the secretive patrons.

"That's a nice bank," Dak mused.

"Yeah," Pavel agreed. "You don't want to know how much money flows in and out of that place on a given day."

"Probably not."

Lebedev pointed at the screen. "I have seen this bank many times. I drive by it every week. You are saying this is where the hidden hotel is?"

"Yes," Pavel answered.

"You're sure?" Dak pried.

The mousey Russian spun around in his chair, doing his best to look hurt. "Of course I'm sure. I wouldn't send you there if I weren't."

"How do I know you're not sending me into a trap?"

"You don't, but you also know where I live, so if it is a trap and you manage to escape, I suspect the first place you'd visit next would be my home. So, we're just going to have to trust each other."

"I'm running low on trust right now," Dak said. "But it doesn't look like I have much of a choice."

Lebedev squared his body to face Dak. "Do you need anything

from me? Any way I can help? Perhaps you take a few of my men with you, just in case."

Dak knew where that road led. It was a slippery precipice with a thousand-foot drop into the chasm of owing a mobster a favor. "No; but thank you. I think I've caused you enough trouble for one night."

"That is your decision, and I respect that."

Dak returned his gaze to the screen, locking the image of the bank into his mind.

"The only thing I know is that the secret hotel is on the top floor. Security is going to be difficult to deal with." Pavel motioned to the monitor. "I don't know much about the layout. Never actually been inside."

There was a second where Dak considered asking him how he knew the hotel was in there if he'd never been inside, but he let the thought evaporate and decided he'd have to deal with that issue if it came up.

"There's one other thing," Pavel added. "This is the trickiest part. There's no way you can get in without a seal."

Dak's heart sank into the pit of his stomach. Another hoop to jump through? Just once, on one of these missions, he wanted things to go swimmingly, but he knew that was never going to happen. If he'd wanted things to be easy, he would have gone into another line of work. Except that doing so would have exposed him to Tucker much faster than the low profile he kept with this gig.

"What is this seal? And how do I get one?"

"Don't look so crestfallen," Pavel said with a little too much glee. "It just so happens I know where you can get one."

"You do?" Dak felt a tremor of suspicion rising in his core.

"Yes." Pavel crossed his arms.

"And how much is that going to cost me?"

"Nothing. Just put me on your nice list, yes?"

"Fine. Where do I get the seal?"

"Today is your lucky day, my friend." Pavel swiveled around and pulled open a drawer. He took out a black disc that looked much like a coin, about the same size as a silver dollar. Pavel held up the seal in the light, as if inspecting it for the first time. The dark metal seemed to absorb any light that touched it.

"Do I want to know how you got one of those?" Dak asked.

"Probably not," Pavel admitted. "But I didn't kill anyone for it if that's what you're thinking."

It was what he was thinking,

"One of the people who work there stole it. They were looking to make some quick cash, so I made them an offer."

"You bought it?" Dak said, dubious.

Pavel shrugged. "I guess they didn't know how much it was worth. They're part of the hotel cleaning crew, so they see all sorts of things left in rooms, dropped on floors, even under vending machines. One time, she said she found a baggie of cocaine on the elevator. Someone had dropped it, I guess, probably after a long night of hard partying."

"What's this going to cost me?"

"You've paid enough," Pavel said, dismissing the question with a wave of his left hand. "Just don't tell anyone where you got it if you get caught. If they figure out you're not a member, they'll kill you. But they'll probably torture you first, so do me a favor, and don't mention my name. Got it?" He held out the seal then yanked it back to wait for Dak's agreement.

"Fine," Dak relented. "I won't tell them you gave it to me."

Pavel accepted the promise and placed the disc in Dak's palm.

Dak stared at the inscription on the coin. An emblem of a phoenix rising from the ashes adorned the surface. Its curved wings climbed to the same height of its head; the feathers made from flames. The Latin word *Hospes* was emblazoned below the image of the mythical creature. On the top, what looked like a barcode had been etched into the metal.

"It means 'guest' in Latin," Pavel pointed out, indicating the word with his index finger.

"My Latin is a little rusty now and then."

"Well, they don't speak it there, so you should be fine."

That hadn't been what Dak was worried about, but in hindsight, he could see why the Russian thought that was his point.

"Thanks for the intel," Dak said, turning toward the door. "And for the seal. Keep yourself useful, Pavel," Dak said as he sauntered toward the door without looking back. "I might need you again someday."

Pavel gulped and nodded. "Yeah, sure, whatever you need."

Dak paused at the door, looked over his shoulder at Lebedev, and said, "Thank you. I appreciate it." He didn't make the mistake of saying "I owe you one," but the thought crossed his mind. He quickly swept it aside. "If I'm ever in Mumbai again, I'll be sure to look you up."

Lebedev gave a single nod. "Just don't kill any more of my men if you do. Okay?"

Dak let the right corner of his mouth curl up into a smirk. "I make no promises."

Dak sat on his motorcycle, staring at the extraordinary Paladin Banc building from a block away. It was even more spectacular in person than in the images he'd seen at Pavel's. In a few hours, he knew the sun would rise in the east. If the buyer truly were still in town, Dak's guess was that he'd be leaving early in the morning. He hoped the German hadn't already left, though a nagging feeling in his gut kept needling him, telling him that the man was already gone—and Dr. Laghari with him.

He thumbed the black coin in his hand and looked down at the phoenix carved into the metal on both sides. *Such a strange piece,* he thought. Dak had never seen metal like that, except for gunmetal, but even that wasn't as dark as the seal in his palm. He wondered where they had these things minted, how many were in circulation, and who decided who received a coin and who didn't.

That last part sent a chill through Dak's spine.

A cabal of shadowy underworld elites who controlled an entire network of black-market goods, services, and buyers wasn't something Dak had ever conceived, but based on what Pavel told him, it was a well-established system of high-end degenerates. Like a high-stakes blackjack room solely for evil people.

In hindsight, it made perfect sense—once he really thought about it. The various black markets had to be run by someone, at least the marketplaces themselves. While the people—mostly buyers—set the prices with demand, there still had to be a way that all of it worked, that these wealthy sickos found each other. Much like the network of mercenary nests all over the world, *someone* managed things. Even though that particular underworld example was one Dak possessed a good deal of familiarity with, he still didn't know how all of it worked, and who kept tabs on all the connections.

Dak knew one thing to be true. Someone was always watching, no matter if you were an ordinary citizen eating a sandwich on a park bench or a drug smuggler bringing in half a ton of cocaine.

For the ordinary citizen with the turkey on whole wheat, it was the government or local law enforcement watching. Homeland Security, the IRS, and for sure the NSA were all watching, too.

But the underworld had its own monitoring tech. And any would-be Pablo Escobars of the world would be tracked similarly by those on the other side of the law: rival cartels, international crime syndicates, and guilds of high-dollar thieves.

Dak didn't understand that last part where the additional risk came into play. He once read about how Pablo Escobar brought in $420 million a week, smuggling fifteen tons of blow into the United States every day. *Incredible numbers.* Even with all that money, Dak wondered how it was worth the risk, how any similar operation was worth it.

He didn't think there was any amount of money that he'd happily take to have the constant threat of someone shooting him in the back, trying to take everything from him. That sort of life, a life of mistrust and constantly having to watch his back, wasn't something that appealed to Dak.

He almost laughed at the irony.

Here he was, in India, running from his past, constantly having to look over his shoulder. The difference between him and Escobar was that Dak wasn't making $420 million a week. *Well, and I'm not a mass-murdering drug lord,* he thought.

Escobar was only one man. Dak wondered how many dozens or hundreds or thousands more just like him existed in the illicit trades. The veil of what looked like a normal world to the rest of the population was merely an illusion, a thin mist covering the masses in the valley below as the people on top dealt in whatever commodities they desired: drugs, weapons of mass destruction, even people.

Dak strapped the helmet onto the motorcycle and climbed out of the saddle. He adjusted the pistol in his hidden holster beneath his black button-up shirt and started down the sidewalk. He'd opted for a business-casual look, wearing khakis with the shirt untucked. Somehow, he didn't think wearing a T-shirt into a place where some of the world's wealthiest miscreants hung out was a good idea. Then again, going in there in the first place was probably also not a great plan.

At this time of morning, there wasn't much going on except for the early delivery trucks rumbling by on their routes to take produce, beverages, and other supplies to markets or restaurants.

Dak had the vacant sidewalks all to himself, though, as the only other people out at this time of day were the occasional vagrants.

He walked briskly to the next corner then crossed the street, made a left, and crossed again over to the plaza the enormous building occupied. Dak stopped at one of a dozen front doors and took a quick look around. He noted the cameras on the eaves overhead, at least ten that he could see right away. No doubt, one or more of those fed right into the security room on the top floor, where someone surely monitored the feeds twenty-four hours a day.

He pulled the door open and stepped inside. Cool air washed over him, tickling his skin and filling his nose with the smell of vanilla and jasmine. A man who looked like he was in his mid-forties sat behind a reception desk along the far wall. The man was staring at a computer screen when Dak entered the building, and he immediately perked up at the arrival of such an early morning visitor.

Dak didn't hesitate and walked across the marble tile floor toward the desk. He took in the surroundings as he made his way to the information center. Huge black columns towered forty feet up to the ceiling. Dak let his gaze linger on the pillars longer than the rest of the giant lobby. Unless he was mistaken, he could have sworn that the columns were constructed either from the same material as the seal in his pocket, or they were simply made to look that way. The round support structures seemed to absorb the light radiating from basketball-size bulbs dangling beneath long, silver rods.

Before Dak reached the desk, the man behind the counter offered him a weary grin. His black mustache twitched slightly. His navy blue security uniform hung loose off his skinny frame, and the blazer looked as if it were a size too big for the guy.

"How can I help you?" he asked as Dak stopped short of the counter.

"Hello, I'm here for a room," Dak said.

The security guard puzzled over the statement. "I'm sorry?" He put on a confused expression, but Dak saw through it.

"I would like a room, please," Dak repeated.

"Sir, this is a bank," the guard insisted.

Dak made a show of looking around the lobby, taking in the sights as if interested in the architecture and design aesthetic. He brought his attention back to the guard and nodded. "Yes, I know it's a bank." Dak fished the seal out of his pocket and set the object down on the counter. "I'm interested in making a withdrawal on the top floor."

The man swallowed, a look of comprehension finally dawning on him. "I see. Then allow me to show you to the elevator."

"Much obliged."

The man pressed a button on his radio and spoke. "One for the top floor," he said. Then the guard walked around the counter and motioned for Dak to follow.

Dak wasn't sure if the guy was supposed to simply leave his post like that, especially in a bank, but then again, this wasn't like any bank he'd seen. There were no teller windows, no ATM machines, no giant steel vault in the back. He didn't see any other guards, either, and it was difficult to tell if this guy carried a gun or not. Then again, this wasn't exactly the local bank on Main Street.

While he'd heard of high-end money centers that dealt with only the richest clients, offering them a place to do business away from the masses, those establishments had only existed in his imagination until now.

The guard led Dak along the wall to a corner where the lobby continued around to the left. They stopped at the first of a row of four elevators with shiny silver doors, and the man pressed the button. The door opened immediately and the two stepped inside.

Once on the lift, the guard turned to Dak and asked for the coin, holding out his palm. "Your seal, please."

Dak didn't like the idea of letting the disc out of his possession, but if he refused it might look as though he'd never done this before and thus give the impression that he wasn't really a member.

He reluctantly pressed the seal into the man's palm and watched as the guard held up the disc to a transparent black panel above the numbered white buttons. Dak noticed the lack of the number 30 on the buttons—the options only went up to 28 and down to a parking garage level. Again, he held back his questions. The slightest misstep would give him away.

A green light blinked behind the black surface.

The guard handed the seal back to Dak with a polite smile and a nod. "Enjoy your stay, sir."

"Thank you," Dak said, still uncertain what was going to happen next.

The security guard stepped out of the elevator and the doors closed. A second later, the lift began its ascent to the top floor. Dak had no idea what to expect next.

When the elevator doors opened, Dak couldn't force himself to step off right away. He simply stared into a place that was nothing like the bank downstairs. It was like looking into a different world.

Dark crimson walls surrounded the lobby. A concierge desk straight ahead featured a golden counter façade. The floors were decorated in black marble tiles, and Dak noticed the one feature the hotel shared with the bank lobby was the black pillars lining the walls.

Dark brown leather couches and club chairs sat on either side of the direct path to the concierge. A man with silver hair sipped a glass of red wine on one of the sofas. A woman a third his age, seated next to him, sipped on a glass of champagne. They talked with another man who sat across from them. He was younger, perhaps mid-fifties, with dense, dark hair. All three of the patrons wore expensive clothes, and the young woman's neck sparkled with a necklace overflowing with teardrop diamonds, the largest of which stopped at the V in the top of her black dress. Her golden hair draped over her right shoulder and shimmered like a waterfall as she laughed at something the Middle Eastern man across from her had said.

Dak walked out of the elevator, realizing he'd lingered a few seconds too long, and strolled toward the concierge desk where a stunning young Indian woman stood behind a computer. Her hair hung just below her ears, and slightly longer on one side than the other. Her black dress looped around the nape of her neck, clinging tightly to her athletic form. She flashed bright white teeth as Dak approached, and for the first time in recent memory, he didn't know what to say. He immediately realized that his plan had a gaping hole in it.

Seconds before he reached the concierge counter, he thought the only thing that made sense was to ask for a room.

"How may I be of service?" the concierge asked. Her sultry tone stirred Dak's blood, which wasn't a bad thing considering how tired he was. He needed something to wake him up.

"I need a room, please," Dak said. He wondered if the woman would be curious as to why he was rolling in a few hours before sunrise, but then recalled that she was probably accustomed to patrons checking in at all sorts of random times. The clientele for this joint didn't exactly keep banker's hours.

"Certainly, sir. I'll just need your seal."

He flashed her a half smile and laid the coin down on the counter. The concierge picked it up and set it down on top of another scanner, similar to the one in the elevator. It reminded Dak of the scanners at grocery store checkouts, where people swiped bar codes to ring up their tally.

A light within the transparent cover blinked green.

The woman smiled, handing the disc back to the guest. "Welcome, Mr. Thibadoux. How many nights will you be staying with us?"

"Just one," Dak said, dropping the idea of cracking a joke correcting her about only staying for the morning.

"Excellent. We have a room in the east wing." She produced a black card from a drawer and slid it across the counter to him. "Will you be needing anything else, Mr. Thibadoux?"

Thibadoux? Dak wondered where exactly Lebedev's little friend managed to find this card. He hadn't said anything about a Thibadoux, though to be fair, he'd been skimpy on the details in just about everything. Still, Pavel's information had gotten Dak this far. Now, the only question was how he could locate the buyer.

Then Dak had an idea as the laughter from behind him caught his ear.

"I'd like to have a drink or two before retiring for the night," Dak said.

"Certainly, Mr. Thibadoux. The bar is just around that corner. Feel free to enjoy your beverages there, or here in the lobby lounge, or in your room."

"Thanks. I will."

"You're quite welcome," she said, flashing the same smile he figured she showed everyone. She'd been expertly trained to make it seem like it was just for him, but he could see through the charade.

Dak scooped up the card and stuffed it into his front pocket and made his way around to the right, then left around the corner. Once there, he continued into the bar, where the short corridor opened into a one thousand-square-foot room enclosed by tall windows in black steel frames. The bar to the left contained hundreds of bottles, most of them high-end liquor for the most luxurious of tastes.

The windows that made up the walls gave a spectacular view of the city, and a doorway led out to a rooftop bar with several seating areas offering even more stunning vantage points. Inside, more leather chairs and sofas occupied the corners and spaces along the walls. The smell of cigars lingered in the room, and Dak found the source in the far-right corner where a balding man, with white bristles circling around the back of his head, puffed on a long stogie. Two younger women sat with him, one on either side. Both of the Indian girls did their best to look like they were having a good time, but Dak saw through it. His guess was the wealthy man could, too. He simply didn't care if they were having fun or not. It wasn't about them.

Dak's stomach turned at the thought, and he quickly turned away to the bar, ignoring the other hotel clients strewn around the room with their drinks and conversations.

He made his way to the counter and waited until the bartender—a tall, pale man with a long beard and matching coiffed brown hair—

approached. He wore a brown leather apron that looked like something a woodcrafting teacher would wear, with a white shirt and black pants underneath.

"What can I get for you, sir?" the man asked in an English accent.

Dak spied the bourbon selection and gave a nod in the general direction of a bottle that caught his eye. "Blade and Bow, neat please."

"Excellent, sir."

The man turned and plucked the bottle from the shelf. In a smooth motion, he selected a clean tumbler from a pyramid of glasses to his left, flipped it over, and began pouring the drink. He didn't stop until the glass was half full, then stuffed the cork back in the bottle. He whirled around, careful not to spill the drink, and set it in front of Dak, who held up his seal for the bartender to take.

"Thank you," the bartender said with an appreciative grin. He scanned the disc over another one of those transparent coverings. No green light appeared this time, but the bartender didn't seem concerned about it. "Enjoy your drink, Mr. Thibadoux."

Dak figured the beverage would be billed to his room. He wondered how long it would take before the mysterious Thibadoux found out someone was using his seal to get access to this place. Then again, there was a very real possibility that Mr. Thibadoux was dead, and that the man's demise was how Pavel's friend had come to acquire the rare coin.

"Thank you," Dak said with a nod as he picked up the drink and turned away.

Be unmemorable, he reminded himself in his mind.

He considered walking over to the window and having a look out at the view of the city below. Tall buildings sprang up all around the bank, and more were being built. Cranes towered into the sky in several spots, and Dak knew that in the next year or so the skyline of Mumbai would be forever transformed.

He passed on the notion of going over to the window, opting to instead walk back to the lobby where he'd spotted several open seats near the elevator.

Dak took a sip, casually turning back toward the corridor, and made his way back to the front of the hotel.

He wondered how many rooms there were, imagining it couldn't be more than a few dozen at most. Curiosity begged him to go check out his own room, and he realized that he hadn't bothered to ask what room he was in. He took the card key out of his pocket and noted the number on it—3138.

That makes sense, I guess.

Walking back into the lobby, the concierge smiled at him again. He raised a glass to thank her and veered toward the elevators and the seats on the left, opposite of the group sitting in the area to the right.

He found a comfortable leather chair farthest from the conversation and eased into it, keeping his back to the wall and the rest of the top floor in his view, as he always did when sitting down for a meal or a drink.

The cushions underneath and behind sucked him in, almost wrapping around him in a leathery hug. He felt immediately relaxed, and a touch drowsy. *Probably best I don't check out the room, just in case I'm tempted to take a snooze.* He theorized that if the chairs were this comfortable, the beds had to be out of this world.

The people on the other side of the room noticed him but didn't say anything. He was grateful. The last thing he wanted to do was strike up a conversation with a bunch of these types. His sleepy mind, however, wouldn't allow him to let go of the fact that these people were degenerates of the highest order. He wondered what their vices of choice were: drugs, sex slaves, something else he couldn't even imagine?

He shivered at the thought.

Their laughter only heightened his inner rage, but he knew there was nothing he could do about it. He forced himself to stop paying attention to their conversation and took another sip from his glass. The act was more for the feeling of comfort, or of normalcy, calming him in the face of an onslaught of tension. Dak had been in the trenches of real warfare, with gunfire blazing all around him. Since his time in the military had come to an end, things hadn't eased much. The only thing that changed was the battlefield.

Dak sipped his drink, idly daydreaming about the past. Nicole's face appeared more than he'd have liked, and an old flicker of pain tempted him to finish the rest of the whiskey in one big gulp. Fatigue didn't help, and his thoughts began to swirl around in his head, a churning like the tide against the shore.

The blonde across the way cackled drunkenly at something the Middle Eastern man said and slapped her date on the knee as she rocked forward.

Ugh, that laugh, Dak thought. At least as long as she stayed here, there was no chance he'd fall asleep in the chair. That shrill, sharp laugh could wake the dead.

Based on Pavel's information, the buyer was going to leave sometime around sunrise. Dak didn't like to base things on ballpark estimates like that. He'd never been much of a gambler, except for when he indulged the itch to hit the poker table from time to time. He found himself wishing sunrise would be in the next twenty minutes, but knew it was still at least more than an hour away.

The minutes ticked by, and from time to time, Dak caught himself nearly dozing off as the fog in his mind mixed with exhaustion—a sleepy cocktail for even the most vigorous of night owls. Fortunately, he had a smartphone with a VPN and was able to play a few games to keep his brain semi-sharp while he waited for the fish to swim by. Occasionally, he stood up and stretched, only to fall into the near-sleep state he'd been fighting since arriving at the hotel.

A server brought drinks from the bar to the three at the table, bringing them freshened versions of their beverages of choice every twenty minutes or so.

Amid the blurry visions of Nicole, the wild ideas swimming around, and the fatigue, one other thought needled him as he stared at his phone. *What if they've already left?*

Dak typically tried to be a positive person, but with every passing minute, the stark reality that the buyer had already left became a more likely probability. Frustration built up inside him, and more than once he considered the ridiculous notion of walking over to the concierge and asking if the rich German guy with an Indian woman was still around.

He knew better.

While he'd never been to one of these places, he knew how they worked. Just like the mercenary nests all over the world, the handlers never divulged secret information. If they did, the soldiers of fortune who came in looking for work wouldn't be able to trust the source, and the jobs they took would be questionable at best.

Despite the shadowy nature of the merc nests, they were built on trust. Part of that trust was that the handlers, and the people offering the contracts, were dealing with some of the most dangerous killers in the world. The backlash against any sort of shenanigans would be swift, and probably brutal.

No, the concierge won't tell me a thing, Dak realized for the umpteenth time as he suppressed the urge to go speak to the woman at the desk. Despite the social interaction going on across the way from where Dak sat, and the people chatting it up in the bar, there was no way the concierge was going to tell a patron anything about one of the others unless permission had been granted.

So instead, he stayed where he was, waiting, watching, and doing his best not to listen to the conversation going on thirty feet away. There were things, though, that they said that Dak couldn't ignore. He heard talk of extraordinary amounts of money more than anything. The two men were in the midst of a pissing contest regarding their high-end asset acquisitions, along with high-stakes gambling takes.

The Middle Eastern man said something about a loss of four million in a single night, which he promptly got back then doubled within hours the following morning. He claimed it was on a sixteen-hour binge at the craps table.

Their conversation detoured to talk of other patrons, a more gossipy side of things. Despite the hour, the woman's excitement only heightened at the chance to discuss something juicier than gambling or business.

"What about the German?" the blonde asked abruptly, looking first to her date, and then to the man across from them.

The Arab shrugged. "I don't know much about him," the man said. "This is the first time I've seen him. I have to admit, though, he does have good taste in women."

Dr. Laghari, Dak thought. *So, they were here.*

"What does he do?" the woman wondered out loud as she picked up a fresh glass of champagne and took a long sip.

Her date fielded the question. Taking his arm from around her shoulder, he reached out and picked up his cocktail. "He's into a lot of things," the man answered. "Owns several businesses, including a biotech startup in Frankfurt."

"Biotech?" She puzzled over the statement. "What's he doing in biotech?"

"No one really knows. I've heard anti-aging research, but it's anyone's guess. He's one of the world's wealthiest people, off the books of course. Just like the rest of us, you won't find much information beyond a simple Wikipedia page about his public holdings, and as with us, the net worth is hidden behind a veil."

These guys must be drunk, Dak realized. Their tongues got looser by the drink, and what had initially been quiet voices swelled to new volumes.

The blonde didn't seem satisfied by the answer, and she briefly pouted, internally wondering about the mysterious German.

"I wonder what he had in the case," she blurted.

"I don't know," the Arab laughed. "Why don't you ask him when he leaves? I heard they were flying out sometime this morning."

They're still here!

The information injected a surge of energy into Dak's veins. He caught his breath, and his heart raced.

The woman laughed at the suggestion, slapping her date on the shoulder with a delicate hand. "I don't think that's a good idea, Marcus. You're so silly." She took a drink, then continued, "It did look heavy, though, the way his bodyguard was carrying it. Did you notice that?"

"Not really," her date admitted. "I try not to pay too much attention to other people's business when we're in one of these places, my dear. I would advise you do the same."

Dak knew better than to think she would heed the advice, but none of that mattered now. The German, and Dr. Laghari, were still here.

The epiphany brought with it renewed energy and focus. Dak's skin tingled, and he suppressed that sensation he'd learned to squash before going into battle. Keeping a cool head was paramount, and he couldn't allow himself to look like some child waking up on Christmas morning when the German and his entourage appeared, which from the sound of it could be any minute.

Dak wasn't surprised to hear the buyer had a bodyguard, and he figured the man had more than one in his employment.

There was a bigger problem inherent to the situation, one that Dak had tried to consider before entering the building. He still didn't have a plan as to how he was going to take out the buyer and his men while rescuing Dr. Laghari and the statue, though at this point Dak wasn't even really thinking much about the idol. If he lost it at this point, he didn't care. It was just a piece of metal to him. Sure, the Jain statue had cultural and spiritual significance for many people, but that paled in comparison to the life of a human being.

He'd even considered a scenario where he could corner the German and his men, force them to let Laghari go, and allow them to take the statue so long as they didn't harm her.

In his wildest imagination, though, Dak didn't see how that was going to go down, and he diverted to other plans.

Here, in the hotel lobby, he wouldn't be able to take aggressive action. While it didn't appear to be a well-fortified operation, two unmarked closed doors on either side of the room offered a different conclusion. People of such high importance and wealth wouldn't solely rely on their own personal security teams. A place like this could be a powder keg ready to explode, and all it would take was a single disagreement between two galactic-size egos.

Unless Dak missed his guess, he believed the hotel security teams were hidden behind those two doors, one on either side. He had no idea how many there might be, or what actions they were ordered to take in case of an incursion, or even a bar fight between billionaires. Something was behind those doors, though, and Dak didn't care to find out what it was.

That meant confronting the buyer and his men in the lobby was a no-go. On top of the other issues, he would be outnumbered and have nowhere to take cover except for the furniture, and that wouldn't last long.

After running through every conceivable scenario he could think of, Dak decided the best course of action would be to wait until the buyer and his group left the building, follow them outside, catch them by surprise, and rescue Laghari.

With his mind made up, Dak resumed playing one of his puzzle games on the phone while he waited for the mark to appear. Now, though, he felt stronger. The fatigue melted away in seconds, and his focused sharpened back to its normal levels.

Another ten minutes passed before the group on the other side of the lobby decided to call it a night—or morning. They stood up and continued their discussion as they walked by the concierge desk, heading down the hallway on the left.

Dak watched them until they circled around the curve in the corridor and disappeared, their voices fading until he could no longer hear them.

He was glad for the silence. Having listened to them for far too long, he found the now-empty lobby offered a surreal peace.

That peace only lasted a few more minutes—until Dak heard people approaching from the same hallway. He checked the time on his phone. His senses heightened again with a resurgence of adrenaline, and he sat up a little straighter in anticipation.

The sounds continued to crescendo until, at last, he caught sight of a figure as it appeared from around the bend. He let out an annoyed sigh as he realized it was the blonde woman from before. She made her way back around the concierge desk, and for a second, Dak thought she might be coming straight toward him.

She veered off, though, and sashayed over to the spot where she'd been sitting. Apparently, she didn't want to waste good champagne. The glass she'd been sipping from still sat on the coffee table in front of the sofa. She picked it up, whirled around, and made her way back toward the corridor.

That's when Dak saw them.

Two bodyguards—one blond and one with dark brown hair—in black blazers and T-shirts with matching cargo pants, appeared around the turn. Right behind them, another man, probably in his mid-forties or early fifties, followed behind them, accompanied by a younger Indian woman. She looked tired and distressed. Her hair dangled around her ears in tangles, like it hadn't been brushed in several days. Deep circles hung under her eyes. Even looking so disheveled, Dr. Laghari possessed a natural beauty that could have rivaled any of the world's best.

Four more bodyguards followed her and the German. Dak figured all the men were armed, including the buyer. He took a sliver of solace in the fact that they weren't shoving Laghari around or holding her at gunpoint. Then again, they didn't have to. If she tried to escape, who would she call for help? This was an establishment built on total personal sovereignty of its clientele. That meant they could do whatever they wanted with what they deemed their property or assets. It was a house of indulgences, and nothing would be denied, not even by the sugary sweet concierge behind the desk.

The thought that she permitted such atrocities to happen right under her nose sent a tremor of nausea through Dak's gut, but he forced it back down. This was his chance, probably his one and only opportunity to save Laghari. He couldn't screw it up now.

One of the guards stopped and left two room keys on the counter without saying a word, then turned and caught up to the others.

Dak pretended to stare at his phone, tapping on the screen as he would have if he were still playing his game, and waited as the group passed by. He kept his eyes on the phone in case one of the men made eye contact and became irrationally suspicious. As they marched by, though, no one seemed to notice him, and the convoy continued to the other end of the lobby to the elevator.

When the door opened, Dak barely flicked a sidelong glance over at the lift, then returned his gaze to the device cradled in his hands as he watched the buyer and his team with peripheral vision. They entered the elevator, positioning Laghari in the middle of all the men so she couldn't escape. *Not that she has anywhere to go,* Dak despaired. They were on an elevator for crying out loud. *Do they think the curator is going to somehow take out all six armed guards, and the buyer, with nothing but her bare hands, then magically escape the building alive?*

The second the doors closed, Dak stood and walked briskly to the second of the two elevators. He pressed the button and waited as he watched the other lift descend rapidly toward street level. Anxiety built up in him, rising from his gut all the way up to his throat, tightening his esophagus with a vice grip. With every passing second, the sensation worsened. *Come on. What's taking this stupid thing so long? There's no one else in the building using these at the moment.*

Finally, after what felt like minutes, the elevator dinged when it arrived, and the doors opened. Dak stepped on and mashed the button twice, just to make sure the signal registered. He looked through the doors as they closed and noticed the concierge still manning her desk. She apparently didn't care about people coming and going from the hotel, as her eyes remained fixed on a computer monitor off to her right.

The lift dropped, and in his head, Dak counted the minutes and seconds' head start the buyer and his squad of goons had over him.

The fatigue he'd felt for the last few hours was gone. Dak's second wind had kicked in, though he knew that would only last so long. Eventually, he would crash, but not until after Dr. Laghari was safe.

Dak didn't recall the elevator ride taking as much time on the way up, and he started to wonder if the engineers who built it designed that into the specs, though he had no knowledge of such things.

"Come on," he urged. "Faster." He briefly regretted saying those words in a moving elevator as visions of the cables snapping and emergency brakes failing sent him tumbling down the shaft to a horrific death at the bottom. And then, just as he shook off those premonitions, the bell dinged, and the doors opened to the lobby.

Dak hurried out, instantly scanning the room for signs of his quarry. Fear snaked through him. The lobby was empty. There was no sign of Dr. Laghari and her escort anywhere. Dak wasn't the kind of person to panic, but he couldn't deny the feeling that crept up on him like an assassin from the shadows. He'd lost her. And now, Dak had no way to track the curator down.

Dak breathed heavily, racking his mind for an answer. This couldn't be how it ended. He wouldn't let it. He stared through the giant windows, scouring the streets and sidewalks beyond for any sign of the group.

The sky remained dark outside, with only the faintest glow on the horizon as a clue that daybreak was coming. The streets remained quiet, though, and Dak remembered that it was a weekend day. Traffic would be lighter this morning than during the week, and it explained why there were still only sporadic signs of life in the city.

Desperation wrapped around him, squeezing his lungs. Panic tightened his gut. He was the guy who always had an answer for everything, always found a solution to problems no one else could. Dak got things done when all the odds were stacked against him.

Now, however, he was at a complete loss.

His heart ached for the terrible future that awaited the curator— an innocent woman who'd just showed up for work on the wrong day at the wrong time. She'd been going about her business, locking up the museum, doing what she was supposed to do. Now, she was headed to some foreign land, probably to be sold, or at best, to be kept as the buyer's personal prisoner.

The deathly silence of the closed bank drove home the finality of Dak's failure. *How could it end like this?*

He'd failed in life, more times than he could count. Failure, he'd learned, was a tool for becoming better at something. It was the crucible that forged human beings into enhanced versions of themselves, teaching them to level up at one skill or another. Those who didn't embrace that fell to the whims of the fates.

Dak had seen many of those types of people come and go in his life. They were the ones who always blamed bad luck for the ill twists and turns in their lives. It was easy to see that their mindset and their lack of persistence and patience were the real culprits.

Now, when all hope was lost, he tried to remind himself of that, that all wasn't lost and that there was always another way.

A light tapping sound interrupted his thoughts, and for a second, he wasn't sure what it was. *Too quick to be a clock.* The noise echoed throughout the cavernous lobby, bouncing off the ceiling and hard floors. For a split second, Dak wondered how loud it must be in here during normal business hours, with people walking around in hard-sole shoes or talking to each other or into their phones.

The source of the sound struck Dak in a blink, and he hurried around the corner, a new idea burning in his head.

The same security guard he'd seen before stood behind the information desk, staring at a check sheet with a pen in one hand.

Dak slowed down before the guard looked his way. Collecting himself, Dak flattened his jacket and put on his most unmemorable smile. "Excuse me, did a group of people just leave here? I believe there were several men and a woman. They dropped something personal, and I'd like to return it to them. I hope they haven't already left the building."

"Oh, thank you," the guard said. "Yes, they just left, but you might be able to catch them. Their car was supposed to pick them up around there, on the side of the building." He pointed toward the far wall, and that's when Dak saw them. "There they are."

"Thanks," Dak managed, and took off toward the door.

He burst through and cut to the right; any plans he might have imagined slipped over a precipice into a deep abyss. No time for a plan now.

Instead of running straight toward the two SUVs where the buyer's crew was loading into the vehicles, Dak detoured to the left, back toward his motorcycle. There was no way he could get to the SUVs in time, but with the bike, he could make up ground quickly.

Dak kept the two vehicles in his periphery as he crossed the first street, then the second to the right. The driver of the first vehicle closed his door, and within seconds, the convoy accelerated away toward the next intersection. Dak reached the bike just as the two SUVs turned to the left. He slid the helmet on his head without strapping it, fired up the motor, and twisted his right hand.

The powerful bike charged forward and onto the street. Dak's ears filled with the sounds of the wind, muted by the densely cushioned helmet, and with the rocket between his legs. He fiddled with the strap and got it looped through before he hit the next intersection and then swung left down the street he'd seen the convoy take.

"There you are," Dak said to himself.

Dak hung back, keeping a safe distance behind the two SUVs. He had them in his sights, but that meant he was in their sights, too, and a sport bike speeding up to catch them would set off alarms to the buyer and his drivers. Then again, if they saw the single headlight in their mirrors, that might have the same effect.

Visions of a car-motorcycle chase flashed in Dak's mind. While he could be far nimbler on the bike, there were too many risks in taking that approach. He couldn't simply pull alongside the convoy and shoot the drivers, or at the tires. Doing that would put Dr. Laghari in danger. A blown tire at high speeds could be deadly, and Dak doubted the buyer and his goons were seatbelt guys. Not that those were a guarantee.

The other problem was that the men in the vehicles were armed, and there were way more of them. While he could engage in a shootout on the expressway, he had no protection on the bike. And then there was the challenge of firing back at the buyer's security team without hitting Laghari.

Unfortunately, Dak was running out of options, and he knew a decision had to be made as to which way he'd handle the rescue.

He closed the gap between him and the convoy but kept back enough to not draw suspicion, or so he hoped. Dak passed a sign pointing to the expressway, and he knew it wasn't far. Once the SUVs made it to the on-ramp, there was no way he could follow behind them without them thinking something was up.

At the next intersection, the SUVs turned right. Dak sped up to reach the corner in time to keep from losing them and then slowed down as he rounded the turn. His heart sank as he saw the vehicles accelerating away toward the on-ramp.

They were going to get away.

He shook off the negative thought and slowed down at the next stop light and waited, giving the convoy time to put some distance between them and him. There was still a chance he could catch them, but it would have to be before they reached the airport. They'd be going to a private airport. No way someone like this German buyer would use a commercial one. Dak knew how these types operated. One of his friends flew wealthy elites around all the time, often from New York to Florida. Discretion was paramount, and not just for the curious eyes of the public.

When the SUVs were out of sight, Dak twisted the throttle, and the motorcycle surged forward. He reached the on-ramp and steered onto it, speeding up along the straightaway leading to the expressway.

The wind whistled louder in his helmet, and he felt the rush of warm and cool air pockets wash over him as he charged up the ramp onto the highway.

Dak spotted the convoy more than a thousand feet ahead, but they were in his sights, and now there were other cars to cover his approach. Traffic remained light, which gave him maneuverability, and he weaved around a white delivery truck and tucked in close behind it as the driver of the truck sped along, passing the few other passenger cars and commercial vehicles.

Every ten seconds or so, Dak eased the motorcycle to the right to get a view of his quarry up ahead. He still wasn't sure how to get Laghari out of the buyer's vehicle in one piece while taking out the guards at the same time.

Then he had an idea. It would be tight, and Dak wasn't sure how he'd be able to pull it off, but he had to try.

He looked out again around the corner of the truck ahead of him and scanned the horizon to the right and left. Dim hints of dawn spilled into the dark sky to the east, the deep blue colors surrendering to faint whites and yellows.

There. In the distance, probably three miles away, a small plane climbed into the sky at a steep angle. The blinking lights on the wingtips might as well have been a beacon. They were almost there, which meant Dak didn't have long. He was only going to get one shot at this, and the window was going to be as tight as any he'd worked with before.

With a twist of his hand, the motorcycle flew forward. Its rider held on tight, gripping the tank with his knees as he dove behind another vehicle, drafted them for a few seconds, and then merged over into the next lane.

The first SUV in the convoy of two signaled with its blinker and switched from the center lane to the left lane, preparing to exit in the next few miles, or kilometers, as it were.

Dak closed in on his quarry, zipping around another car, narrowing the distance to six hundred feet, then five hundred.

He eased up on the throttle behind a plumbing van and waited several seconds before poking his nose around and stealing a look ahead. He could see the tower of the airport off to the left and rows of private aircraft lined up in front of rounded hangars.

He passed a sign signaling the exit up ahead, only another kilometer away.

Time to make his move.

Dak squeezed the throttle grip and turned it hard. The bike shot around the sedan in front of him, probably drawing a few irritated looks or words from the driver he'd been tailgating. Dak caught up to an 18-wheeler rumbling along in the left lane and waited ten seconds before he swerved back into the middle lane. The wind whipped his shirt up behind him, probably exposing the top of his holster to the drivers he passed, but he doubted they'd notice.

He veered back into the left lane ahead of the big truck just as the exit ramp appeared up ahead. Dak squeezed the gas as far as it would go. The sport bike's motor roared as he sped toward the exit.

The SUV in the rear flashed its turn signal, copying what the first driver had done. *At least they know how to use a blinker,* Dak thought, his mind begrudgingly returning home to the States, where it seemed like only half the drivers on the road did that.

The gap between him and the last vehicle closed rapidly, and Dak forced himself to ease off the throttle just a tad so he wouldn't catch up too fast. He flipped on the turn signal and veered onto the exit less than two hundred feet behind the convoy.

A sign on the side of the road indicated that the airport was to the right. Down at the bottom of the hill, a red stop light glowed.

That's my chance, Dak thought. He reached around to his back and grabbed the pistol tightly, pulling it from its sheath with ease. Ducking down behind the short windshield, he kept the gun out of view behind the tinted screen over the fuel tank, allowing the bike to coast down the hill.

He knew shooting the tires would be futile, having considered it several times on the short trip from the bank to here. Those luxury SUVs would, no doubt, be equipped with run-flat tires, capable of going up to fifty miles with a leak.

With the tires a no-starter, his mind quickly turned to another option, which was going for the engine blocks. That could work, but there were no guarantees he'd hit vital engine components, thus shutting down the vehicles' mobility.

The only plan that worked in Dak's mind was the one that would be trickiest to pull off. But he didn't have a choice. It had to work.

He slowed down, keeping his distance from the two SUVs, though there was little doubt in his mind that they'd seen him by now. That was okay, as long as he played it cool and didn't get too close. To keep up appearances as a normal, early morning commuter, he switched on his right turn signal as he approached the stop light and the convoy. He gripped the pistol tightly in his left hand, using both brakes to gradually bring down his speed but without stopping. Then, Dak switched the pistol to his right hand, squeezed the clutch, and down shifted into third, then second gear before exchanging hands once more.

The buyer's vehicles stopped at the red light and waited. Dak rolled behind them, the distance closing with every passing second. He steadied himself on the bike, guiding it slightly to the right-hand side of the lane.

"Okay, Dak. Let's hope this crazy idea works," he mumbled.

Then, he twisted the grip and sped up, turning the motorcycle onto the shoulder to pass the second SUV in line.

His plan was simple in theory. Take out the driver of the first truck —the one with Priya inside. The SUV might roll through the intersection and hit the railing on the other side, but the hostage would be safe, and then Dak could use the confusion to take out the buyer and his men. The element of surprise was always the most powerful tool in anyone's arsenal, and it gave Dak the best chance of success to eliminate the enemy while confusion gripped them.

The motorcycle rolled up to the right-hand side of the second truck's bumper, and Dak prepared to launch his attack.

Just as he was about to drive past the SUV, the light changed, and the buyer's driver stepped on the gas, speeding through the intersection. The second vehicle followed, and Dak found himself losing ground as he coasted down the ramp.

"Oh, come on," he complained. He twisted the grip and sped up in pursuit. The engine whined, and the tailpipe let out a loud roar. The quicker sport bike caught up to the second SUV in an instant, and Dak passed the back-left side with ease.

His plan, however, had changed. He'd intended to take out the drivers while the trucks were sitting still at the stop light, but now that wasn't an option, and he doubted attacking a couple of vehicles with a pistol in front of the airport security gate would be well received.

If he was going to make the move, it had to be now.

Dak sped by the second SUV in line and caught up to the lead car within seconds. He knew the driver of the first truck he passed would be immediately suspicious of the motorcycle passing on the right-hand shoulder.

Dak didn't care. *It's now or never.* "Ugh, clichés," he muttered, cursing himself for even thinking it.

The motor under his body screamed, and the needle inched closer to the redline. With one more twist of the throttle, the bike surged ahead, pulling level with the SUV as the convoy gained speed. When he was even with the driver-side window, Dak looked over at the man behind the wheel, who peered out at him with curious bewilderment in his eyes. By the time he saw the rider raise a pistol, it was already too late.

Dak squeezed the trigger three times in a single second.

The window shattered as the bullets ripped through glass, boring into the driver's face and out the back of his head.

Dak let the throttle go for a second, and the motorcycle instantly slowed as the SUV served left, right, then back to the left, careening off the road. It smashed into an embankment just as the second vehicle caught up to Dak.

He twisted around and fired his pistol, sending rounds through the windshield as the bodyguards inside desperately tried to react and ready their weapons.

The two men in the front seat caught most of the bullets. The projectiles tore through flesh and vital organs. The driver jerked the wheel to the left in an involuntary and irrational decision and then overcorrected, sending the SUV barreling across the lanes and into an embankment.

Dak didn't have time to appreciate his handiwork. He twisted the throttle again, guiding the motorcycle over to the first crash on the left.

Thankfully, the road was empty, and there were no signs of any other cars approaching. Yet. He knew that luck wouldn't last.

Arriving at the first accident, he saw people moving around

inside, but they were disoriented from the crash and had yet to open any doors. The car had been moving at a decent speed but nothing so dangerous that it would have killed anyone inside, or so he hoped.

The motorcycle slowed as it reached the grass along the road's shoulder, and instead of parking it or coming to a full stop, Dak swung his right leg over, balancing on a single peg until the machine started to wobble. Then he pushed off and jumped, letting the bike roll on its own as he hit the ground at a full sprint, rushing toward the SUV like a steam train as he ripped the helmet from his head and tossed it aside. The motorcycle wobbled a few times behind him before diving into the grass.

Dak closed in on the wrecked vehicle, his pistol extended at arm's length. The first bodyguard opened the back door and set his foot on the ground. Dazed, the man climbed out of the car with a gun in his right hand. The pistol hung just below his hip, the arm limp. He tried to raise his weapon to fire, but the muscles didn't obey. Dak squeezed his trigger three times. The muzzle flashed in the waning darkness of dawn. The gunman caught two of the rounds in the chest while the third narrowly missed his head and drilled a hole through the window behind him.

A door opened on the passenger side, and Dak heard orders being barked in a hazy German accent. The buyer's anger filled his voice, but there was no panic to it. Much like a great field general in the heat of battle, the commands were concise and issued with a sharp intensity.

The instant the bodyguard staggered back against the door and began slumping to the ground, Dak juked to the right, sprinting around the other side of the SUV. The other guard scrambled out of the vehicle, and Dak nearly ran headlong into him at point-blank range when he rounded the SUV's back-right corner.

The enemy's pistol popped one, two, three, four times in rapid succession. Dak dove back behind the bumper for cover just as the bullets cracked by, smashing into the earth only a few feet away.

Rolling to his feet, Dak spun and pushed his shoulders against the bumper. He recounted the number of shots he'd fired, calculating in a second how many he had left in the magazine. Across the road at the other crash site, the last guard alive fell out of the front passenger side door. He hit the ground hard and rolled over. Dak had time to deal with him. The greater danger was only a few yards away, and he was outnumbered with the buyer probably armed in the back seat.

With the number in his head, Dak ducked down and looked under the carriage. He saw the guard's feet as the man crept toward the back of the vehicle. Dak aimed his pistol sights at the man's right foot as it touched down on the grass as he passed the back door. His finger twitched. The top of the bodyguard's black shoe exploded. The man instantly screamed in pain, and he dropped down onto his side, clutching the foot with one hand while firing his weapon wildly by accident, sending bullets into the dirt.

Dak shifted his sights and squeezed again. This round went through the side of the bodyguard's face and he immediately stopped moving.

Without hesitation, Dak rolled around to the right-hand side of the vehicle and kept his gun trained on the dead man for an extra second. Then he stepped over to the back door. Holding the pistol in front of him, he yanked open the door and retreated a foot, aiming the weapon into...an empty back seat.

34

A terrible omen surged through Dak's body. *Where is the German? More importantly, Where is the curator?*

He looked back at the bodyguard on the other side of the road, but the man still lay motionless on the ground. He ducked his head into the vehicle, craning his neck to look into the third row, but just like the rest of the interior, it was empty.

"Missing something?"

The German's voice cut through the early morning air like an arrow. Dak took a step to the side, bringing the front of the SUV into view. Beyond the hood, bright headlights bounced off the trees and shrubs along the embankment and shone eerily onto the German's face.

The man's disheveled, peppered hair fluttered in a cool breeze. His eyes blazed with furious malice.

His left forearm wrapped around Dr. Laghari's neck. In his right hand, he held a Glock, with the muzzle pressed firmly against her head.

"Let her go," Dak said. "There's no way out of this now. You kill her; I kill you."

The man laughed at the offer. "I don't think so, cowboy."

"That's the only way it's going down. You can do this the easy way or the painful way. That's up to you."

The German shook his head. "Who are you?"

"Just a guy," Dak answered, "trying to keep a bad guy from doing bad things."

"Oh, a do-gooder." He bobbed his head around in multiple directions, squeezing Laghari's neck tighter.

She grimaced, and Dak could tell she was having trouble breathing.

"You're hurting her," Dak warned. "And the more you hurt her, the more I'm going to hurt you." He kept his pistol sights squarely on the man's forehead. At this range, the shot would be tight, but it was one Dak had made hundreds of times before on the range, and more than a handful of times out in the field.

"You Americans, always so full of righteousness. You think you can police the world, when in the end, your nation is brimming with as much corruption as anywhere else."

"Glad to hear you have a grasp of our culture, along with the language," Dak grumbled.

"Tell me, boy," the German spat. "What is your name?"

Dak shrugged. "I'm the guy who's going to kill you if you don't let her go. My name won't matter when you're dead."

The captor huffed at the threat. "I'm holding all the cards here. Drop your weapon, and maybe I won't kill you."

"Doesn't sound like much of an offer to me. And forgive me if I don't believe you."

An idea bubbled in Dak's mind, but he pushed it aside for the moment, giving the situation time to evolve.

"I don't care if you believe me or not," the German fumed. "I will kill this girl if you don't drop your weapon right now."

"No, you won't," Dak said. "You know she's your only bargaining chip now. You kill her; you die. It's simple. We both know it. This isn't the first time I've been in a situation like this. As you can see, I'm still alive. And so are the hostages I freed. I'll let you figure out who died."

The German held his stance, but his eyes narrowed. Dak could see the decision weighing in his eyes, the options fading with the dark of night.

"You are strong," he said. "And you look like a man who was in the military."

"Something like that."

"I wonder if you were part of a Special Forces unit. Rangers? Green Berets, perhaps? One of those SEAL teams everyone hears so much about?"

Dr. Laghari squirmed, trying to loosen his grip on her neck, if for no other reason than to catch her breath and swallow. Her eyes teared up, and Dak couldn't tell if it was from the choking or fear. Or both.

Dak clenched his jaw, unwilling to answer.

With no response from his opposition, the German went on. "I met a group of men like you once." He spoke with a scathing tone. "They were a Delta Force group based in Iraq."

The second the man mentioned the unit, Dak's ears pricked up. A fire sparked inside him, and questions rose in his throat, but didn't make it past his lips.

"I can see from your reaction that perhaps you were part of Delta Force. Yes, that would make sense. You're not like them, though. They understood business. I suppose it was more than a year ago, although I can't really say. These kinds of transactions happen so quickly, and then I move on; life takes over. I'm sure you understand."

Dak humored him with a single word. "Transaction?"

"Yes," the German confirmed. "They were on a mission in the mountains, or so they said. They claimed they discovered an ancient treasure horde somewhere in a cave."

Now Dak's curiosity was fully roped in. "What did you have to do with any of that?"

"Oh, they needed a buyer. You see, selling priceless antiquities is difficult for men like you. One of them found a way to contact me, and I arranged a meeting. I bought everything from them, though I must admit I got the artifacts for a steal. I sold them for twice as much on the market."

Dak's blood boiled. He couldn't believe it. Was this really the man who bought up the stash his former team had stolen from the cave in Iraq? He had to know.

"This team," Dak mused, "you're certain they were Delta Force?"

The German grinned devilishly. "I can see from the expression on your face that perhaps you knew these men. Despite my low offer, it was more money than any of them would have ever seen in two lifetimes. Although I'm certain a few of them probably squandered it away by now."

You could say that.

"How many?" Dak asked, instead of voicing the thought.

The man's head twitched slightly, and Laghari shifted, again trying to clear her airway.

"That's an odd question." He inclined his head an inch. "There were five of them," the German conceded. "An odd number for an odd question. It makes me wonder...if one was missing."

"They left me to die in a cave," Dak confessed. "That treasure didn't belong to them. I told them so. They closed off the entrance and abandoned me to die."

"But you didn't die." The man spat the words with vitriol.

Dak shook his head one time. "No. But they did."

The realization struck the German like cold water to his face.

"Now," Dak continued before the guy could say anything else, "here's the thing. I don't know her. If you shoot her, I'll feel bad about it for a little while, but I'll get over it. And when you execute her, I will execute you. The other way this could go down, is you drop your gun, and you spend some time in jail. A wealthy guy like you won't spend twenty minutes in a jail cell, though, so that ending doesn't really work out for me."

"This is true," the German agreed.

"Although, morning is coming and with it, more traffic. I suspect this road will be pretty busy here in next ten to twenty minutes." If Dak was honest, he couldn't believe they hadn't seen a car yet, even if it were a road that led to a private airport. "All it takes is one curious driver to see a couple of white guys standing here with guns pointed at each other, and one of them holding an Indian national hostage. I give it, what, five minutes before this place is crawling with cops and whatever SWAT units they have."

The German's right eye twitched, and Dak knew the man had reached his edge. He'd seen it before in similar situations. As the hostage taker stood on the precipice, with two lives in their hands, they often chose to do something stupid. *Would he kill Dr. Laghari?* Dak didn't know the answer, but he knew what would happen if things went down that way. His finger remained tense on the trigger.

Headlights bounced along in the distance to Dak's right. "Looks like traffic is getting here early. Better make up your mind before it's too late."

The words had barely escaped Dak's lips when the German suddenly shoved the hostage forward. The woman stumbled toward Dak, effectively cutting off his entire view of the man. Dak leaped to the right. Two gunshots rang out as one. Dak hit the ground hard with his shoulder and rolled to a stop, extending the pistol way from him, aiming at the German.

Dak peered through the smoke trailing out of his barrel.

The buyer's right arm dropped to his side. The man's eyes drifted down to his chest, where a crimson stain bloomed across his shirt. He stared at the wound for a strained heartbeat, then another. He raised his eyes, balance leaving his control, and wavered side to side, then forward and back. He touched the wound with his left hand, smearing blood on his finger. The man looked puzzled, perhaps curious as to how he came to this tragic end.

For a second, Dak thought the man might fall. Then, with the last ounce of strength he could summon, the German lifted the gun slowly. The weapon looked heavy in his hand, and Dak knew what was coming—one last desperate attempt to kill.

"You shoulda taken my offer," Dak said.

The man shouted something unintelligible. It was a haunting, ghastly sound somewhere between a war cry and a wolf howling in a rainstorm.

Dak's finger twitched. His gun discharged, sending the bullet through the front, then out the back, of the German's skull. The life left his eyes, abruptly hollow and unseeing. After an unconscious struggle against gravity, the dead man fell to the ground near the shrubs.

It felt like Dak hadn't taken a breath in the last four minutes. He knew that wasn't true, but now he took in huge gulps of air in rapid succession. He turned onto his side, checking back across the road. The bodyguard who'd initially survived the crash still wasn't moving. Dak needed to make sure.

He directed his attention to Dr. Laghari, who stood trembling only ten feet away. She stared at the body of the German, her eyes betraying disbelief at the sight.

"Dr. Laghari?" Dak ventured. "Are you okay?"

She swallowed hard, grabbing at her neck where her captor had been squeezing. "Yes," she said, gasping for air. "I'm...I'm fine."

"Stay here. I'll be right back."

"Where are you going?" Concern filled her question.

"Just making sure we won't be having any more trouble."

Dak stood, looked both ways, then trotted across the street. The car he'd seen before had turned into the airport gate about a quarter mile away, and there was no sign of any other traffic. He stopped by the bodyguard who'd fallen out of the SUV. The man held a pistol in a limp grip, and Dak made quick work of it by kicking the weapon away.

Then he bent down and checked the man's pulse, then held his hand under the gunman's nose. Nothing on either.

Dak surveyed the crash site, noting the bodies in the vehicle's front seats.

He hurried back across the road, stuffing the empty pistol into its holster as he arrived back on the other side of the road.

"Did he hurt you?" Dak asked. "Other than choking you just now." He moved close to her, grabbed her gently on the shoulders, and looked her up and down to make sure she was okay.

"I'm fine," she said. "He...he didn't hurt me. They—" Her voice faltered.

"It's all right," he said. Dak wrapped his arms around her. He wasn't sure why. He didn't know the woman from the prime minister of Italy, but it felt like the right thing to do.

He held her for a moment as she sobbed into his chest. Her hair smelled of flowers, but he couldn't figure which kind. It reminded him of Nicole's hair, and the way she smelled so good whenever he held her.

To his surprise, she looped her hands around him. Dak didn't pull back. He stood there, letting her weep. Relief spilled over him, and he finally felt his tension ease.

"I don't suppose the idol is in the wreckage," he hedged.

She started laughing amid the tears, then nodded. "Yes. It's in there. They stowed it in the cargo area."

Dak felt her right hand shift abruptly, and then a pain shot through his lower back. He felt his legs weaken. He jerked away from her, shoving her backward. He stumbled, reaching for his back.

When he looked into her eyes, Dak saw the truth he'd been missing since arriving here in Mumbai two nights ago.

The tears in her eyes were gone. Only streaked remnants remained on her cheeks. Dak grasped at the knife in his back. His fingers slid over the wound, and his blood made it difficult to grip.

"Yes, the artifact is still in the truck," she said. "It's coming with me to the airport." She took a step toward him, and he stumbled backward on to his tail. The abrupt landing sent a fresh pain signal through his body, and he grimaced. He grabbed his pistol as she approached, and for a second, Dr. Laghari retreated.

Dak pointed the gun at her, his eyes narrowed against the stabbing sensation in his back. "It was you," he sneered. "It was you all along."

Everything that happened over the course of the last few days rushed through his mind—the lack of video footage at the museum, the dead thief in the house where a makeshift cage had been built... all if it had been a ruse.

"You killed him," Dak said. "It was you. You owned the house. All this time, I thought he built that cage for you."

"No," she said shaking her head. "He couldn't have come up with a plan like this. And obviously, he couldn't see through mine." She tossed her hair to the side. "So, what are you going to do? Shoot me?"

Dak squeezed the trigger in response, but the weapon clicked impotently.

Her eyes flashed wide for a second, then her expression eased at the realization. "Out of bullets? That's too bad for you. I wouldn't move around too much. It will make the wound that much worse."

Dak responded with a sickly laugh, smattered with a few coughs.

"What's so funny?" she asked.

He shifted over onto one hand and reached into his pocket with the other. He produced his phone and turned it around to show her the screen. A red button on the bottom of the black screen showed there was a call in progress. The number at the top was local.

"What is that?" she wondered, apprehension building.

"Just a call to an old friend," Dak said. "Detective Naik? Maybe you've heard of him. Not much of a conversationalist," he struggled for the words. "But the man is persistent. I'll give him that."

The sounds of sirens pierced the early morning, hammering home Dak's insinuation.

"No," she spat. Fear streaked across her face.

She spun around and ran to the SUV. She grunted as she grabbed the dead driver by the collar, then jerked the body out of the seat. Ignoring the blood on the door and seat, she climbed in, shifted the transmission to neutral, and started the engine again.

Dak was surprised the motor revved to life, but the damage to the front hadn't been significant.

She backed away from the shrubs after slamming the door shut, sped away toward the entrance to the airport.

Dak let out an exhausted sigh and with a groan, yanked the knife out of his back.

"Well, I did not see that coming."

Dak winced against the pain, his teeth clenched hard to fight it off. Visions dipped in and out of his mind, churning in the current filled with images of Nicole, his childhood, his family, and the former teammates from his Combat Applications Group.

He forced away the hallucinations, but the knife wound in his back continued to throb, and bleed into his already soaking shirt.

How could he not have seen it before? He cursed himself again for not even considering that Laghari might be behind everything. She'd set up everything, right down to the routine she must have allowed Gavin Harris to observe.

He ripped off the right sleeve of his shirt, wadded it up into a tight knot, and shoved the fabric into the wound. He grimaced again as thread touched nerve, but it would slow the bleeding for now.

He struggled to his feet and looked down the road. Dr. Laghari was gone. At least she thought she was.

Dak scowled as he gingerly hurried over to the nearest dead bodyguard. He pried the pistol from the man's hand, stuffed it in his belt, and trotted over to the motorcycle.

Picking up a fallen bike was no easy task on a normal day, much less with an open knife wound in your back. It took every ounce of energy Dak could muster to leverage the thing upright. He took half a second to make sure the tank hadn't leaked or flooded the engine then pressed the ignition button. He half expected it to bottom out, but instead the motor revved to life.

The sirens drew closer, but still no sign of flashing lights. By the time the cops got to the scene of the crash, Laghari would be in the air and there'd be no bringing her back.

Dak twisted the throttle. The back tire spit out dirt and grass behind it. Dak muscled the handlebars back and forth as the tail end kicked left and right until he corrected it. Then the motorcycle shot out onto the road. Rubber bit into asphalt, and Dak felt the machine surge ahead. In seconds, he hit top speed, screaming down the road toward the airport gate.

Laghari's SUV had already turned through the gate, and he could see it speeding across the tarmac toward a white Gulfstream in the far corner. The plane sat in front of a domed hangar, and it looked like a fuel truck sat next to it, though the bland colors of the truck made it difficult to see against its backdrop of trees and fencing to the right of the hangar.

Dak slowed down as he reached the gate and swerved onto the driveway. He hadn't had a plan for getting through the guardhouse, but upon looking into the guardhouse, he immediately knew he didn't need one. Through the punctured, spider-webbed window, Dak saw the guard slumped to his side, still in his chair, with multiple gunshot wounds in his chest.

Anger cut through Dak's pain. *She just killed an innocent civilian. And I thought she needed my help.*

He hit the gas and weaved around the long metal rail blocking the path in and then gunned it. Dak shifted through the gears in quick, smooth rhythm. The SUV was halfway across the tarmac and closing on the plane in the corner.

Dak hammered down on the throttle, shifting into the top gear. The wind in his eyes made it difficult to see, even staying tucked down behind the windscreen. The sound in his ears was like standing on the beach in the middle of a hurricane. None of that mattered.

Dak closed the gap between him and Laghari rapidly, the sport bike chewing into the distance like a ravenous asphalt monster.

With a few thousand feet to go to the hangar, Dak drew closer every second. A hundred feet behind the fleeing SUV, he reached back cautiously with his left hand and drew the pistol from his belt. At this speed, the bike basically steered itself. Like a missile with a saddle on it, all Dak could do was guide it.

Fifty feet from the SUV, he raised the pistol over the windscreen, doing his best to keep it steady along the millions of bumps the motorcycle exaggerated under him. He lined up his sights and fired. The bullet smashed through the back window.

The driver reacted just as any civilian might with a bullet going through their car. Startled, she jerked the wheel to the left, then right, nearly losing control before correcting it and stepping on the gas.

The SUV charged forward, but Dak only let off the throttle for a second before twisting it hard to the bottom again.

Only forty feet from his target, he aimed the pistol again and fired. The bullet burrowed into the back door. This time, the driver surprised Dak. She slammed on her brakes and he was forced to let off the throttle, gently apply the brakes, and shift his momentum to avoid crashing into the SUV.

He sped by her as she accelerated again, but couldn't get off a shot. Keeping the bike stable with such an erratic move proved nearly impossible, and he narrowly missed a painful and catastrophic wipeout.

Dak leaned to the right, steering the bike around in a big loop to get behind the SUV again.

They were barreling toward the hangar, and Dak knew Laghari had passed the point of desperation. *What's her plan now?*

Even if she made it to the plane, there was no way he'd let her get on—making this entire chase moot in his mind.

Still, she powered on. Dak turned in a wide arc and changed his plan. If he tried to get behind the SUV, she'd make the same move again, and while he was good on a bike, he'd rather not be forced to make a quick maneuver like that a second time.

He calculated his speed, her speed, and the distance between them in half a second, then pulled the clutch, shifted down one gear, and poured on the gas.

Dak aimed the nose of the bike at the broad side of the SUV, putting himself on a collision course with it. He raised the pistol, holding it just over the windscreen. Way out of range, Dak fired three shots anyway. His goal wasn't to hit the driver, though that would be a happy accident. Rather, he needed to cut her off from the airplane. With a pilot on board and another member of the airport crew fueling the aircraft, Dak didn't want to endanger any more lives if at all possible.

He had no way of knowing which rounds struck the car, but at least one of them did, and the driver suddenly veered away to the left.

Dak fell in line behind her. Their speed had been reduced, but she was accelerating again. He fired another shot through the back window. This one went right through the windshield, narrowly missing the driver by less than a foot.

Laghari jerked the wheel to the right, then left, letting off on the gas again so Dak would smash into the back, but he anticipated the move and had already let off the throttle before she could make the maneuver.

Again, she accelerated away.

Dak had nearly forgotten about the knife wound in his back thanks to the adrenaline pulsing through his veins. Now, though, it throbbed. The strip of cloth he'd stuffed in the wound was still magically hanging on, though he figured that was more due to his own aerodynamics than random chance.

He grunted against the pain as Laghari once more steered the SUV back toward the hangar. She'd lost ground on her futile journey to the plane, but it seemed she wasn't going to give up yet.

"What are you thinking?" he wondered and risked a look at the aircraft. The fuel tech had disconnected the hose and was running away from the scene toward the fence beyond the building. Seeing the high-speed chase along with gunfire must have been all the motivation he needed to get out of there.

The pilot, too, took off, scrambling down the steps leading to the jet and racing toward the rear of the plane to seek safe shelter.

The woman behind the wheel pushed the SUV to its limit. Dak glanced in his right mirror and saw police cars pouring onto the tarmac from the gate. Now she truly was screwed. Even if she made it to the plane, there was no chance of taking off. The pilot was gone. The cops would block her in.

Priya Laghari had no way out.

That didn't seem to register as she kept her foot on the gas.

Dak had to end this.

He gunned the throttle and charged forward again, cutting around to the right-hand side of the truck. Laghari swerved to the right, and Dak slowed down again, falling back for a second. Having grown up in the South, he'd seen this movie before when watching NASCAR.

Taking a lesson from one of his favorite childhood racers, Dak leaned his head to the left, steering the bike the same direction. He accelerated, as if about to pass, then at the last second, let off the throttle just as Laghari jerked the wheel to sideswipe him.

He lagged back only a second, then powered ahead, pulling up alongside the driver. He kept a safe distance, at least twenty to thirty feet from the SUV, but it was enough.

Dak saw the look in her eyes as she realized she'd fallen for the trap. He raised the weapon and squeezed the trigger. Five rapid bursts from the muzzle peppered the SUV with bullets.

He saw the window shatter, at least a few of the rounds striking the target in the shoulder and ribcage. Maybe one in the neck.

Her body shook with every bullet's impact, and after the initial shock, Dak saw her head roll to the side, then back to the center, then to the left.

He let off the throttle grip and let the motorcycle slow down on its own and thought the SUV would, too. Instead, the vehicle continued lumbering toward the hangar. It weaved back and forth as Laghari struggled to maintain consciousness. She'd be losing blood, and as someone who'd probably never been shot before, Dak knew utter fear was taking over rational thought.

The motorcycle rolled to a stop when he applied the brakes. He planted his feet on the ground to stabilize it.

"What are you doing?" he muttered, watching as if in slow motion as Dr. Laghari—death drunk—guided the SUV toward the plane. "Stop," he ordered under his breath. Then again louder. "Stop!"

He didn't hope she could hear him. Maybe he simply wished the universe would and perhaps intervene with a giant invisible hand that forced the vehicle to halt.

Nothing of the sort happened.

Dak knew what she was doing now, and there was nothing he could do to stop her.

He merely watched as the SUV roared forward to smash headfirst into the fuel truck. In a bright flash and a thunderous boom, the tanker exploded, consuming both Laghari and her ride in a searing flame of orange and yellow. The concussion from the blast blew through Dak, who'd already braced himself for it as he stood there with the bike saddle between his legs.

Within seconds, black smoke spilled into the air from the raging inferno.

Sirens blared across the tarmac, and Dak looked over his shoulder at the approaching fleet of police cars. Fire engines growled out of their housing, their sirens announcing their approach as well.

Dak swung his leg over the seat, removed the key, and inserted it into the side of the bike to unlock the saddle. He lifted the seat up and discreetly placed the pistol inside a black box next to the tool kit before lowering the saddle back down and locking it in place.

He waved to the cops as they approached, signaling that he was friend and not foe. Then, Dak turned his head back toward the burning trucks. Beyond the pillar of smoke climbing into the air, the dim light of dawn pushed back the night, and he caught a glimpse of the first rays of sunlight piercing the darkness.

Dak lay in the hospital bed and watched the television with absent disregard. After the incident at the airport, an ambulance brought him to the emergency room, where surgeons patched up the knife wound in his back and gave him some medication for the pain.

He'd resisted going to the hospital, explaining to Detective Naik that he couldn't be taken there. If he visited a medical center, they would keep records on him and he'd be easier to track. Telling people his name wherever he went was bad enough, but leaving a paper trail was a big no-no in his mind.

Then again, a part of him almost wanted Colonel Tucker to find him. Maybe then Dak could put an end to this once and for all.

As things stood, he was here, in a hospital bed with a wound that might have qualified as a scratch to the rest of the men in his operations group. In a strange sort of way, he was glad his old military buddies weren't there to see him like this.

Dak had been kept there all morning for observation, but the doctors had cleared him to leave after noon, and he planned on getting out of Mumbai as soon as possible. He'd resisted falling asleep, but the medication they gave him, combined with utter exhaustion, pushed him over the precipice and into the land of dreams.

He slept for four or five hours, which was about half as much as he really needed, but it would do for now. There'd be time to sleep when he was somewhere else, a place where no one had any records on him.

He rolled his head over and looked at the clock on the wall. It was getting close to noon, and he knew the doctor would be coming by soon for one last visit before releasing him.

Footsteps clicked on the floor in the hallway outside, echoing in through the half open door. Dak turned and looked to the entrance. There was no mistaking the sound of a cop walking down a hall. The methodical, deliberate steps were different than nurses or doctors, and Dak had no other visitors coming to see him—or so he hoped. He suddenly felt exposed as a wave of doubt crashed over him, and he wondered if Tucker had already found out where he was and sent one of his assassins to take Dak out, or perhaps do the deed himself.

Dak shrugged off the notion. Tucker wouldn't risk that. *No way he shows his face here.* Dak knew the man didn't have the guts to take him on face to face, at least not yet. The day would come, though, that Tucker would have his chance, and then he would face judgement for his sins.

A knock from the door sent a rush of relief through Dak, as he'd already searched the room for some kind of makeshift weapon—only able to find a plastic fork he hadn't used with the hospital breakfast a nurse brought earlier.

A second later, Detective Naik stepped through the door. "Hello?"

"Hey, Detective," Dak managed, twisting a little to ease the pressure on the wound in his back. He'd received stitches and a bandage covered it. The doctor told him there was no significant internal damage, and that the organs and tissue were fine. He'd been lucky, the doctor said.

"How are you feeling?" the Indian asked, smiling at Dak for the first time in his recollection.

"I've been better. I've also been worse."

Naik laughed, approaching the bed slowly. He stuffed his hands in his pockets and looked at the monitors for a second before speaking again. "I owe you an apology," he said. "I didn't think it was a good idea for the museum director to bring in someone from outside. While I can't officially condone your actions, especially the shooting, sometimes we have to turn a blind eye to such things when it serves the greater good. No?"

"Are we agreeing on something?" Dak asked. "Feels weird."

"I know," Naik huffed. "But to be fair, we never really disagreed either."

"That's true. I guess I just thought you didn't like me."

"Whether I like you or not is irrelevant. I try to uphold the law." He grinned wickedly. "Okay, at first I didn't like you. Now, you're okay."

Dak mirrored his smile. "Thanks, man. Same here."

Naik nodded. "I also owe you thanks. We were able to recover the artifact from the wreckage."

Surprised splashed across Dak's face. "Really?"

"Yes. Luckily, the statue was in a steel case. Fireproof. After the blaze was extinguished, we were able to extract it. It didn't have a scratch on it."

Dak was glad to hear it. At least one thing had gone according to plan.

"What about the buyer?" Dak wondered out loud. "The German."

"Ah, yes. You certainly made a mess with him, and his body-guards. His name is Franz Heimler. He owns—or rather, owned—several major businesses in Germany. His net worth is estimated close to a billion dollars, though I suspect his actual holdings are worth far more. We've learned that he's been under multiple investigations for half-a-dozen illegal activities, and we suspect he could be connected to a much larger organization that spans the entire planet."

Dak's eyebrows looked like they'd been pinned to the middle of his forehead. "Wow."

"Yes. Wow." The detective sighed. "Well, I just wanted tell you goodbye. I suppose you'll be leaving Mumbai soon?"

Dak nodded once. "Yeah. I have to hit the road. There's a price on my head, and I don't like to sit around too long."

"From your past life, yes?"

"Something like that. I pissed off someone I used to take orders from. He blames me for his fall from grace, or whatever he calls it. One of these days, I'll find him before he finds me. Then, maybe I can settle down."

Naik offered one last parting smile. "I hope you do. Thanks again for your help, Dak Harper. Next time you're in town, though, maybe you should come see me first. Okay?"

Dak chuckled. "You got it."

"By the way," Naik said. "The museum is going to give you a handsome reward for retrieving the statue. They should be in touch soon."

"Nice. Thanks for the heads-up."

The detective gave a nod, then turned and walked out of the room, his shoes clicking on the floor until the sound faded away.

When the cop was gone, Dak felt alone again in the hospital. It was a feeling he'd gotten used to over the last few years, but that didn't mean he liked it. He missed Nicole but knew giving that relationship another go would have to wait.

He glanced over at the phone on the little rolling table next to him and considered calling his employer, Boston. The kid would be glad to hear the artifact had been recovered, though it was strange he'd sent Dak to help out in a scenario that presented no real payout for himself.

"Kid's got a good heart, I guess," he muttered to himself.

Deep down, Dak wondered about his own heart.

His mind hearkened back to one of his favorite songs by a band out of Nashville called The Floating Men. The lyrics danced in his mind as he stared out the window, and he sang them quietly as he stared at a fluffy white cloud in a clear blue sky.

"I'm a good man, just done a couple of bad things along the way."

THANK YOU

First of all, I want to thank you for reading this story. I had a great time creating it, and I hope you enjoyed every minute.

There are millions of books you could have chosen to spend your time and money on, and you chose mine. So I appreciate that. Be on the lookout for book 3 in the Relic Runner series, Country Roads.

Thank you so much. And if you haven't read the Relic Runner Origin story, you can check it out here: readerlinks.com/l/1372903

Also, visit ernestdempsey.net to get a free copy of the not-sold-in-stores short stories *Red Gold, The Lost Canvas,* and *The Moldova Job.*

You'll also get access to exclusive content and stories not available anywhere else.

While you're at it, swing by the official Ernest Dempsey fan page on Facebook at https://facebook.com/ErnestDempsey to join the community of travelers, adventurers, historians, and dreamers. There are exclusive contests, giveaways, and more!

Lastly, if you enjoy pictures of exotic locations, food, and travel adventures, check out my feed @ernestdempsey on the Instagram app.

What are you waiting for? Join the adventure today!

Ernest

ACKNOWLEDGMENTS

As always, I would like to thank my terrific editors for their hard work. What they do makes my stories so much better for readers all over the world. Anne Storer and Jason Whited are the best editorial team a writer could hope for and I appreciate everything they do.

I also want to thank Elena at Lı Graphics for her tremendous work on my book covers and for always overdelivering. Elena definitely rocks.

Last but not least, I need to thank all my wonderful fans and especially the advance reader team. Their feedback and reviews are always so helpful and I can't say enough good things about all of them.

ALSO BY ERNEST DEMPSEY

The Milestone Protocol

Adriana Villa Adventures:

War of Thieves Box Set

When Shadows Call

Shadows Rising

Shadow Hour

The Adventure Guild:

The Caesar Secret: Books 1-3

The Carolina Caper

Beta Force:

Operation Zulu

London Calling

Paranormal Archaeology Division:

Hell's Gate